Children of the Oak

By Sinead Cox

Copyright © 2015 Sinead Cox

All rights reserved. Except for the use in review, the reproduction or utilization of this work in whole or in part in any form by electronic, mechanical or other means, now known or hereafter invented, including xerography, photocopying and recording, or in any information storage or retrieval system, is forbidden without the written permission of the author.

This is a work of fiction. Names, characters, places and incidents either are the product of the author's imagination or are used fictitiously, and any resemblance to the actual persons, living or dead, business establishments, events or locales is entirely coincidental.

For Patricia and Seamus.
You never doubted me! I'm so blessed to have you as my parents.

I love you Mum and Dad.

Acknowledgements

When this idea was only forming, I took a walking tour around the walls with my family. We thoroughly enjoyed the experience and I was truly inspired by some of the stories that our wonderful guide, Garvin Kerr, imparted to us. It helped my idea to grow arms and legs and become a story itself. Thanks to Garvin, and of course, our beautiful city for being the perfect muse.

A special thanks to my patient Mother who has always believed I had 'a book in me'. Your encouragement and support has been unstinting. My love for writing was influenced by your own talent with words. My Dad's imagination also played a role. Whether it was walking barefoot to deliver papers as a six year old, his life as a mermaid or gargling in the pram whilst my Aunt Isobel chucked him under the chin, he always had a tall tale. Unfortunately, my Father passed away before I completed my story and I can only hope that he would be proud. We all miss you Dad.

To my sisters, Martine, Margaret and Tricia: thank you all so much for your support and your belief in me. When I first mentioned my idea to write, each of you helped to build up my confidence and self-esteem. With my family, including my wonderful nieces and nephews, by my side, I can do anything!

I offer my thanks to all of you who supported me in different ways and by different means – you know who you are! There really are warm, kind and sincere people who the rest of us would be lost without. Sometimes a simple *thank-you* is more than enough; so to all of you lovely people, thank-you!

Finally, I hope this is only the beginning and that you enjoy reading my characters as much as I enjoyed creating them.

Sinead

Foreword

I chose to set my story in Derry~Londonderry, not only as it is my home, but because it is a beautiful city steeped in history.

Derry~Londonderry, more recently and proudly referred locally as *'Legenderry'*, is located in the North West of Northern Ireland. The River Foyle fondly caresses the city and physically separates the Waterside from the Cityside. Not only does it have the mountains of Donegal overlooking it like a silent guard but the core of the city is surrounded by magnificent walls.

These walls are made from a type of stone called schist and have outlasted many battles including sieges. They were built in the early 1600s and can boast the fact that they have never been breached. This has led to it being christened informally as the 'Maiden City'. It also makes them one of the best examples of intact walls in Europe.

Although Saint Columb made it his home in 545 AD, it is believed that the area was an attractive place for people to settle for many thousands of years. If only the land could talk!

To explain why I chose the name, *Children of the Oak*, I must refer to the Irish version of Derry, 'Doire'. This translates as *place of the oaks*, which emphasises the strength and character of this special place.

I refer to the Apprentice Boys in my book. This group played their part during one of the sieges in 1689. They closed the gates of the walls to stop an army of James II gaining entrance to overthrow King William of Orange's Protestant rule.

However, battles are only part of this city's chronicle. A whiskey distillery, the linen industry, a busy port for migration to America and the surrender of a fleet of German U-boats after the Second World War, all contributed towards shaping the modern *Legenderry*.

The history of this city has great depth and feeling. My book does not relay this but it is inspired by events which helped create an exciting adventure for my characters to get swept away by.

Chapter 1

As the mist crept up and over the banks of the River Foyle, a lonely figure stood atop the famous walls. A strange light appeared to hover about it, drawing importance to the very stillness of its presence. The face was cloaked in shadow and the outline of the body was blurry, as if not fully formed. And yet it stood, silhouetted against the mist as it began to envelop even the proud walls. Just before the body was lost from view, sheathed by the moist veil, a name burst forth from the very walls themselves, *Spellbinder*.

In an instant, the mist evaporated and the figure was gone. Streetlamps flickered on and off until once again they bathed the walls in a faint glow. The nightlife of the city continued, unaware of the figure only moments before; horns blared and footsteps echoed as people hurried to catch taxis after a night's entertainment. Chatter and laughter were carried along by the gentle breeze and even a few songs rang out enthusiastically if not tunefully.

Only one person stood in awe. So it was true. When the historic walls were four hundred years old, the Spellbinder would return to the walls of magic, whose very bricks were steeped in mystery. When that time comes, all will not be as it seems as enchantment will be cast over those who dare to cross the Spellbinder's path. This anniversary was the call for the return of magic to the walled city of Derry. The Spellbinder would battle for all that is good so that the city and its people could continue to flourish. If he failed, then evil would gain control of the magic and use it to destroy the city and even the very world's existence. And so, the time for this battle had come.

Knowing the myth was not only reality but about to take place the following day, the lone observer closed their eyes in a moment of fear of what was to occur. The myth about the Spellbinder used to be widely known but long since forgotten through the modern age. Ask anyone from the city about the Spellbinder today and confusion and ignorance of the name would be the response. As far as she knew, she, Dearbhla Doherty, was the only living local person who, not only had knowledge of the myth, but now wholeheartedly believed in it. How could she not, after just witnessing the scene prophesied in ancient writings.

A shudder ran through her body which had nothing to do with the light drizzle that had started to fall. A sense of foreboding was the cause. What was she going to do? If nobody else knew about the Spellbinder and the series of events foretold from hundreds of years ago, then how could she even warn the people about it? She would be taken away in a straight jacket or laughed right out of town. Even she had only turned up tonight out of pure curiosity. She never believed it could actually be true and she had read every written word about it. How could she expect anyone else to take her word for it when she had to witness it with her own eyes?

In truth, she had loved the myth about the walls being bound by magic. It had been so refreshing and exciting to believe her beloved city was a foundation of old magic. She had treated it like a fairy tale which was precious to her in a childlike grasp of wanting the world to be a more wondrous place of spells and castles, happy endings and good triumphing over evil. Yet now, it seemed that her favourite fairy tale was being retold in flesh and bone, 3D, Technicolor, surround sound. Reality. No, she was on her own with this one. The only thing she could do was to be prepared. Tomorrow she would spend all day in the city centre and see if anything happened. If it did, she would attempt to prevent something bad happening. If this was as far as it went, as in the presence she saw tonight, then she'll only have lost a day loitering in the town. No harm done. If anything did kick off, at least she would be there to witness it and perhaps have a starring role in her very own fairy tale instead of just reading about them. Groaning, as the rain fell heavier, she decided it was time to go.

Chapter 2

Returning home, she quickly turned on the heating. Dearbhla was shivering from not only shock now. Her clothes were damp from the rain and she needed to warm up quickly. She ran herself a bath and added some bubble bath to help relax her tense muscles. Soaking down into it, she let out a contented sigh and closed her eyes. The bubbles seemed to whisper words of comfort reassuring her fears and easing the knot of worry that had lodged in her tummy.

Ever since she was a girl of eight, she had read the tales of the Spellbinder. Seventeen years later she could still remember them. Her Granda had sat her on his knee and together they had shared the words etched into rolled up parchments. For some reason, he couldn't actually read them and she had revelled in that. Stained and worn with age, they seemed like a treasure to her even as a young child. She knew they were special, different to the usual fairy tales her Mother read to her at night. At first, her Granda was reluctant to keep them. She had succeeded in wearing him down as only children could.

Her Granny had been clearing out the attic, making space for 'new junk' as she had put it, getting rid of the 'old junk'. One of the boxes Granda had lifted down was an old fashioned crate. It held a battered brown leather suitcase. The leather was cracked with age. It had a dent in its side but was still intact. Covered in a layer of dust, two initials could just about be seen. She had excitedly wiped her hand over the dust to reveal them. Faded golden lettering could still be read, J.D. Granda had explained it had been his own grandfather's suitcase, whose name had been John Doherty. She had marvelled at the thought of such an old case and all the places it might have been. Her hands had stroked over the case in wonder that her great, great granddad had owned this.

She had asked her Granda to open it quickly as she hoped some kind of treasure was waiting to be discovered inside. Obligingly he pushed open the two locks and with a bit of effort lifted up the lid. Dearbhla remembered being disappointed there had not been any jewels or gold coins. Instead of treasure, there were old maps of the city and a strange looking medallion. She reached in to grab the medallion which was the same size of an old penny. It had a disc shape and an inscription in it she could not make out. There was a hole in the middle. She handed it over to her Granda who turned it over in his palm but seemed puzzled by it. Then her eye caught an old book. It was very thick and bound in leather. The cover was battered as if it was well handled. Strangely there was no title anywhere on the cover. When she tried to lift it, she needed both hands as it was quite heavy.

The black book seemed like any other book except the pages were trimmed with red. She tried to open it, but couldn't. Frustrated she turned it over and over looking for something that was keeping it shut but saw nothing. This made her even more determined and so she studied it more closely. When she lifted it closer to her face she noticed a tiny bit of brass on the top left corner of the binding. Running her finger lightly over it she realised it was a button. Pressing down, she held her breath. Nothing happened. She pressed it again, harder this time, but still it didn't budge. She shook it in irritation but refused to let her Granda take it when he tried to. Luckily her Granny called him away to help her lift some other boxes.

When she returned her attention to the book she gazed at it intently hoping it would just pop open. Running her finger along the full bind, she felt another slight lump in the leather. Wiping away the dust she saw an exact copy of the button. She pressed it down but there was no response. Then she tried pressing both of the buttons, using both her hands, at the same time. A catch released and the book opened. Slowly she lifted back the cover and was amazed at what she saw. It wasn't a book. It was a box disguised as one to hold the treasure inside. Rolled-up parchments lay snugly together. There were four in total and each was tied up with leather strips.

Chapter 3

When her Granny and Granda returned to see what she had found, she jumped up and started to dance around, crowing that she had found the greatest treasure of all: a magic box. Her grandparents laughed at her enthusiasm and congratulated her on her great find. Dutifully, they gasped with wonder in all the right places as she described how the book was actually a box with hidden scrolls. Up until now, they were playing along but once Dearbhla showed the rolled up paper inside, her Granda grew more serious and asked if he could have a closer look. When Dearbhla nodded excitedly, he lifted the first one out and carefully turned it around in his hands. Then he gently slid the string off one end as the knot was too tight to unravel. He laid it down on a nearby table and slowly, ever so slowly, began to unroll it bit by bit.

Spreading his hands lightly over it to keep it in place, he frowned at the words written in a flourishing hand script. The black ink had blotted in certain places suggesting it had been exposed to drops of water at an early stage. The parchment also contained some symbols that he could not recognise. More intriguing was the fact that it was not written in English. It seemed to be another language, yet he couldn't make out any Latin or Irish words. Indeed, it appeared to be a nonsensical language, 'gobbledy gook', with no pattern or logic to its construction. The sentence-like sequences was all that it shared with our language.

Dearbhla was growing more impatient to see the writing or treasure map or whatever secret it held. She asked her Granda repeatedly to tell her what it said but he just stood half bent towards it with a look of concentration on his face. Sighing, he straightened and moved away from the table. The parchment quickly rolled itself back up and Dearbhla caught it with both hands before it fell off the table. Dearbhla asked again with frustration in her tone,

"Granda, what does it say?"

"Not a thing. It must be somebody's idea of a joke. It doesn't mean anything, love."

"What? No. It can't be. It was hidden away. You're wrong."

Dearbhla slowly unrolled it and copied the way her Granda had spread it out. Her little hands found it harder to keep it in place and so the bottom kept rolling up on itself. She ignored it and concentrated on the first few lines.

"But Granda, it's English! I can read it. Look!" She slid it over closer so he could see. He leaned over her and looked again.

"Dearbhla," he said, shaking his head, "It doesn't make any sense. It's not English. But you can keep it and play with it and use that wonderful imagination of yours!"

He smiled kindly and ruffled her hair with his large hand. Dearbhla's thoughts turned wistful as she returned to the present day. She really did miss her grandparents.

As she soaked deeper into the bath, a voice boomed out,

"Gather to me, Children of the Oak."

Dearbhla's eyes flew open and she shot upright in the bath. A little shiver ran down her spine and she glanced about the bathroom looking for the source of that voice. Her breathing was rapid as her hands grasped each side of the tub. One minute she had been thinking of the moment she had found the secret book, the next a voice was right in her head calling for…what was it? The Children of the Oak..? Feeling cold now, she climbed out and put her towelling robe on. Opening the door she stepped onto soft carpet and made her way over to the bed. She rested a minute and allowed her heartbeat to steady. When she opened the door, she almost expected someone to be standing in her room. The voice had been so clear and loud; authoritative. She knew she hadn't imagined it. It was a message; from who, the Spellbinder? Had he noticed her earlier during his arrival? Why did it sound familiar? That phrase, 'Children of the Oak', seemed familiar too. She couldn't think and pushed it aside. She was beginning to feel overwhelmed and nervous. Getting ready for bed, she kept the lamp on. Not that she thought something was going to happen; no, no. She just felt better knowing that if she suddenly woke up the room would be in light and she could easily see. No, she wasn't scared, just prepared.

Chapter 4

The next morning made a surprise attack. Sleep had stolen her waking thoughts and daylight was setting the next challenge. Good. Too much time to think was not a great thing. She knew where she needed to be. She hoped the next visit would involve some help and useful information. As it was she was pretty much on her own. Surely if she showed up and was recognised then things would go smoothly. In fact, maybe this was as far as the legend would go. If not, then she would be entering a whole new predicament. Let's face it, a whole new world; a world where magic actually exists and her expertise in that area was a solid zero.

Getting ready seemed so mundane in comparison to what she could be about to face. However, she went through her morning ritual without much concentration. Looking in the mirror, she carefully studied her expression. A frown had settled between her brow, giving her a serious and worried look. Her face was pretty in a conventional way. None of her features drew attention. Dearbhla had a small pert nose and thin lips which hid rows of fairly straight teeth. Her top right front tooth had a chip in the edge which seemed to be the only visual imperfection. That was a gift from her younger brother whilst playing a game of cricket on the beach. He had been twelve and she was fifteen years old at the time. That was ten years ago and she still hadn't gotten it fixed; sentimental reasons. That chipped tooth was her battle scar from living with a boisterous and energetic brother. Her blue eyes were slightly widened, possibly from fear, and as she contemplated that fear she thought about ringing her brother Paul to talk this over with someone. Shaking her head she quickly dismissed that moment of panic. It would just complicate things and anyway she had no time to get into it with Paul. He would only make it into a great joke and convince her she was crazy. No, she was definitely on her own.

She brushed out her shoulder length auburn hair and tied it up into a high ponytail. Glancing at her reflection, she nodded, yes, functional if she had to run for her life. She ran downstairs and grabbed a black blazer and put it on over her blue skinny jeans and a black v neck t-shirt. They were chosen for comfort along with black suede boots, flat heeled, of course. She threw her brown leather bag over her shoulder and neck. Dearbhla made sure she had her *book* containing the scrolls and the medallion. It was time to go.

Her precious car was in the garage getting some tender loving care, which was going to be costly, so she walked hurriedly to the nearest bus stop. Luckily, she only had a five minute wait until it pulled up beside her and on she got. She sat near the back so she could watch everyone getting on and off. What was going to happen? How was she going to help all of these people? So unsuspecting of anything that was destined for today. She knew deep down that this was going to be. The Spellbinder had returned and the events to follow would change her forever. She closed her eyes and took in a deep breath. Opening them she slowly surveyed the other passengers.

An older lady was clinging to her handbag with one gnarled hand while the other tightly held an umbrella. A mother sat with one toddler on her knee while her older child sat beside her. The mother looked tired and hassled. The toddler wouldn't sit still and kept bouncing heavily on her. The older child would flick the younger one's ear and set it off all over again. Two teenagers sat cuddled up to each other. They wore school uniforms and were obviously on the wrong bus but the girl giggled and the boy hugged her closely. Each had a life filled with happiness and sadness to come but at least it would be their story. If the Spellbinder couldn't do what he needed to today then their stories would be cut short. No, she couldn't let that happen. She would do everything that she could to save her city and to allow the many stories to continue. She wouldn't give up. This was what life was about; all the wonderful diversity of people. Everyone had their part to play and without even one person it just wouldn't be the same. That's what she would fight for.

The city was busy. Everyone was going about their own business for a usual weekday; nothing strange or unexpected.

Dearbhla climbed down off the bus and walked along Foyle Street. She remained wary and alert as she made her way to the gate at Shipquay Street and stood there for a few moments. Looking around, she took everything in. Faces blurred as her eyes darted about from one to the other. What was she looking for? She wasn't sure how she would recognise the Spellbinder but she was pretty confident it wouldn't be as easy as seeing a man in a pointy hat with a long white beard and hair to match. Her wizard-like description would make this much easier but something told her it wasn't going to be that simple!

Dearbhla squeezed her eyes shut and took a few calming breaths. The important thing was not to get overwhelmed by it all. Okay, so he wasn't going to look like *Merlin* but he would probably stand out in a crowd. If he was powerful, she'd probably be able to feel him before she would see him. The sensible thing was to wait where she could pass some time with a good view.

Dearbhla made her way up the steep hill of Shipquay Street and crossed over the road to an old department store called Austins. It was a grand building which exuded class and pride. And so it should. It had outlasted most other retail shops and did so with persistent dignity and determination. Since 1830, this Edwardian building has been appreciated due to its large windows, columns and balconies as well as its attractive copper dome shaped roof. As she entered, she saw the majestic staircase. This is what had always made Austins stand out to her. Even as a child she had appreciated the beauty of the dark wooded staircase, with each step lovingly covered in a dark green carpet. She chose to walk up the old fashioned staircase at the left hand side while others chose the more modern and recent installation of an escalator.

Memories flooded her system stirred on by the sense of smell from the age of an old building. When she would climb the stairs as a child with her mother, she had felt such pride. It had made her feel important and special using such a staircase. The last curve of the stairs entered the main foyer of the store. Descending it, you almost felt that all eyes were drawn towards you, marvelling at your elegance. It was as if it wanted to give you a few moments of being *Cinderella*; part of the magic. Yes, Dearbhla thought to herself, no matter what age you were it still made you feel special. She fondly stroked the bannister as she reached the top floor.

This was the café where she hoped to pass some time. Making her way over to the far window, which had a great view of both the Diamond and Shipquay Street, she sat down with her tea and got comfortable.

Chapter 5

At the same time, a group of sixteen and seventeen year old students were arriving at Foyle Street on a school visit. They bundled excitedly out of the hired bus and immediately began organising themselves over at the steps. There was a selection of pupils from nine of the schools in the city. The pavement was alive with all the colours of their uniforms; the air was vibrating with the chatter and laughter of pupils freed from the confines of each of their school buildings. Finally, all of the supervising teachers had exited the bus and began calling out to their respective students to gather to them. Reluctantly, they did just that although some needed a bit more encouragement than others. Especially since the boys were seeing an ideal opportunity to get some attention from the girls.

One in particular seemed to be focusing his attention on a girl standing off to the side behind her teacher.

"Mark, get over here now!"

Mark snapped out of his study of the pretty girl he had spotted. "Sorry Miss, I was daydreaming."

The rest of his classmates sniggered and his friend, Ben, poked him in the ribs, "Yeah? More like checking out the local wildlife, eh Mark?" Ben poked him a couple of more times for emphasis.

Mark spun away from him and then grabbed Ben's hand twisting it behind his back.

"*Owww..!* I'm only winding you up." Ben tried struggling but it was no good. Mark was too strong for him. It only seemed to make it hurt more.

Seeing this, Mark made sure he held it twisted long enough to see Ben's eyes water.

"That's enough, boys! You're showing us all up in front of the other schools. I don't want to have to send you back to school but I'll do it. *Behave!*" said Miss Dunston although the last part of this was delivered in a low hiss.

Mark released Ben's hand. Both of them duly apologised so as not to get sent back, missing out on a glorious excuse for a doss. He glanced over at the girl and she shyly smiled at him. There was something about her that made him want to stare at her all day. He didn't understand it. It wasn't what the rest of them thought. He *didn't* fancy her. There was just something about her that didn't feel right yet he couldn't work out what it was. Shaking his head he fell into step with Ben.

"Okay, everyone just follow me and make your way to Shipquay Gate. No diversions, *of any kind!*" shouted Miss Dunston over their heads. She pinned Ben with her glare leaving him in no doubt who she thought had the most flight risk.

Ben smiled innocently, which transformed into a smirk as soon his teacher's back was turned. "So, ah, who wants to ditch this lot and head to the chippie?"

"No you don't. If I have to do this project, then so do you. I'm not going to do your work as well," said Mark. Just to emphasise this, he grabbed a handful of Ben's jumper and pulled him along, "Keep up, my wee mucker."

A sea of uniforms almost moved as one until they reached the gate. The teachers did a quick head count to make sure they hadn't lost anybody and then they all continued on towards the steps to take them up onto the historic walls. When they assembled near the cannon, the pupils were told to sit down on the ground so they could listen to the instructions. Groans and grunts of unenthusiastic teenagers were ignored by their weary teachers. After all, what did they expect, velvet recliners; leather beanbags?

"Sir, I am not sitting on that ground. It's all dirty. No way!" said a pupil from one of the girls' schools.

"Orla, sit down and shut up. I don't have time for this," said Mr Bradley, not amused that he had ended up on this visit when it should have been one of his colleagues, who was conveniently sick. He could have been enjoying three free periods in school with a mug of hot tea and catching up on some paperwork. Instead he was stuck on top of these walls with whiny Orla who was always moaning about something.

"But sir, this isn't fair. I'm not wearing tights and I'll be freezing. Not to mention all the creepy crawlies that will be trying to climb up me."

At this comment, several of the other girls jumped up screaming.

"Eww… That's disgusting; I'm not sitting either if there are bugs about."

Mr Bradley rolled his eyes and looked as if he wanted to feed their dead bodies to an army of the most horrendous bugs on earth. "Grow up girls. Why do you have to cause a scene when those girls from the other schools just sit down and get on with it?"

"I dunno Sir. Maybe they're used to slumming it with bugs!" said Orla nastily.

Some of the boys laughed at this while the other girls just muttered to each other and ignored her.

Mr Bradley threw up his arms in surrender and walked away before he did something that would lose him his job. At that point Miss Dunston walked over and made a suggestion.

"Why don't you take your blazers off and sit on them?"

Everyone waited to see which way this was going to go. After a few tense moments, Orla shrugged her shoulders and did just that.

"Okay, but I'm not happy."

Those pupils nearest to Mr Bradley heard him murmur, "No, you never are Orla." He sighed and went over to Miss Dunston. "Thanks Sarah. I was just getting angrier by the minute. She's like this all the time."

"No problem, Jake. I have a few like that myself. We should get started before another distraction arises." She walked off towards her group and ran through the instructions she had already given them in school. As usual, there were some blank stares as if they had never been told about this trip never mind the project details. Closing her eyes and taking a deep and calming breath, Miss Dunston recalled her mantra: *I love my job and love a challenge. This is just a blip.* "Okay guys, I'll start again..."

Ben just so happened to be one of those who had a blank and confused look fixed on his face. He nudged Mark beside him. "What is she on about?"

Mark tried ignoring him but the persistent elbow in his side was getting sore. He elbowed Ben back twice as hard and had the satisfaction of hearing him grunt in pain. "Ben we've already heard this in class, this morning, yesterday and she even gave us a hand-out with the key points highlighted. Do you even know what subject this is?"

Ben shot a sleazy look over at the girls. "*Learning for Life?*" he said out loud and waggled his eyebrows at them.

"Ben!" hissed Miss Dunston. "Cut it out and pay attention. Okay, get out your hand-outs and then split into your teams. Don't forget there are marks awarded based on how you communicate and work together as a team so there's no room for messing. Well, unless you want to fail!" Miss Dunston pointedly glared at Ben.

"Miss, seriously, I'm going to ace this. I'm *sweeeet*." Just for effect he waggled his eyebrows again at the girls sitting opposite.

"Give me strength. Just get on with it," said his increasingly exasperated teacher.

Mark smothered a laugh. Ben was annoying but he was funny and so this project wouldn't be as boring as it could be without him in the team. As long as he pulled his weight, he didn't mind a bit of banter. Though Miss Dunston, who was usually very patient with Ben, looked about to lose the head with him if he pushed it. He better warn Ben about that as the last thing they needed was their school showing themselves up. They'd never get out on a trip again. "Don't push it with Miss. Stop winding her up or she'll boot you back to school and this day will be twice as long."

Ben looked over at Mark and exaggerated a happy face and clasped his hands together. "Gee Mark, I didn't know you cared! I'll be good." He emphasised this last bit by doing a scout's honour sign.

The rest of the boys and the girls across from them laughed at this and Mark felt the heat creep up his cheeks.

"Reddener..!" Billy shouted out. "Look at that reddener he has!"

Mark muttered what he could go and do. It involved the cannon and a part of his anatomy. And a mess!

They all laughed uproariously at that image and Mark felt he'd salvaged a bit of his pride. He glanced up quickly to see where Miss Dunston was but it seemed something had amused her as she had turned away with shaking shoulders and a muted giggle. He turned his head to the right and the girl he'd noticed earlier was watching him. She didn't smile and looked a bit sad. What was her deal? He frowned and she put her head down and focused on her hand-out. He tried to think if he knew her but she didn't seem familiar although there was something about her…he shrugged it off and got back to his own reading material.

Chapter 6

Orla looked to see where Mr Bradley was explaining something to Molly. She smirked over at the other girls in their uniforms. Clearing her throat at Leanne sitting beside her she used her eyes to point over at the group of girls so engrossed in their work. *Losers*, she mouthed to her friends. They all dutifully cackled and Orla was satisfied when one of the "losers" looked up and caught her eye. She raised her eyebrows and jutted her chin out in an act of "so what are you going to do about it?" The girl slowly raised her right hand up and held it into a fist. Orla, fascinated by the girl's slow and purposeful movements watched on as she couldn't honestly be challenging her to a fight. She quickly looked at her friends and saw that they were watching her as well. Then, the girl mimicked her own defiant expression and with her left hand she seemed to turn something beside her right fist. Orla leaned forward to see what she was turning and then it became very clear what was happening. As the girl was rotating her left hand on an imaginary key, her middle index finger of her right hand slowly raised up to an upright position. Orla stared open-mouthed at this new way of giving someone the birdie. The girl smugly laughed at Orla's response and joined in with her *loser* friends. Orla was mortified and looked away. Incredibly, even her *supposed* friends were cackling at her.

"Shut up. I mean it, shut up." She scowled at each of them in turn and their cackles died down into an uncomfortable silence. If Orla was annoyed, she'd make them all pay.

"Ach, Orla. You have to admit that was hilarious," said an uncharacteristically brave Fiona.

Orla pinned her with an angry glare. "I don't have to admit anything. She's a bug. A bug that needs fumigated. And I think I'm just the right person to do it. You wait. I'll get her. You just wait." Orla was seething with rage now and continued to stare at the offensive "bug" who'd completely humiliated her in front of her own friends and all of the other pupils. The other girl had already returned to her work but Orla wasn't so ready to forget. She began formulating a plan in her head; a plan to end this ugly bug's ball.

Takuma had seen this exchange of bitchiness between the two girls. It had been funny but as he watched the girl Orla's face change into a mask of hatred, he wondered if perhaps it had gone a bit too far. He straightened and stretched his neck to see if he could see the girl Orla's teacher. He couldn't and wondered if he should say something to his own teacher. Biting his lip he pondered if he should get involved and then thought twice about it. No; better to stay clear of girl fights. Let the teachers deal with it. After all they were getting paid to deal with difficult teenagers. He had more important things to worry about; like getting as many 'A stars' as he could. Since moving here from Japan a year ago, he had his life mapped out in as fine a detail as was possible for his age. He knew what he wanted and he knew the work he would have to put in to get there. That helped settle him and he put unnecessary thoughts of the previous incident out of his head which was already working on the best way to get the highest grade in this particular project.

Susie looked over at the boy called Mark. Why did he keep staring at her as if she was an alien? At first, she had thought it was sweet. Now, she thought it was creepy and she didn't like it. It was as if he was trying to figure her out or something. She looked away in case she made eye contact with him again. The sooner they got this project started the sooner they could go and she could get away from the boy with the probing eyes. She hated days like this; away from the safety of the school; mixing with strangers and being exposed to their comments, which were usually negative; just like that catty one Orla. She was a real piece of work. Linda had bested her that time but more than likely it wouldn't be the end of it. The boys in her class were being quiet and watchful. They always became so protective of them in situations like this. She had watched their reaction when Orla had been making her snide comments to her friends. However, they were more alert when Mark was "observing" her. It seemed funny to her that all of the schools were so different and yet they all had the same problems in some shape or form. She bet not one of them was as confident about themselves as they made out. At least she was open about it but probably the most insecure of them would be that boy Ben and Orla. Now that would be a partnership worth filming. Just as well they weren't working on the same team or they'd be spending more time outdoing each other for attention. She on the other hand would be blending into the surroundings hoping no one would notice her.

She let the voices of all the others drift into the background as her gaze wandered over the ancient walls. They held so many secrets. Wouldn't it be amazing to hear all the stories the walls could tell? She sighed and watched the people below getting on with their daily routines. She noticed a figure standing at the corner of a shop at Bank

Place. A woman with short fair hair was staring back at Susie, while a light breeze ruffled the woman's hair about her eyes. She looked out of place and her clothes looked dated. Something about the woman stirred a memory in her but she couldn't grasp it. The woman was squinting against the afternoon sun but she couldn't mistake that she was looking directly at her. She was wearing a brown well-worn leather bomber jacket. It seemed to fit her body perfectly, as if it had moulded to her every curve. She had matched her jacket with khaki trousers and brown boots scuffed and old fashioned in style. The strange woman tilted her head to the left and continued to stare at her. Susie met her gaze and tried to match her face to a name. She frowned deep in thought, when suddenly a loud bang snapped her attention away.

Her heart beat heavily and she scanned the others to find the source of the noise. Everyone was looking around but no one knew what had caused it. When Susie looked back to see the woman, she was gone. Susie strained to see if she could pick out her leather jacket in the people walking around below but there was no sign of her. She'd obviously moved on. That was a bit weird as the woman seemed to know her yet didn't call her name or approach her. Maybe she thought she was someone else and then was mortified when she realised she had made a mistake and just hurried off. Susie started to read the first page of her instructions for the second time…and then a third until she'd refocused herself on the project.

Chapter 7

Dearbhla sat sipping her second cup of tea and had treated herself to a large cream bun with icing on top. She savoured her first bite and congratulated herself on a good decision. This was no time to be watching her calorie intake. Uncertain times called for large endorphin releasing buns to give her a boost. She was armed with a napkin in one hand and the tasty treat in the other. She could die happy right now. Okay, perhaps not, but she was definitely in a better mood than when she had first woken up this morning.

It was hard to imagine that anything was going to happen. Everything seemed so normal. She looked out of the café window and felt almost safe. It was so familiar; every shop, every building; the war memorial in the Diamond area; the walls overlooking their precious core. She polished off the bun and wiped the crumbs from her mouth. Well, one thing was for sure, she couldn't sit here devouring buns all day. No matter how delicious they were.

The sun bore down happily on the pedestrians. Some were strolling along in no hurry to find their destination. Others strode by with no time for dalliance. The sky was azure blue and there was an absence of clouds which in itself was nearly unheard of. Dearbhla may love her city but there was one thing she had contempt for and that was the weather. More often than not it threatened to rain, persistently drizzled or just plain poured. No, the weather was not something she appreciated. That made today a real delight.

Suddenly, a loud bang made her jump and she spilt some tea down her top. Great; a nice tea stain to add to the stress of the day. She fumbled with her top and tried wiping it with a napkin. It didn't help. At least it hadn't burnt her. After having a quick look outside for any disturbance and satisfied with seeing none, she put on her coat and made her way over to the toilets.

Inside, she used some cold water to wipe at the offensive tea stain. Luckily it was coming off so she held herself at an awkward angle under the hand dryer. Now this was more her kind of day. As she was drying her top, a child's voice was singing a nursery rhyme in one of the cubicles. The mother was singing softly along with him. Dearbhla caught herself from singing along. She checked her reflection in the mirror and tucked some stray strands of hair behind her ears. A minute later she realised the singing had stopped. The cubicle door was unlocked and a young boy of about two tottered out. Dearbhla smiled at him but he blankly looked straight ahead. More strangely, he turned towards the door and tried to walk through it. He was too short to reach the handle. Dearbhla paused to listen for his mother to shout for him to wait but she didn't. Unsure of what to do, she gently said to the boy,

"Maybe you should wait for your mummy. You might hurt yourself on the door."

However, the child kept walking into the door as if he could get through it. As if he needed to get through it. Feeling a bit uneasy, Dearbhla looked towards the cubicle and loudly said,

"Hello, sorry but your son is trying to get out the door and I think he's hurting himself."

Just as she finished this the thumping noise of the child's head hitting the door seemed to get louder and more frightening in the silence. Dearbhla swung round to see trickles of blood running down the boy's forehead. Her stomach dipped.

"No. Stop it. You're hurting yourself." She frantically looked around for the mother. No sign of her, so she ran over to the door and held back the child so he didn't make contact with the door. She felt sick as the boy strained against her trying to get free. His blood was smeared on its surface looking so stark against the white paint. She held on tightly but was so scared at what she was seeing. Just then the mother pushed out of the cubicle with a similar blank look in her eyes as her son's. She walked over towards them. Dearbhla sighed in relief.

"I thought you were ill when you didn't come out. Your son's bleeding. He just..."

Dearbhla stopped talking. The woman opened the same door her son had been trying to get out and holding it back with one hand, she grabbed her son's left hand. They left. Dearbhla stared at the door as it shut behind them. What was that? Only for the smear of bright red on the door, she would have believed she was hallucinating. She stood still for another minute and then let out a long breath. That was just too weird. The poor child was really hurting himself. Why was he so determined to get out that door and even when he was bleeding he was still trying?

Opening the door, she walked out into what could only be described as a mass evacuation. Everyone was leaving the café. Not just the customers; everyone. The till operators, the cooks, the cleaners were all walking down the elegant staircase. A stairway packed with people. She turned her head from left to right and her mouth went slack with shock. The worrying thing was not just that they were all leaving at the same time, in the same manner and with the same blank expression on their faces but that they did so in complete silence. Not one word was spoken. No laughter, no screaming, no whispering. Nothing - that is when Dearbhla got a shiver working its way slowly and meaningfully down her spine. It felt as if a caterpillar was trailing her backbone and she could feel every one of its tiny hairs on its chubby body. Her back arched of its own accord. This was fear. This is what she had been waiting for. This was the beginning of her nightmare.

Chapter 8

Ben was getting really bored of the project and was thinking up ways to cause some kind of distraction. He looked about him and was disappointed to see everyone else was in deep concentration. What a let-down. It looked like he was going to have sole responsibility of waking this bunch of nerds up. After all, it was his duty as school entertainer to do some entertaining. He stood up off the ground and dusting himself down, he shouted out,

"Miss. Miss Dunston. *Miss Dunston*!" He waited until she stopped her conversation with the other teacher.

She turned around slowly and after staring at him for a few seconds, she asked almost reluctantly, "What is it Ben?"

"Nothing much, Miss, but I think I was just bitten by a spider." He waited to see a ripple of disquiet among the girls. "I mean it mightn't have been a spider but something definitely bit me." He watched the reaction of uneasiness begin to work its way round the girls and added with just the right amount of uncertainty, "It had eight big hairy legs and a big fat hairy body. And seriously pointy teeth! But could that be a spider?"

At this last comment, most of the girls squealed and scrambled up from their sitting positions. Chaos ensued. The boys were laughing and shouting out unhelpful things like "There it is. I see it. It's on your jumper," while the girls jumped around screaming and crying. Some were doing a fit-like dance trying to rid themselves of the imaginary hairy body clinging onto them. One girl, Louise, was frozen from sheer panic as she suffers from a very real fear of spiders, never mind those of the hairy bodied pointy teeth species. As teachers attempted to calm the situation down and the more sensible girls comforted their friends and explained it was just lies, Ben was doubled over laughing at his little "pantomime". One of the girls had actually fallen in the panic and cut her knee. Blood was streaming down her leg and onto her grey sock. She was yelping in pain and still Ben laughed and laughed. Eventually a hush fell over the group and Ben's laughter rang out twice as loud, seeming to echo off the walls.

Miss Dunston walked towards Ben in a purposely slow way. This was going to get ugly. Yet Ben kept on laughing and was now clutching his side as if in pain.

"Ben." One simple word and there was enough in its tone to make Ben stand up and stop his guffawing. He watched as his teacher made her way towards him and saw something in her eyes that finally made him realise he'd pushed her too far. He heard Mark's earlier warning, *"Don't push it with Miss. Stop winding her up..."*

"Ben. I warned you but as usual you completely ignored me and did your own thing. Well I've had enough. We've all had enough. Because of your antics another pupil has been hurt. You are going back to sch .."

That was as far as Miss Dunston got. The pupils and the teachers stopped what they were doing. The boys stopped sniggering. The girls stopped crying. The blood stopped flowing from the girl's cut knee. All movement stopped. Only a few of the group were not affected.

"What the hell?" asked Ben, "Miss, are you okay? I'm sorry right. I'm sorry. What's going on? Mark? Do you see this?"

Mark pulled himself up and looked around at the rest of the pupils and teachers. They all looked the same. They didn't even seem to be breathing. All held blank stares; staring at nothing or no one in particular. Molly was half crouched as if somebody had pressed a pause button as she was trying to stand up. Luke had a hand raised to David's mouth ready to burst the bubble of gum which had been blown to full size. Mark stumbled over to Ben and stood beside him. Their teacher had stopped in mid-sentence and her mouth was frozen while forming her next word. Mark ran his hand through his hair and grabbed a handful of it. He held on for dear life as if it would drag him back into reality because this could not be happening.

Ben was waving his hand in front of the teacher's eyes. No response. Not even a blink.

"Geez Mark. What's wrong with her?"

"Take a look around you, Ben. What's wrong with all of them?"

Ben did a quick sweep of their group and saw the weird empty looks on their faces and the almost frozen in action stances. It was as if they were all playing a strange and inappropriate game of musical statues, except, it was clear that this was no game.

A few other pupils had been left out of the strange "game" and after failing to get their friends or teachers to react, began moving towards Mark and Ben.

Orla was shaking and looked as uncertain as anyone had ever seen her. "This is totally mad. What happened? What did you do?" she attacked.

"Don't be so bloody stupid. I didn't do this. It just happened," said Ben.

"Well everything was fine until you started mouthing off about a killer spider on the loose. Then it all went crazy! So what did you do?" Orla was not backing down. She was looking for someone to blame and Ben fit the profile.

Ben was starting to get angry and was leaning into Orla, "I-told-you-I-didn't-do-anything!" he enunciated each word sharply. He was a lot taller than Orla and was staring down at her daring her to say any different.

Orla was never one to give up and as far as she was concerned, he'd caused this. "And I am telling you, it's your fault. What did you do?" She raised herself up on her tiptoes and eyeballed him to show she meant business.

Ben pushed her away, "Get your ugly face out of mine." He walked away from her and over to the wall. "Oh crap. We are in serious trouble. Get over here NOW!" he shouted.

Mark and the rest walked quickly over to Ben.

"It's everyone. It happened to everyone. Everyone," Ben uselessly informed them. He shook his head over and over as if not believing the shocking sight before him.

People sat motionless in cars. Pedestrians stood as if turned to stone. They were all frightening in their stillness.

Susie shuffled over to stand next to Mark. She didn't know why but she felt safer beside him. It was as if some deep instinct was guiding her to the boy she had been wary of earlier. She didn't understand what was happening. It didn't make any sense. One minute they had been working on their projects, the next Ben had been acting like a real prat. She had been annoyed at him herself as he had interrupted their work and she knew it would make the day even longer to do what they had to. She had hoped his teacher would really tear a strip off him and send him back where he belonged. Some kind of detention involved as well. Yes he deserved it for stretching this ordeal out longer. She was just getting ready to enjoy Miss Dunston's tirade when the world turned upside down. Now they were left in limbo while everyone else was on pause and happily unaware of being so. She glanced up at Mark. He was looking out over Guildhall Square with a worried expression. Okay, this was bad.

"What should we do?" she asked Mark. She needed hope. Please let him give me hope.

Her question broke his reverie and silent pleading for someone to help. He took a deep breath and turned his attention to the girl with the sad eyes.

"I'm not sure…sorry, what's your name?" Mark asked. He knew her name but it gave him another minute to organise his thoughts for a sensible answer. His gut response was to get the hell out of here but that wasn't helpful. Anyway Orla covered the drama department.

"I'm Susie. And you're Mark?" she looked up at him and into his cloudy eyes.

"Yeah, and that's Ben. Or as he's known in close circles, Spiderboy!" he grinned over at his friend and his eyes seemed to clear.

Ben glanced over and snorted his disgust but was grateful his friend didn't think this mess was his fault; unlike that Orla one.

"Yes and I'm Orla and no-one really gives a crap because *Spiderturd* here has jinxed us all." Orla glared again at Ben even more fiercely now when she saw that the whole town had gone whacko.

They all ignored her. A nervous looking girl stepped out from behind Orla and said, "Hi. I'm Leanne and this is seriously freaking me out." She peeked at Ben and flashed him a quick smile until Orla swivelled to glare at her.

"Whatever, like Sandra said, what are we going to do?" Orla asked, whilst nodding her head at Susie.

Susie rolled her eyes and braced herself to deal with a bitchy twit. "It's *Susie* and I think we should see if we can find anyone like us who can still move and talk."

Takuma inched forward to the group and agreed with Susie.

"My name is Takuma and I believe Susie is correct. There must be others like us. We need to make contact and then try to work out what has happened from there. Perhaps there are people who have more information and we can get help."

"Well, *Satsuma* we know what happened, Spiderturd jinxed us and so he's the problem." Orla was intent on irritating Ben and she was watching him, hoping he would lose it. She nearly got her wish.

Ben lunged towards Orla and gripped both her shoulders. He started shaking her and was shouting in her face, "Listen to me you puke, just shut it." He was still shaking her. Mark grabbed him and pulled his friend away from the troublemaker.

"Leave it Ben. She's stirring the pot. Ignore her," he advised.

Ben shook Mark off him. "I'm okay." He pointed at Orla. "She needs to wind her neck in."

"Or what..? What's Spiderturd going to do?" she agitated.

"I'll wind it in for you!" Ben snapped back at her.

"Oh stop it. This is getting us nowhere. The two of you ignore each other. We need to get moving. Come on," said Susie who was fed up wasting time with insulting chatter.

Chapter 9

They began to make their way in single file down the steps when it happened. The statues woke up. They began to move. People walked out of the gates. No matter where they had been, they were drawn like magnets to the gate nearest them and out they went.

"David. Stop. Where are you going?" Ben tried to stop the other boy but he didn't even glance at him, he just kept on walking. They all did; their teachers, their classmates, all of them. They followed the rest of the people out of the gates.

"Now what's happening?" cried Leanne. "Why are they all leaving?" She ran over to her friend Molly. "Look at me Molly… Talk to me … Why won't you look at me?" Molly stared vacantly in front of her. Leanne dropped to her knees sobbing.

Susie waited to see if Orla would comfort the frightened girl but instead Orla curled her lip in distaste at her weakness. Then she turned away from the wretched scene of a girl falling apart. Susie was furious. She muttered under her breath, "Selfish cow," as she passed by to kneel down beside Leanne. She murmured words of comfort to the girl and put her arm gently around her. "It's okay. Don't cry Leanne. We'll figure it out. We'll get help. Please don't cry."

Mark, Ben and Takuma all looked on and felt helpless. They didn't speak but each gave silent thanks that Susie was there to deal with the tears as they were definitely no good in that area. Every so often a few more people would stream by with a single minded mission to exit the gate.

Susie eventually got through to Leanne and helped her dry off her face. She helped her up and made sure she was okay to walk. Leanne's face was pale and scared. She looked very young. But then, thought Susie, they were all young. None of them was prepared for the incredible event that had just occurred. Yes, they were young but they were going to have to be brave for a while.

"Okay, let's go. We'll make our way up to Austins and see if there is anyone there," Mark said.

They all nodded in agreement; except Orla.

"No. I think we should follow Mr Bradley and the rest out of the gate. We should just stay with them in case they snap out of it."

They all looked over the top of the wall and saw the sea of people just standing still below them in Guildhall Square. Nothing had changed. There were more people but no-one spoke or moved.

Mark turned to Ben, "What do you think?"

Ben scanned the crowd of statues and facing the group said, "I think... that I always knew our teachers were zombies and this just goes to prove it. It's like a zombie convention down there and we're probably the meaty snacks!"

Leanne gasped in horror. "You don't really think they're zombies do you?"

Mark and Susie both shouted, "No!" They looked at each other in surprise.

"Of course not, Leanne; zombies aren't real," reassured Takuma.

Orla was enjoying the fear she saw brewing on Leanne's face.

"Well, how do *we* know? Maybe they've been infected with some airborne virus and we're immune. Or the water supply has been contaminated and they've all got mad cow disease!" Orla said.

Ben started laughing into the stunned silence, as Leanne looked on the verge of a fresh breakout of tears.

"You eejit. The only mad cow here is YOU!"

Ben's comment relieved a bit of the tension as the rest of them couldn't help but agree. Even Leanne seemed to pull herself together.

Orla however was not amused. She continued to babble her theories out loud and succeeded in raising tension levels again.

Leanne was sobbing and had mascara tracks down her cheeks which gave Orla immense satisfaction when she saw them.

Susie had also seen the smeared black eye make-up and was getting more and more aggravated with Orla's ridiculous explanations.

"Okay, Orla. We get the point. None of us know what's going on but standing here exaggerating about it isn't helping. Let's start walking up Shipquay Street." She looked at each of her companions in turn and as they nodded mutely, she led the way.

"I still think we should follow them out of the gate. I mean they all left for a reason. So why are we going further into the town?" Orla muttered as she followed.

Ben glanced over at her and said, "You know I hate to agree with her but she's got a point. Maybe it's not a great idea to go in to where everyone else wanted out of." Ben was specifically talking to Mark. He wanted him to take control. Not that Susie girl. No harm to her but they didn't know her and he *trusted* Mark.

Mark walked on in silence. He was trying to make sense of it all and so far he was failing miserably. He honestly hadn't a clue what they should do. So he kept quiet rather than seem frightened and unsure. He avoided eye contact with Ben and hoped they would find someone 'normal' soon.

Chapter 10

That 'normal' person they were hoping to find was making her way down the treasured staircase in Austins. She moved slowly and carefully as she didn't want to fall the rest of the way. Her mind was surprisingly calm. After all this was the 'something' she had been waiting for. Well, perhaps not quite like this but definitely as big as this. She was alone in Austins. As she stepped out of the grand department store and surveyed the streets around her, she was alone. Dearbhla walked along the street and looked into the shops as she passed. Empty. There were cars abandoned on the road. The doors lay wide open but inside they too were empty. The street lights turned green, then amber and red. Then the cycle began over again, yet no car could move. Drivers and passengers had left. She was alone.

She turned and walked back past Austins and made her way over to the Diamond. She quickly checked for traffic out of habit. Of course, there were cars, just no-one to drive them. As she crossed the road and stood in front of the war memorial, she looked down Shipquay Street and could see a crowd of people standing near the Guildhall. So that's where they had disappeared to. She had begun to think they had just vaporised into thin air. Well, she was new at this. Anything was possible.

She sighed as she realised she was the only person left inside the walls; made sense. She was...*NOT alone!* Her head cocked to the side and she screwed up her eyes to focus on the unbelievable sight of people walking up the hill on Shipquay Street. Amazing; there were actually five, no six people coming up towards her. Dearbhla could feel the excitement wash over her. She was not alone. She would have help to sort this mess out. They must be just like her and have read about the predictions made by the Spellbinder. She exhaled her fear and worry in one large breath. Seven of them were much better odds in fixing this than one. She had never even considered there would be others like herself. This was going to go much more smoothly than she could have dreamed. Maybe they knew even more than she and they could have things back to normal before the end of the day. She began to smile a broad and welcoming smile as the little group caught sight of her and their frantic waving and shouting echoed over to her. Happily she waved back.

Mark was beginning to feel the ache in the back of his legs as he trudged up the steep incline, when the pain just disappeared. He saw someone standing in front of the big memorial directly in front of them. He started yelling and pointing the person out. "There's someone there. Look. They're moving. Just like us."

The others quickly latched on to the wonderful vision of someone just like them. They jumped and hugged each other and waved eagerly. Their energy renewed, they ran the rest of the way up the hill and over to the waiting figure. As they drew closer, they could feel that something was wrong. Instinctively, every one of them slowed to a stop and spied the watchful figure of a woman.

Dearbhla's smile had faltered when she saw the six jumping up and down. It vanished when she recognised the six were wearing uniforms. *Uniforms!* They were kids. She closed her eyes briefly. This could not be happening to her. Kids. Six of them. She scanned their faces, wary of her now. Six terrified kids. This was not good news.

Susie stepped forward first and said, "We were on a school trip and then everyone just froze. Our teachers and friends... everyone walked out Shipquay Gate and they are just standing there, not moving. I...we...we...thought we were the only ones left." Susie found she couldn't say anything more. The woman stared back at her as if she was angry.

Mark moved over beside Susie as a sign of support but he didn't say anything. The rest of the six just stared back at the woman feeling dejected.

Dearbhla pulled herself together and saw how frightened they were. Okay, so they weren't the saviours she had thought they were but the least she could do was talk to them.

"I'm sorry. Please forgive me for being so rude," she looked at the girl who had first spoken and continued, "My name is Dearbhla and as far as I know we are the only ones left inside the walls. You took me by surprise. I thought I was the only one. Then when I saw the six of you coming up the hill it was like a miracle. Except, I thought you were...well...older." She broke off embarrassed. It was true but it sounded pretty feeble and unnecessary.

The girl smiled back at her. "It's okay. We understand."

Orla made a loud harrumph in the background but no-one paid her any attention.

"I'm Susie," she introduced and then proceeded to name the rest of the six. When she came to Ben, Orla interrupted,

"We just call him Spiderturd." She smirked and then stuck out her tongue as Ben whirled round and flipped a finger. That reminded Orla of earlier when that 'Bug' had gotten the better of her. Hmmm she had got her just desserts being turned into a statue or whatever she was. That was fate dealing with her. She would still get her turn.

Dearbhla cleared her throat and thought to herself that this was definitely going to be a challenge. How was she going to cope with six hormonal and stressed out teenagers, never mind when the Spellbinder appeared into the mix. She decided that this might be the best time to tell them what this was really about. Now, how to begin…

Chapter 11

"Why don't we go and sit down somewhere?" she asked with a false cheeriness.

The six all looked at one another.

"Okay, this is nuts. Isn't this nuts?" Ben turned to Mark.

Mark was at a loss. "Why? Should we not be trying to leave and find other people?"

"Yes I believe that is the only sensible course of action to take. We must find others and determine if anyone knows what our situation is," Takuma said, finally getting over his initial shock of finding only one person like them.

Dearbhla shook her head. "No. We can't leave. This is just the beginning." She saw the kids looking at each other as if they were with an escaped lunatic. How could she possibly explain this without sounding crazy? They were scared enough. This might just tip them over the edge. She took in a deep calming breath and tried again.

"Listen to me. I know this sounds strange but this was meant to happen."

Leanne gasped, "You *knew* this was going to happen?"

"Don't be so stupid, Leanne. How could she know? Why are you saying this?" Mark was beginning to lose his patience with the woman. He had been so sure she could help them. If he admitted it to himself, he had even believed they were going to meet this woman. He didn't understand it but he had felt he knew her. The same way he felt he had some strange connection to Susie.

"Have any of you heard of the Spellbinder?" asked Dearbhla.

Five of the teenagers shook their heads while the one called Ben began to nod slowly.

Dearbhla's stomach clenched in hope, that he had at least heard the name. "Where did you hear the name mentioned Ben?"

Ben stuck his chin out thoughtfully and scratched his head. "Hmmm... Let me think...oh didn't he used to play lead guitar in a boyband?"

He held Dearbhla's stare defiantly. She decided it was best to ignore him and continued,

"Just listen to me. These walls all around us in the city are built with magic. I know it sounds crazy but legend has it that when the walls reached four hundred years old, the day would come soon after, when the Spellbinder would return."

She looked pleadingly at the six suspicious faces. None of them reacted to her story. Ben just stood and grinned. He was really beginning to annoy her. Taking a deep breath, she tried again.

"I'm serious. The Spellbinder is part of the magic and today is the day he returns to the city. It is said that he will entrust a mission to the Guardians of the Gates who will battle dark forces of a being known as the Divider in order to save the walls, the magic and ultimately the city." She didn't seem to be getting through to them at all.

There was a pause after Dearbhla had finished. Then Leanne quietly asked, "So if the Spellbinder is good, I take it the Divider isn't?"

Ola sneered over at Leanne but directed her comment at Dearbhla, "Don't tell us, you're the Fairy Godmother who's going to keep us all safe from the big bad Diva!"

Both Orla and Ben snickered and then Ben joined in,

"I suppose we're the seven dwarves and your woman there is *Snow White* of course!"

Orla cackled loudly while Takuma, Mark and Susie shifted uncomfortably. Leanne stifled a hysterical giggle and Ben started whistling a tune to emphasise his reference to the well-loved characters.

Dearbhla tutted and walked away from him while he turned to the other five and said,

"We lucked out! The one person we meet is a total nutcase. We should move on and see if there's anyone SANE about."

Dearbhla stood with her back to the group while they exchanged quiet looks of uncertainty. Ben was annoying but he might be right. The woman was talking about magic for goodness sake. It simply didn't exist, especially in Derry. It was just a normal city that had survived a lot of historical events. Yes it was a brave city. But not magic. They had never heard the names this woman mentioned; never been told of the magic walls. They were just walls. They had been built to protect this town long ago; a defence, not magic.

It was Susie that spoke some sense. "I'm sorry these idiots are making fun of you," she glared over at Ben and Orla, "But you must see this sounds...strange."

Dearbhla sighed and turned to face the young girl. "I know. It makes me sound crazy but it's true and you are the only other people who haven't had to leave the walls. I need your help. Soon we're going to run out of time and you won't have any choice but to help. This sounds dramatic but it is a case of life and death."

Just as she finished a loud and booming voice called out, "Children of the Oak, gather to me!"

All seven of them froze; children of the what?

They looked around to see who or what had said that.

"Why do you not pay heed to my Guardian of the Gate?"

Very slowly and, almost as if in slow motion, a form began to appear in front of them. It shimmered in and out of focus as if it was a television signal.

Dearbhla's heart rate had accelerated twofold when she heard the voice. It was the same she had heard last night. She could feel the hair standing on the back of her neck. She quickly surveyed the teenagers and all stood in awe with the same shock and surprise she was sure was mirrored in her own expression.

Chapter 12

Then in a flash of white light, the Spellbinder stood in all his glory. He was magnificent. He was dressed in flowing robes which had many layers. A purple velvet cloak was draped over his shoulders and its two ends were held together in a wooden clasp. It had intricate designs carved in to it; stunning in its simplicity. It was made from oak.

He was tall and slender yet exuded power and authority. His demeanour was calm as he studied those trembling under his gaze. The Spellbinder was handsome though he had rugged features and a large nose. His hair was short and peppered with grey. He was a contradiction, old yet glowing with youth.

He stood in his splendour and took his time to consider each of them in turn. Dearbhla and her six companions met his stare. His stern features did nothing to relax them. They were on their highest alert and the slightest movement from him would send them into a melee of running limbs in every direction. The further away the better. They seemed to convey this plan through unspoken thoughts and tensed muscles.

He surveyed each of their faces, seeming to read their very thoughts. Finally his gaze rested on Dearbhla. His eyes were captivating. They seemed to swirl and hypnotise with a myriad of colours. As he spoke, his eyes settled into a deep shade of violet.

"My Guardian of the Gate, I have waited a long time to meet you. Today you will realise your true destiny. See me and know your very existence to be fated through time itself."

The Spellbinder walked over to Dearbhla and took both her hands in his. "Speak the name which calls to you from within the deepest recesses of your memory."

As Dearbhla looked up into his eyes, the strangest feeling began from the centre of her body; a warm tingling, which grew and spread throughout. Her very organs were consumed in the warmth. Her arms and legs felt it next and yet still it travelled, reaching her fingertips where the Spellbinder held her hands in his. It continued on until every part of her felt alive with this tingling sensation. She could feel it building inside her and knew it was gaining power. She *felt* powerful.

The Spellbinder held her gaze and she felt something shift inside her and suddenly the tingling and all the heat retreated back to her centre. It rolled around and she doubled over in shock at the force of it moving inside. She pulled at her hands but couldn't break the connection with the Spellbinder. She tried to fight the heat but couldn't get free. Just as she was beginning to feel faint with the heat clawing at her, it moved quickly. It fired a path from her centre to her head. Here it gathered behind her eye. The force of it moving upwards actually caused her body to straighten as if jumping to attention. Once again, her eyes were drawn to the Spellbinder. As she stared back at him the heat rose until she could feel her eyeballs burning. Strangely, it didn't hurt her and she felt invigorated, as if she had been given an injection of pure energy and nothing could ever make her tired again. A white blinding light passed from her eyes into the Spellbinder's eyes. Her body leaned in towards him and her hair flew about her face as if she was caught in a storm. At the same moment she spoke in a loud and clear voice.

"I am the Guardian of the Gate. I must defend the Walled City from the shadows of the Divider. In me lies the splinter of oak that calls upon the strength of our very survival. I am answering the call of time gone by and time yet to come, our call; the call of this city; the call from the walls themselves. Good *must* overcome the evil."

At this and with her body vibrating with power, she broke the connection with the Spellbinder. He steadied her as she was shaken from the burst of such overwhelming and unexplainable intensity. He led her to a nearby step and she collapsed on to it with relief.

As the group of frightened teenagers looked on, still in shock at the event that had unfolded before them, the Spellbinder turned to them and said:

"You are my Children of the Oak. You are charged with the mission of helping your Guardian succeed in defeating the one who would destroy this city and bring his reign of evil into the world. You must find three objects that will give the virtuous control over the magical walls and so saving the city and the world in equal measure."

Mark looked around at his friends and decided it was going to be up to him to ask any questions. The rest of them looked as if they had been turned to stone; even Orla, which was a shock in itself.

"Ah... Sir, what kind of objects? Where will we find them? Oh and what happens if we don't find them?" Mark met the Spellbinder's eyes and quickly looked away. He was one seriously intense man. He was terrified in case that thing that had just happened to Dearbhla happened to him. I mean that looked really uncomfortable and pretty scary, like, demonic possession scary!

Everyone waited for the answer. Ben shot a brief look of admiration to Mark who, in his opinion, had moved up higher in the bravery stakes.

"You must use the ancient scrolls. They will guide you to the objects you seek. Failure is a pathway which holds our collective destruction. The Divider will stop at nothing in his search for these objects. Trust wisely and use your talents to succeed."

Leanne snapped out of her stupor.

"Please, I can't do this. I can't be part of this. I'm just Leanne Noble. I'm sixteen and a half years old. I'm not a hero. I can't even believe this is really happening. I just want to wake up in bed and out of this nightmare. Please. Don't make me do this. I can't do this." She broke off and began to cry.

The Spellbinder walked over to Leanne and encircled her in his arms. It seemed to calm her and as he held her away from him, he said, "Leanne Noble, sixteen and a half years old, you will be a hero. Today you shall be remembered henceforth in the history of warring good and evil. You have been chosen, my child. This is your destiny." He raised her chin with his long fingers. Then he turned to each of them and said,

"Know this. Today has been foretold in your past bloodlines. Every one of you who stand before me was meant for this battle. Look deep within your hearts and you shall know it to be true. I tell you this; those who join me in the war against the Shadows will walk in the safety of light forever. If you falter, and choose the Shadows, prepare for their merciless grasp."

Susie stifled a shiver and met the Spellbinder's gaze. Did he think someone was weak enough to choose evil over good? Impossible! Okay, they all had their little quirks but no one here would willingly want evil to win. This was too big; too life changing.

The Spellbinder let Leanne go and said, "I must leave you now but I will return when I am able. Much magic is required to give me these precious moments with you. Remember, trust each other and yourselves. Your gifts will aid you in victory." He turned to look at Dearbhla and as they all watched in awe, he shimmered out of focus and then was gone.

Chapter 13

Orla was the first to react.

"Okay, that has to be the weirdest thing I've ever been part of. It's like we're living in a movie. What is he on about, use our "gifts"? What bloody gifts? I mean, I know mine is obviously intelligence but the rest of you have zilch on the gift front!" She began to pace up and down, emphasising each of her insults with waving arms.

Ben snorted and immediately replied, "Orla get over yourself. You're about as intelligent as your ma….which is probably an insult to your ma 'cos nobody could be as thick as you. I, on the other hand, have a long list of gifts I can bring to this fight; brains, brawn and the ability to run *really* fast!"

Everyone smiled at this which was what Ben had been aiming for. Susie crouched down beside Dearbhla and asked her if she was feeling alright.

"Yeah, Susie, thank you. I feel a lot better. I just felt a bit sick but am fine now. What about you?"

Susie turned away from Dearbhla's pale face and looked over at the others.

"I can't believe this is happening, but it is, so we're going to have to get organised and come up with a plan before this Divider comes on the scene."

"You're right. Help me up." Susie stood up and then pulled Dearbhla up from the step.

"I need to get out the scrolls I have. The Spellbinder says that they will guide us to the objects."

Dearbhla walked over to an abandoned silver Ford and set her handbag on the bonnet. The six teenagers followed and huddled close around her in a semicircle. She took out three scrolls and a medallion. Ben lifted the medallion and turned it over in his hand trying to decipher the writing. He held it up to the sunlight but still couldn't seem to make it out.

"What's this for?" he asked Dearbhla.

"I don't know. There is no mention of it in the scrolls so it might not even be important. I found it with the scrolls hidden in a box in my grandfather's attic. That's why I brought it. It may be of some use."

Ben had passed the medallion on to Takuma who took his glasses off and held it right up to his eyes but the words were illegible. He was looking at it as Dearbhla continued,

"I know that the scrolls all hold information in them but the first one is this." She held it up for them all to see. It was worn and stained with age. It was a cylindrical shape and Mark could see it was tied closed by what looked like a piece of leather. Dearbhla carefully untied the binding and began to unroll the scroll. Susie held the top part down while Dearbhla held the bottom part. Then she turned to the newly appointed "Children of the Oak" and asked,

"Well. Can you read it?"

Orla strained closer to it, moving in front of Ben.

"Move your big head Orla. All I can see is yellow."

Orla shoved against Ben, "Shut up!"

"Oh and you need your roots done. *Oomph..!*" Ben doubled over after Orla delivered a well-aimed elbow at his midsection.

Dearbhla took in a deep breath and let it out slowly. How was she supposed to get anything done with this lot? They needed a babysitter. She needed an action hero!

"Stop it you two! Go on Dearbhla. We can see it."

Dearbhla looked over at Susie thankful that at least one of them had sense. Then she hesitated as Susie's words sunk in.

"You can read it?"

"Yes of course. Can't you?" Susie glanced up worriedly at the older woman who was nodding.

"Can all of you read it?" she asked. To her utter astonishment they all nodded their heads. This meant they really were the true Children of the Oak. Only she had ever been able to read the scrolls. For anyone else it was illegible or 'gobbledy gook' as her Granda had called it.

"This isn't just luck that you didn't leave the gates. Each of you is meant to be here. The Spellbinder was right. Okay, let's see if it gives us any clues to what we're supposed to be looking for." As she scanned the old swirling script handwriting, a word caught her attention:

Gatekeeper...

She now knew that that was her role in this quest or mission. Furrowing her brow, she leaned in closer to the scroll and traced her finger along the words which had caught her attention.

"This is it. This is our first clue." She waited until her team had settled and there was quiet. Then she read out loud,

"**Deep within the bastion of those that fought before you in centuries gone by, find Meg. Free her from the wolf spitting cleansing fire and use the silver sun to feed the spectre of twisted wood.**"

Dearbhla rocked back on her heels and blew out a breath.

"Okay, this isn't going to be easy!"

Orla snorted in disdain. "Whatever gave you that idea? I mean this whole thing is a freaking fairy tale…"

Orla broke off as she caught Ben ready to make a comment, "You shut it! You are the least useful of the lot of us so I vote we feed you to the big Diva when he shows up and that should keep him busy for at least a week. We'll have time to find the objects and save the world. Just think Ben, you'll go down in history as a hero; the boy who gave Diva indigestion for a hundred years. And by the way, my roots don't need done!"

Leanne smothered a nervous laugh and glanced over at Ben. His face was reddening with anger and he took a breath getting ready to retort. Dearbhla beat him to it.

"Enough. I'm so sick of you Orla. All you do is find fault with everything. What? I'm not your teacher or your mother, thankfully. You are the most annoying, negative, bitchy moan I have ever come across…no, don't you even think about it, Ben. You're as bad. We need to find these objects or we are in deep trouble. Cut it out and help me work out this clue."

Takuma winked over at Susie and she smiled back. At last, someone to put Orla in her place. She turned to share her delight with Mark. He was standing with his back to her and staring over at the war memorial in the Diamond area.

"Mark? Are you okay?" She gently nudged him in the back but he didn't reply nor did he move.

"Mark. What's wrong?" She moved to stand beside him and tried to see what had caught his attention. She saw nothing.

Still he stood staring with his eyes squinted against the winter sun.

"Mark, talk to me!" She shook his arm and slowly he turned to look at her.

"Run. Run. *Run*!" His voice was urgent and got louder as he repeated that one word.

Confused, Susie only managed to say, "Whaaaaa…" Mark grabbed both her arms and swung her away from him.

"Run. Get out of here. *Move..!*"

The group had watched this with mild interest. At his last shout, every one of them moved; fast. Something flew over their heads lifting the very hairs on their head it was so close. It swooped back over again causing them to duck and protect their heads with their arms. Ben stumbled and bumped into Orla. She was on the edge of the pavement and this knocked her off balance. She twisted her ankle and fell off the road and on to her knees. More things were swooping overhead and seemed to block out the sunlight. Ben ran to Orla and helped her up. She sniffled and moaned in pain. Both her knees were cut and bleeding heavily. He threw his left arm around her waist and half dragged her along. They had fallen behind the rest of the group. Suddenly, a dark figure loomed in front of them. It seemed to grow taller and wider as they watched in stunned silence.

Chapter 14

The figure unfolded itself from what looked like a black cape. Arms that were stretched out in front, slowly moved to lie at his sides. His head was covered in a black wide brimmed hat with a green feather sticking proudly out of it. Slowly and purposely his head began to lift upwards and his body straightened as if synchronised. Orla huddled closer into Ben and he tightened his hold on her waist. They waited in fear to see the face of their enemy. This had to be the one and only Divider.

Everything about his arrival screamed 'threat'. Ben strained his eyes to catch a glimpse of where Mark was but all he could see was this dark figure. It was as if it blocked everything else from sight but that was impossible. The first feature that stood out was his grin. A wide, arrogant tilting of the mouth showed no reassuring quality at all. Ben could feel Orla shivering with shock and fear. He tried to comfort her by squeezing her side but knew it was a wasted gesture. He was terrified. This was definitely the great 'Diva', as Orla had christened him. But she would have to change her nickname, if they survived this meeting, for he was definitely no diva. He was evil personified. Every pore of his being oozed darkness and terror.

Ben watched in fascination as the Divider raised his eyes at last. That was when Ben shivered. And he couldn't stop. His very bones were bathed in coldness. It washed over him until the shivering in his muscles was so intense he thought his spine might break. As he breathed out he could see the misty cloud leave his mouth. Even the air had cooled in this creature's presence; for he was not human. No human could emanate such wickedness. This was the creature of nightmares; the very harbinger of doom. His eyes were pools of darkness, murky and unnatural; cold and lifeless, so at odds with his human form. What lurked in that "body" had no soul. Ben was sure of it. The Divider threw back his head and laughed loudly at the two shivering humans in front of him.

"Finally, we meet. You are not what I imagined warriors to be like but I find I am amused by you. Tell me, what names do you go by?"

Ben and Orla had stopped shivering the very moment the Divider began speaking. It was as if he had released them from their fear in order to respond. Ben willed Orla not to speak in his head. The less he knew the better for them. However, Orla had other ideas.

"I'm your worst nightmare and this here's Spiderturd. And you better just watch out. We're stronger than what we look. I foresee your ass getting kicked all the way back to the fourth dimension or fairyland or wherever the hell you're from." Orla glanced at Ben in disbelief at what she'd just said while Ben was sure his own hair had turned white from fear. She obviously had a death wish.

Caught between being frightened at what she'd said and not wanting to back down from a fight, Orla tried to look back defiantly at the Divider.

His eyes narrowed during Orla's tirade and then his smile widened and he met her stare with scorn.

"I see you have spirit, little Orla."

Orla gasped at the use of her name and Ben swallowed and briefly closed his eyes. This was it. Time was up for them. He hoped that Mark and the others would make it.

"But I take great pleasure in breaking the spirit of humanity. In fact it's a hobby of mine. You will discover that I am no fairy tale monster. I am all your worst nightmares rolled into one. Prepare for my Shadows and weep for your souls. I will own them all. Fight your friends. They are weak and filled with fear. Look around you." At this he raised both arms and half turned to the left and then the right. "They flee and leave you. It is you who stand before me. Brave as warriors while they hide and snivel like the cowards they are."

Ben took his arm away from Orla and stepped forward.

"Is that right? Well then how come they're standing right behind you, Bird Boy."

The Divider's eyes widened and he swirled about in a cloaked mass until he had vanished from sight.

Mark let out the breath he'd been holding and caught Ben's attention.

"Bird Boy..? Did you really just call that monster, Bird Boy?"

Ben shrugged and tried for nonchalance. "Well the Diva had a giant feather sticking out of his hat so when the cap fits."

There was a collective groan at this and Mark laughed and shook his head. When he had realised that Ben and Orla weren't beside them, he had immediately turned back. He couldn't get to them. It was like there was an invisible barrier preventing him from going near the Divider. All they could see was darkness as if there had been an eclipse. He couldn't even see the rest of the girls. He just stood there fumbling about turning in circles. Then something had changed and the darkness began to dispel slowly. That was when he'd seen the girls looking scared and disorientated. He'd quickly made sure they were okay and then ran back to find Ben. Then he'd seen the Divider from the back. The whole atmosphere was like ice and he had nearly turned on his heel and fled. One thing stopped him. The sight of his best friend and Orla shivering in fear and clinging to each other had made him so mad. He had inched forward and then saw Ben's face. His expression of terror had faded to annoyance at something the Divider said. Then it switched to hope as he caught sight of Mark.

Leanne and Susie ran over to Orla and supported her on either side. She leaned heavily on them as the pain in her knees was throbbing and the after effects of standing up to the Divider had left her weak and tired. Dearbhla watched as they led Orla over to the open door of a black Seat Altea and sat her on the passenger seat.

"Orla, we need to clean you up. The chemist is right over there. You stay and we'll go get some stuff to fix your knees." Susie spoke gently to the other girl. She could see that she was still in shock at her confrontation with the Divider. Her usually well-groomed blonde hair was dishevelled and framed her pale face. Two spots of red colour stood out on her cheeks and she was chewing on her bottom lip. That was the first time Susie had ever noticed a visual sign of nervousness from the normally arrogant and confident Orla. She didn't reply to Susie but looked up at her and stared her straight in the eyes. Her blue gaze still held a hint of the panic she'd felt when she had fallen and thought she was going to be a human takeaway for Bird Boy. Then she turned her gaze to Leanne and said,

"Well, I hope you appreciate that I saved your pathetic carc*ass*. You were about as useful as a chocolate teapot. At least I stood up to him. He called *me* a warrior. You're stuffed when he gets to you. Now the least you can do is scurry off and get stuff for my knees." She glared at Leanne with loathing and watched Leanne run off crying.

Susie was so angry but knew it was pointless to say anything. Orla was messed up and she would never understand her. They were genuinely concerned about her and then she opens her mouth and leaks out poison like that. Poor Leanne needed to face her bullying and nip it in the bud. Otherwise she was going to make her life a misery. Susie walked away from Orla and the car and stood beside Dearbhla.

"What a melon!" said Ben, who had overheard. He made towards Orla and Mark grabbed his arm.

"Leave it, Ben. She's a bitch. We knew that. What did you expect?"

"Yeah, but I didn't leave her. I could have but I didn't." He shook off Mark's hand and continued over to Orla. He hunkered down beside her seat and rested his right arm on the doorframe.

"What do you want? I suppose you're over here for something?" Orla huffed.

"Nope... a simple thank you would do me."

"Pah! Get lost! It was you that pushed me over in the first place. Probably trying to run away...you can take a hike, Ben." Orla folded her arms and turned away from him.

"Okay. Fair enough. Next time I'll leave you to it and I'll take great pleasure in hearing you scream your head off before he takes it clean off your manly shoulders." With that, he heaved himself up using Orla's knee as a booster.

Her scream echoed along the deserted street.

"You numpty... *Owww*, I'm in agony. You pig, it has started bleeding again. Ahhhh, you lousy bas…."

"Okay Orla. We get it. He shouldn't have done it. Ben that was uncalled for." Dearbhla walked past him and went to help the young girl with a mixture of irritation and sympathy. After all, she pushed people until they reacted irrationally.

"Put pressure on the cuts and we'll get you painkillers; strong ones." She leaned over Orla and put a comforting hand on her arm. Then she turned and shook her head at Ben.

Ben had strolled over to Mark whistling and grinning. Mark couldn't believe what he'd just seen.

"Ben, you are a bert. What are you playing at?"

Ben stood side by side with his friend and looked over at Orla. He wiped his hand on Mark's jumper and checked it to see if he'd cleaned off all the blood.

"She asked for it. That little cow goes around with a face like a busted cabbage and thinks she can treat us like we're something from the sewer. Well, if our lives are in danger, all bets are off. If she dishes it out then she can cash it in with equal measure."

Chapter 15

Susie had hurried in to find painkillers after Orla's angry words with Ben. She returned with Leanne who had a tight smile on her freckled face. When she had heard the scream, she had almost fainted from fear. She had been about to make a run for it when she collided with Susie running into the shop. Her heart beat had returned to normal after Susie had explained what had happened. She had agreed it was awful to Susie but secretly she had felt such pleasure at what Ben had done. It served that wee selfish madam right. She constantly tormented everyone, especially her. Well, Ben had taught her that not everyone would take her intimidation. Ha. Ben was another one who thought he was all that but that was why he was a good match for Orla's bitchiness. He wouldn't be afraid to show her up. She followed Susie out of the shop with their first aid items and went over to the patient; over to the very loud and ungrateful patient.

Susie handed Orla a bottle of water and took out two painkillers for her to swallow.

"Here. Take these and they'll help with the pain."

Orla made no comment as she took the pills and watched as Leanne began gently washing her blood stained legs. As she got closer to the cuts, Orla hissed and jerked both her legs away from Leanne.

"Watch it you clumsy cow. You're supposed to be helping not making it worse. I want Susie to do it. You're hurting me on purpose."

"I barely touched you. Och, Orla you're such a drama queen." She threw down the wipes she'd been using and looked at Susie. "Go on. The queen has spoken." She moved away from the car and crossed the road to look in the window of a clothes shop.

While Susie muttered under her breath and administered first aid, Orla sat smugly and sipped on the bottle of water she'd been given. She loved being the centre of attention and that was enough for now. She would never admit to the rest of these losers that she had been scared out of her wits by the Divider. She had felt sick when he had lifted his head and she had seen his eyes. Even though her body shook and her blood felt as if it was ice cold, she had spoken to him as if he was nobody. Why had she done that? She hadn't planned it. The words had just fallen from her lips and the moment they had she had been afraid they would be the last she would ever speak. She had been grateful to Ben for helping her and staying at her side but she would never let any of them know that. They would think she was weak like them and then treat her differently. No. Better for them to think they knew her. They didn't. They saw what she let them. She didn't want them to think she was an important part of their team. She didn't do teams. She worked better alone. If the time came when she could do this by herself and escape, she would. She was not happy about being pulled into this insane game of saving lives. She was more into saving her life and she would do everything to keep it that way. Even if it meant sacrificing someone else, she would make that choice. Preferably it would be Ben. He was a pain in the butt. Of course, he had helped her. She would pay her debt and help him. Then she would look for the first chance she could get to scarper.

Dearbhla was standing off to the side of Ferryquay Gate. She had gone there when Orla had been mouthing off to Leanne. How Leanne kept it together, she'll never know. She was supposed to be the sensible adult and she had moved herself away before she reached for the troublemaker and gave her more to worry about than two cut knees. As she looked down Carlisle Road, which was directly ahead of her on the other side of the gate, something seemed to move. She scrunched her face up to see if she could make out the shape that was slowly shuffling its way in the distance. Suddenly a thought struck her and she whirled on her heels and ran back to the car.

"Where's Takuma?" She shouted it out so that they could all hear. As she checked each of their faces, she saw the same expression cross them.

Ben and Mark exchanged glances and then they split up and ran back towards the Diamond area. They met up in front of the memorial.

"Where the hell is he? I thought he was with you lot when Bird Boy came." Ben bent over and started coughing. "I can't take all this running crap."

"I can't remember. When the Divider came, it went dark. When I could see again, I saw the girls but I never even looked for Takuma. How long ago was that?" Mark looked desperately at his watch but it was pointless. His watch had stopped the minute everyone had turned into a bunch of sleepwalkers.

"Mark. Ben. We've got company! Get back here," shouted a worried Dearbhla.

Mark and Ben stood still for a minute until they heard screams and then they ran. Leanne and Susie were supporting Orla and staring down the street. Dearbhla was standing in front of them and turned as she heard their footsteps. Mark took in the expression of astonishment on Dearbhla's face and thought, what now? As they got closer to where the girls were, they saw something completely unexpected. Walking unsteadily towards Ferryquay Gate were two very popular, local figures. Well, more like statues. The strange sound of their feet hitting off the ground filled the air. As they drew closer to the gate, the statues halted. The statues normally stood on top of a roundabout at the bottom of Carlisle Road. They were iconic in the city and known as 'The Hands Across The Divide' symbolising the tentative but important links between the different cultures living in the city. They faced each other with one arm extended towards the other and hands barely touching. Now they stood facing the Gatekeeper and the Children of the Oak who were staring right back in shock and disbelief, with each of their extended arms reaching towards *them*.

"There's a sight you don't see every day!" said Ben as he looked the statues up and down.

"What do they want, Dearbhla?" asked Leanne as she clung to Orla's arm.

"I think they want us or that is they want the clues we have. This has to be the work of the Divider. As for Takuma, I think he's been taken." She looked at the rest of the group.

"Kidnapped? Oh no, poor Takuma. He must be terrified."

"It's fine, Leanne. We're going to deal with these two stoners and then we'll get Takuma. Don't sweat it." Ben winked at her and walked over to Dearbhla.

"Right, like, how do we do this? I mean, how do you stop stone statues?"

Dearbhla sighed and turned to look at the young boy.

"Ben I haven't a notion. I never expected this. I thought we'd be dealing with flesh and blood, not this! Anyway, they're not actually stone. They're made from bronze."

Ben looked at her as if she was crazy and totally missing the point but he relented.

"Fine…how do we stop these guys trying to take us into another bronze age?"

Mark joined them, "Wise up, Ben," and then turned to the other girls.

"You three go find somewhere to hide and take the scrolls with you. Is that okay, Dearbhla?"

"Yes. I think so." She walked over to Susie, who she trusted above all of them, and put her bag strap around her neck and shoulder. "There. Do not let these out of your sight. Without the scrolls, this is over and this city is finished."

Susie fixed the bag more tightly around her and nodded.

"I understand. I won't let you down. Be careful." She looked over at Mark who nodded and she could see the fierce determination in his eyes. He would fight to protect them. Well, so would she. This was their city and they weren't giving it up without a *Legenderry* battle!

Chapter 16

A loud clanging noise stopped them in their tracks. As the three girls turned around, they saw the statues raising the arms usually pinned by their sides, and repeatedly striking the thin air of the gate passage. Clang! Clunk! It was spooky to see their blank expressions. They were grey all over and the ripples of wrinkles and lines on their faces and clothing were frightening in their stillness. Both statues had no fluidity in their movements. They were stiff and clumsy; almost like robots. The carefully sculpted hair on their heads did not lift in the breeze. The clothes they were attired in did not flutter or shift with their bodies. Everything about them was mechanical. No emotion; nothing to appeal to. What was worse, there was no way of hurting them. But they certainly had the means of hurting them. These exceptional pieces of sculpture represented such hope for the future of the people of Derry~Londonderry, yet here they were out to destroy the very city they were designed to protect. That was a twist which obviously delighted the Divider. The girls ran off towards Austins all hoping they wouldn't have to see them too close up.

The metal clanging sound persisted as they continually struck the invisible force field that had been generated all around the walls and their gateways. Mark spoke to Dearbhla.

"What can we use to fight them with?"

"I don't know but we should find any object we can use as a weapon; something to hit them with and maybe knock them over." Dearbhla encouraged the boys to go ahead and find something. As they ran off and opened up car boots and looked into shops, Dearbhla inched closer to the statues. She was hoping that the force field would hold but she knew it wouldn't be long before the Divider figured out some way of getting them in. They had to get rid of these mini dividers so they could search for Takuma.

She felt so guilty that it had taken so long before they even realised he was missing. Not a great start. After all, he was someone who had promised to be useful; unlike Orla. It was because they had all been pulled into her selfish little world that they had overlooked the fact that quiet and reliable Takuma was gone. Dearbhla groaned in frustration. That was it. That was the last time she would get sucked into a silly girl's self-obsession. She silently pleaded to the Spellbinder that Takuma was safe and that they would find him soon. If anything had happened to the bright young boy she would personally hunt the Divider down and rip out his beady eyes. The clanging sound was grating on her nerves. She shouted out in a mixture of infuriation and tension.

"Shut up. Shut up!" It didn't make a bit of difference. They didn't even hesitate, just kept on beating the invisible barrier.

Mark ran over to her out of breath. "What is it? What happened?"

Dearbhla smiled ruefully at the young man. "Nothing, I just lost it for a second. Did you get anything?"

Mark grinned and held up a shovel in one hand and a cricket bat in the other.

"Not bad but I think we need something more than that to do permanent damage." Just at that, Ben came strutting over like a cat that got the cream.

"Well boyo what's your weapon of choice?" asked Mark.

Ben smiled and took his right hand from behind his back.

Mark laughed. "Are you planning to give him a wee touch up?"

Ben shrugged it off. "Say what you like. Throwing paint in their eyes and they cannae see! Result!"

"Good thinking Ben but I don't think it'll matter. It's the Divider who's controlling them. They don't actually have eyes."

Mark snorted and added, "You need something to whack them with. Watch and learn." Mark swung the shovel in a wide arc and then repeated it with the bat.

"I'd say you'll have more chance using that spade to shovel up your sh…s'cuse me…*crapola* than beating on the bronze brothers." He then revealed what was in his left hand.

Ben stared at the older woman and his friend. They were laughing uproariously at him.

"What? What are youse cackling at?" He was getting annoyed at both of them. They were picking at everything he was doing.

"Ben, you are an eejit. They're not going to burst into flames you know."

Ben set the fire extinguisher down feeling deflated. Dearbhla could see the two boys were going to get a bit heated because of all the stress. She stepped in between them.

"Sorry Ben. It's worth a try. We don't know what will stop them so we might as well cover all avenues. We should back away and find a better spot to fight from; any ideas?" She purposely looked at Ben to ease his damaged pride.

Mark sobered up and prodded Ben with the shovel.

"You better make up your mind quick 'cos the Bronzed Babes have found their way through."

Ben and Dearbhla jumped around and saw the two statues lower their arms and step across the gateway into Ferryquay Street, four metres in front of them. Mark threw Dearbhla the bat while he held the shovel with both hands. Ben dropped the extinguisher and used a thin piece of wood to pry open the paint tin.

"Time's up fellas. It's going to have to be here and now."

Ben and Mark nodded at Dearbhla and glanced at each other.

"Let's do this!" shouted Mark.

The statues clunked awkwardly towards them. They began to separate and one fanned off to the right, while the other spread out to the left side of the road. Ben walked towards the one on the left and dunked a full tin of blue paint over the statue's face and head. The statue's strange steps had a hitch in it and yet it never faltered. The paint dripped down its face and the front of its human like frame. Ben fired the paint can at its head and watched as it bounced harmlessly off it and onto the ground. He hurriedly grabbed the fire extinguisher from beside him and took out the safety pin. Then he raised it up high and kept walking backwards facing the statue, racking his brains at how he could hurt this hunk of junk.

The other statue had advanced on Dearbhla and she began thumping the bat at his outstretched arm. Every time she hit it, it knocked the statue off his inelegant stride. He swerved to the side but continued to pursue her. She couldn't reach his head as the bat wasn't long enough. In frustration, she pounded on his arm several times and could feel her own arms tiring. Punching on such a strong alloy meant every time she connected with it, her bones were getting jarred. She looked over at Mark, who was circling the same statue and as she kept it busy, he launched a full scale attack on its head with the mighty shovel. The sound of metal on metal echoed around walls of the surrounding buildings. Mark was determined to do some damage but all he was succeeding in doing was wrecking his own bones. He was jangling all over from the effect of hammering on a chunk of metal. He stood back for a quick survey of the situation. It was dire. Neither statue was backing down. They were in trouble and where the hell was the Spellbinder when you needed him?

Mark took a minute while resting his arms to see how Ben was getting on. He seemed to be just walking backwards staring at the statue.

"Ben. Use that thing on him. Hurry up."

Ben glanced over at Mark and shouted, "Duh! It's not going to work. We need a different plan."

"Mark, give me a hand with this thing," shouted a panicked Dearbhla. Her face was flushed and she could barely lift the bat. Her muscles were aching and she was beginning to wish she was one of those "zombies" in Guildhall Square, oblivious to all this craziness.

Mark put as much force as he could into beating the shovel at the side of the statue's neck. If he could just get it off balance he might get it on the ground. There was no way it could get up again. It wasn't flexible enough. His granny had a hard time getting up off the sofa. This buster hadn't a chance. He'd have to say it though, these boys were made well. There wasn't even a scratch on them after the pummelling they were taking...well apart from the brother who had a fresh coat of paint! Ben was now spraying the white foam all over that same statue. Geez, where did he get his brains from?

"Ben! You need to knock him over. They won't be able to get up!" He hoped Ben had heard him over all the noise. Dearbhla was going for gold with the bat. He'd remember not to get on her bad side. She was definitely getting rid of some pent up rage.

"Dearbhla, take it easy. This isn't working. We'll have to think of some other way." He lowered the shovel and no sooner had he done that than the statue swung round and caught him in the shoulder. He lost his balance and then ducked in time as the statue came for him again.

Ben saw that attack and kept a wary eye on his statue and then called to the other two, "Lead him over to the shop. I know what we can do." He started walking over to the shop which was a few metres away. The statue seemed to pick up speed and followed him.

Mark was still trying to avoid the grasping fingers of his statue.

"Mark. Come on let's go after Ben and see what he's up to." Dearbhla ran over to him and took a handful of his jumper and pulled him along with her.

She was surprisingly strong, thought Mark. He was willing to go too. Anything to stop that useless feeling of hitting a hunk of metal and his arms were feeling heavy and achy. As he glanced behind, sure enough the big alloy was trailing them.

They caught up to Ben inside the shop and weirdly the two statues had stopped just inside the door. It was quite a sight. One statue was dripping with paint and white foam. The other hadn't a tell-tale sign of the physical abuse it had suffered. Afraid their rest time would soon be cut short, Mark asked Ben what the big plan was.

"Cooking oil!" he replied with a satisfied grin.

Mark rolled his eyes and was about to comment when Dearbhla beat him to it.

"Genius!" She grabbed Ben by his shoulders and kissed him on the cheek. "Let's find it and hurry!"

Mark stood with his mouth agape and stared after Dearbhla as she sprinted off down the middle aisle of the shop. He turned to Ben who was slightly flushed but very happy with himself.

"Am I missing something? How is *that* a good idea? First it was paint, foam and now oil?" Before Ben could answer, the terrible twins started advancing on them.

"No time. Just find it." Ben then took off to the first aisle and so Mark ran to the last one.

Ben scoured the shelves on both sides. His painted friend was walking towards him and even though he looked ridiculous splattered in white foam and blue paint; he managed to emanate violence in his refusal to give up. He noticed he was moving much faster than before. How did that happen? As he drew closer, Ben started hurling stuff off the shelves into his path, hoping to slow him down. Then he heard Dearbhla's shout.

"I've found them in the middle aisle."

He ran round the back of the shop and skidded to a halt. There in front of him was the other statue. He backed away and turned. Aw crap! Dummy Duo was facing him. He was boxed in; piggy in the middle, except he was going to end up like mashed spuds. His back was pressed into the shelves and he turned from one to the other. What a way to go, killed by metal twins. He closed his eyes.

Chapter 17

"Ben! Scoot under. We're ready."

He snapped open his eyes and saw the welcome faces of Dearbhla and Mark. They were both armed with bottles of cooking oil. Smiling he launched himself off the shelves and dived under the outstretched arms of the statues. His jumper snagged on the fingers of the one on his right but he twisted and tugged until it tore and he was free.

"Do it!" he shouted and ran to get armed with the precious oil.

Dearbhla and Mark didn't hesitate. They squirted the oil all over the floor in front of them as the statues began to clunk towards them in their uneven gait. They moved back covering every inch and ensuring the statues had no dry bit of flooring to escape. Dearbhla spied Ben popping up behind the statues and oiling the floor there. This was such a good idea. As she used up the last drop, she ran to get an armful of bottles. She flung one to Mark and they did their best to plaster as much of the shop floor as they could. Then they watched. The dynamic duo hesitated and seemed to know that something wasn't quite right.

"Come and get us now you big melons!" shouted a gleeful Ben.

All three of them witnessed the effect of oil on the statues. One slipped and flailed his arms in the air. Then it went down face first and hit the ground. It lay there like a dead weight and did what it does best, be as still as a statue. The other one glided along the floor as if ice skating but in the most unstable style possible. It gathered speed towards Dearbhla and as Mark pushed her out of the way, it slid all the way over to him. Ben shouted to duck and Dearbhla yelped. Mark kept calm, smiled at the giant alloy and as he was face to face with him, he pushed as hard as he could. The statue had no balance and as Mark shoved him his top half leaned backwards as his feet slipped forward. It toppled backwards and fell heavily in front of its twin. It joined his brother and lay immobile coated in cooking oil.

Ben jumped up and punched the air. "Yes! Sweet one, my wee mucker..!"

Mark laughed and turned to Dearbhla. She high fived him and laughed in relief.

"Thanks Mark. I owe you one. I thought he'd flatten me there."

"Well. You're too important to lose. You're the Gatekeeper after all."

Dearbhla smiled, "No Mark. We're all important. We need one another until this thing is over. That's why we must find Takuma. We can't go on when we are missing one of us. I don't know why but I have a gut instinct that we won't succeed unless we're all together."

Mark nodded and then thought about it. "We should go find the girls and then we'll hunt for Takuma. Okay?"

"Sounds like a plan," she agreed. Then as they left the shop and met up with Ben, who had managed to get a lot of the oil over himself, she hugged him.

"Ben that was quick-thinking. Well done."

"Ah well, you know it just comes natural to me." He brushed down his shoulders and flicked his wrist. He looked over at Mark.

"You the man!" said Mark in an exaggerated American accent.

They bumped fists and were filled with excitement and the buzz of defeating their first obstacle It had been a close one but it proved they had the ability to think on their feet.

Ben ran a few steps in front and waved his arms enthusiastically. "C'mon. We saved the day so let's tell the girls what a hero I am!"

Mark agreed and fell into step with him.

Dearbhla half laughed and followed the two boys over to the old department store. Hopefully the girls were just inside. They were all going to have to listen to Ben's blow by blow account of their fight. She hoped they didn't get too cocky as this was only the start of it. They needed their wits about them. What they had been through proved the Divider was capable of anything. Never in her wildest dreams had she anticipated that kind of scenario. She had assumed it would be a group of people who were like them, except they would be under the Divider's employment, so to speak. Stalking statues was another level entirely.

From the top floor of Austins, the girls waited anxiously. They had climbed the stairs with an injured Orla rather than the lift. Leanne refused to take it as she was concerned they would be stranded if it broke down. Orla had mocked her and been prepared to get in by herself, until Susie had reluctantly agreed that there was no outside help if they got stuck; especially if the boys and Dearbhla didn't escape the statues. That had gotten Orla's attention so she had played the wounded victim up every flight of stairs. At one stage, Susie had been restraining herself from pushing the whinging and ungrateful girl back down them. Both she and Leanne were supporting most of her weight and still she was complaining they were going too fast or they were holding her arms too tight or the air wasn't filtered for a queen such as herself. Contemplating it, Susie had wished she'd stayed with the others to face the demon statues than being in this doll's company for one more minute.

They had finally reached the café and had gone over to sit by the window. It allowed a view of the street that the fight was taking place on. She hadn't been able to see everything but she had seen they couldn't stop the statues. When they had run into the shop, she had been freaking out as she couldn't see a thing and was at a loss to know how she could help. Luckily, just as she was beginning to formulate a plan in her head to mount a rescue mission, she had seen them emerge.

Susie turned away from the window and sighed with relief.

"They did it. There's no sign of the statues and all three of them look safe and...*happy!*"

Leanne sat down heavily on the nearest chair. At least that part was over. She was so worried in case they would have to get up close and personal with those scary big thingamajigs. It was so unfair. She wasn't brave at all. Why couldn't she be practical like Susie or even cheeky and forward like Orla? She was none of those things. In fact since this had happened, most of the time she felt like bursting into tears. Orla was right; she was useless and still had no idea why she was part of the team. The Spellbinder must have made a mistake. Maybe there was another Leanne Noble and they had gotten mixed up. Maybe she was standing outside the walls in a trance instead of in here. Leanne put her head in her hands and felt like crying all over again. She knew the rest of the group pitied her and thought she was the weakest one. They probably secretly agreed with Orla but were just being nice so she wouldn't completely collapse in a heap and cause a scene. Well forget it. From now on she was going to stand up for herself and be more assertive. They would value her and ask her opinion and she would make them realise she was stronger than what she looked. She took her hands away from her head and instead used them to smooth down her long red hair. She pulled out a hair bauble from the inside of her blazer pocket and scraped her mass of curls into a high ponytail. Then she stood up and walked over to the other two girls.

"Okay. We need to go down and get the rest so we can find Takuma. He must be really frightened so we had better get a move on." She made eye contact with Susie who nodded and put a reassuring hand on her own arm. Then she turned to Orla and said, "Hurry up. All our lives are at risk. It's about more than just you Orla." With that, she turned on her heel and walked off towards the staircase. She waited at the top and listened to hear if the other girls followed. She sensed Susie was right behind her. As she descended the first two steps, she heard Orla give a loud harrumph and then follow, muttering under her breath; something about being bossed around by a loser. Leanne smiled and continued down the stairs feeling more confident than she had in a long time.

Chapter 18

As they reached the bottom floor, they saw the boys and Dearbhla entering the double doors at the front. Ben made a sweeping gesture and bowed.

"Yes. You may kiss my feet later girlies. I knocked those hunks of metal on their asses." He looked sheepishly round at Dearbhla and his friend Mark. "Well, with a little help from these two wallflowers! Mind you, my wee metal muckers were mighty fond of Mark. I thought I was going to have to leave him there to entertain them."

Mark snorted. "Lies, though the one you painted asked me if I'd put a word in with your ma for him!" He grinned and then ducked in time as Ben threw a punch at his face. Then he caught Ben in a headlock and swung him around telling him he wouldn't let go until he calmed down.

Dearbhla stepped forward getting ready to deliver a sermon when movement at the corner of her eye stopped her.

"Shh...There's someone else here." She watched as Ben and Mark pulled apart and the three girls came in closer.

They waited for a few seconds and then started to move further into the store. A figure appeared from beside a display of handbags and luggage. It walked towards them as they stopped.

Dearbhla said quietly, "This time it looks human but we have to be prepared for anything."

No-one answered her. They all stared at the approaching figure, each silently praying that it wasn't going to try to mutilate them.

The figure halted about a metre away and stared back at them. Then the woman smiled a slow and easy smile.

"Oh, I know her!" exclaimed Susie. "I mean, I've seen her before, earlier today, before all the trouble started."

Dearbhla eyed the other older woman and had a sense that she too was familiar with her but couldn't seem to place her. The woman looked friendly enough but at this stage they didn't know if she was on their side or another one of the Divider's dogsbodies.

As if sensing their caution and slight fear, the woman began to speak.

"No need to be afraid, guys. I'm a friend of yours. I'm a pal of the Spellbinder." She cocked her head to the side and, something about that motion, stirred a memory in Leanne.

"Oh yeah, I know her. That's Amelia Earhart. I'm sure of it!"

The group turned to stare at Leanne as if she had lost her mind.

"You've lost your marbles, Lee," said Ben in disgust. "She's been as dead as a dodo for years."

Orla laughed thankful of an opportunity to get at the puny girl who was getting entirely too big for her boots. "Oh now she's seeing dead people. Okay Septic Sue what's she here for?" She sniggered with Ben and could see the other girl was getting embarrassed.

Mark looked at Orla with distaste and asked her, "Do you even know who Amelia Earhart is?" He glared at her but she didn't even flinch.

"Ah get with the programme, Mark. I don't care who she is. The point is she's dead and Septic Sue here thinks she's communicating with the other side. Oooohhh!" She went into another fit of giggles and Ben was fighting to keep a straight face.

Dearbhla hushed the lot of them and greeted the woman. Then she asked her an important question, "Can you help us find Takuma?"

The woman didn't answer. Instead she walked over to Leanne and spoke directly to her, "Thank you honey. I am Amelia, though my friends know me as Meeley, and I'm kind of honoured you recognised me."

Leanne smiled warmly back at her new friend and was delighted she had such a good memory for faces. The best thing was that it shut Orla's piercing cackle up. She turned to look at the group and beamed at them. Maybe they'd have more faith in her in the future.

Amelia, or Meeley, was a striking woman in her early thirties. She was of slim build and had an aura of pure confidence. She smiled again understanding their scrutiny and in doing so revealed a gap in her teeth. She was dressed casually in what was on closer inspection, flight gear. She had neither helmet nor goggles but wore a brown leather bomber jacket, trousers and sturdy but scuffed boots. Her hair was cut short but framed her features, pretty yet strong. Not beautiful in a model way but definitely memorable and attractive. Her manner exuded warmth and she had the ability to reassure by just being near.

"May I ask Leanne, is it?" she enquired to the young girl.

Leanne nodded eagerly and held her breath.

"How did you know it was me? I mean, I haven't been around in a long time; long before your time." She grinned again and Leanne found she was grinning too. It was hard not to in the presence of such a brave woman in history.

"You're the first female pilot to cross the Atlantic on a solo flight. You landed here in 1932 because of some bad weather and ended up in a field."

Amelia hooted out a laugh. "I sure did and scared all the cows in the process."

Orla stood and gaped while the others hardly dared to breathe in case they missed a detail.

"I went to a celebration of your life and achievements. It was held in a local hotel and there have been so many talks and presentations about you. I even went to the museum we have where you landed. There were loads of photos and that's how I knew your face. You look exactly the same as you did in them."

"Nice of you to say so. Such a fuss about me and my little plane. Good to know I haven't been forgotten. My younger sister Pidge would get such a kick out of this."

"There's a street here in the town named after you!" added an excited Leanne.

"Get outta here. I wish the gals in the ninety-nines could hear this."

Orla muttered to Ben, "Geez this is sickening. She'll be asking for her autograph next."

Ben smothered a laugh but was still incredulous that a dead person was holding a conversation to them about her life in 1932. If only his phone would work so he could record this. He'd be minted. The media would fight over him and he'd make a swift fortune. Happy days!

"What's the 99s?" asked an interested Susie.

"That's the group Amelia," she caught Amelia's eye, "I mean Meeley helped form. It was a support group for all the female pilots and helped encourage them to go further in that career."

Amelia nodded in approval.

"Couldn't have put it better myself. Now I could stay and chat all day, especially with you, but I gotta give you some information regarding your young friend. He's safe."

At that last statement, they all let out a sigh of relief. Apart from Orla who was still miffed that this actually was a dead pilot talking for all she was worth with Septic Sue.

"Are we supposed to believe a woman who's well past her sell by date?" said Orla.

Dearbhla glowered at the younger girl while Amelia chose to ignore her question. "Meeley, do you know where Takuma is being held?" Dearbhla asked.

Amelia shook her head. "Sorry kiddo, can't say that I do. But I can tell you that you lot better get going. The longer you hang around the more time you're giving the Divider to catch up. I'll be calling in on you again but until then I've got an appointment to keep with my little red plane."

She caught Leanne's eye and winked. "Must scamper off now but you have brave deeds to accomplish. Go get 'em!" With that she saluted the group and walked back towards the luggage. As she reached the handbags, she faded and disappeared from sight.

Chapter 19

Mark let out a high pitched whistle. "Whoa. That was amazing. Leanne how did you even for a minute think it was Amelia? That was so quick of you. I wouldn't have had a clue. This could have been much more embarrassing."

Ben agreed. "Yeah imagine appearing from the dead and nobody knowing who the hell you are. Awkward!"

Leanne was enjoying being the saviour, so to speak and felt her worth on this journey was beginning to shine through. However, Orla wasn't going to join in the praise brigade.

"Yeah, you're so right. What a regular Miss Who's Who in History we have. I mean what use is it spotting dead people? She wasn't exactly helpful. We still don't know where Takuma is and we know zilch about what the first clue means. Am I right?"

"Maybe not, but she told us that Takuma is safe and up 'til now we weren't even sure of that. Let's have another peek at the clue. Perhaps if we search for the first item we need, we'll find Takuma close by." Dearbhla beckoned them over to the nearest cosmetics counter and brushed some of the objects sitting on it aside. Then she waited until Susie took the scroll out of the bag she had strapped around her earlier. Once she had unrolled it and spread it across the counter, she immediately focused in on the clue.

"Okay. We know it has to be somewhere within the walled part of the city otherwise it wouldn't be on lock down so... any ideas where this bastion is?"

She watched the expressions of confusion replace the confidence gained a few moments ago.

"I bet Takuma would know this!" said Ben. "He looks like a stu. Total bookworm, eh Mark?"

"Ben, you think anyone that can read is a "total bookworm". You don't even know the fella."

"Aye right. Listen I watched him when we were on the walls. While we were getting the craic, he had his nose stuck to his work, waster."

Dearbhla interrupted the boys' rambling conversation. "We need to focus. Let's break it down. What is a bastion? It's some kind of point from where soldiers fight, right?"

Ben shrugged his shoulders. "Means nothing to me. I thought it was a name you called somebody like Orla!" He laughed at her dirty look and elbowed Mark.

"You're right. All forts have them. They're strongholds in order to defend the city in this case. So that means it must be actually on the walls themselves." Susie was glad she had paid attention to the project she was assigned on the city's history.

Dearbhla felt her excitement grow. "Brilliant. That's where we go then. We need to get on the walls and look for this Meg." She rolled the scroll back up and handed it to Susie. "I want you to hold on to these. I'll get them from you later, okay?" She made sure Susie understood.

The sensible girl nodded and did as she requested. Obviously, Dearbhla thought there was going to be more trouble. That alone made Susie's hands tremble as she closed up the bag. She felt overwhelmed by it all and put her hand to her head, feeling nauseous and faint. Then she felt different; invigorated and fresh, giddy almost. She could feel a smile spreading over her face as if by its own accord.

Mark came over to stand beside Susie. He had noticed the slight tremor in her hands and wanted to reassure her in some way but found he couldn't. He was scared himself but would never admit it, especially not in front of Ben. He would never let him forget it. He struggled to say a word or two of comfort but when Susie looked up at him, he saw something in her eyes that stunned him. *Stupid!* They were all so stupid. He lunged towards the bag but was too slow. Susie had seen when he had known. She easily sidestepped him and laughed in glee when he fell forward and bumped into Orla.

"Watch it, messer!" Orla pushed him away and stalked up to Susie. "How come you get to keep the scrolls? Are you the wee pet?" She was getting revved up for a few insults when she made the mistake of looking into Susie's eyes. That's when she saw it.

Mark came up behind Orla and lifted her bodily out of the way. She yelped and struggled but he swiftly set her down and moved in front of her.

"Give me the scrolls Susie!" he demanded.

"Nope!" whispered Susie

Dearbhla and Ben looked uneasily from one to the other as they watched the exchange. Orla's yelp had snapped them into awareness.

"I said, give me the scrolls." Mark held out his hand and his tone became more threatening.

Susie giggled and leaned her head forward. Very slowly and succinctly, she repeated, "Nope." Then she dissolved into giggles again.

Dearbhla began to feel anxious. This was unlike the quiet and thoughtful girl she had come to rely on. Something wasn't right. She slowly walked up to stand next to Mark. "What's wrong Susie?"

Susie wouldn't look at her. She bowed her head and kept giggling in a childish way that was beginning to get creepy.

Orla backed away and positioned herself in between Leanne and Ben. They watched in fascination as Susie raised her head and shouted, "Come and get me, my master. I have what you seek."

Leanne gasped and shuddered. When had Susie been their enemy? She thought she was so nice and yet here she was stealing the scrolls for the Divider. Oh this was not good.

Mark leaped towards her and tried to reach for the bag but Susie was no longer there. She had vanished in a plume of darkness. "Damn it. I should have been quicker." Mark pushed an unsteady hand through his hair.

"What the hell was that?" a shocked Ben asked.

"Little Miss Goody Two Shoes just stiffed us, that's what," said a very satisfied Orla. "It's always the quiet ones you have to watch!" She pointedly stared at Leanne who let it slide over her as she was too annoyed at the latest turn of events to reply.

She glanced over at the Gatekeeper and saw the disappointment and anger in her face. She knew she would blame herself but how could any of them have known. Susie had been such a vital part of the group. She helped pull them together as a team. Yet all the time, she was deceiving them and working along with the Divider. It didn't make sense. She decided to voice this sentiment to the rest of the group.

"Does anyone else think this is a bit off?" The others turned their attention to her. "I mean, Susie was one of us. The Spellbinder told us to trust each other. If she had been a faker, he would have warned us, wouldn't he?"

"I don't know, Leanne. She just took the scrolls and vanished in a puff of smoke. How else can that be explained?" Dearbhla sat down on the bottom step of the staircase. "I honestly don't know what to do. I've failed and we've barely begun." She shook her head in disgust and felt like curling up into a ball and crying.

Mark looked over at their leader and felt a wave of sympathy. Her shoulders were drooped and as he watched she buried her face in her hands. He walked over and sat beside her. He nudged her with his shoulder and said, "Cheer up. It could be worse." This drew her head up and she looked at him disbelievingly.

"And just how could it be any worse? We've lost Takuma, Susie and the scrolls. We have nothing, absolutely nothing to bargain with."

Mark thought for a minute and then decided to take control. "So we screwed up. We're doing our best. Look, everyone else is out of it. We're fighting for our city, so let's fight."

Dearbhla couldn't see a way out of this. "How do we fight? We have nothing!"

"Well, I'm not going to give up. What other choice do we have? We might as well try. Stick to the plan. We'll head up on to the walls and find the bastions. Maybe by then the Spellbinder will pay us a visit."

He smiled excitedly at Dearbhla and the others. Ben was hovering to his right and gave his verdict.

"He's right. We have to at least try." His face turned gloomy and he held a fist over his heart. "Takuma and Susie would have wanted it." Dropping his head he sniffed a few times for dramatic effect.

Mark swiped at his legs. "They're not dead, you numpty."

"Mm…" Ben eyed Orla and muttered to Mark, "Wish Bird Boy had swiped that one and we'd have been thanking him!"

"I heard that, *Benji*. Why don't you run on ahead and sniff out any scents. That's about all you're good for. Mark's little lapdog." She tossed her head to the side and smiled when she saw Ben follow her. This time it was Leanne who caught his arm.

"She's just winding you up. Ignore her." She smiled up at the tall and lanky boy. He blew out a breath and mouthed "bitch" to her, throwing his eyes at Orla. Leanne raised her eyebrows in agreement. He squeezed her arm in thanks and walked over to the double doors at the front.

"I can't bear this hanging around. Let's go." He stepped outside and warily scanned the street. Suddenly a thought occurred to him and he hurriedly looked up at the sky. His heart had skipped a beat when he remembered the flying freak about their heads. As he pictured Takuma's face, he shivered. He genuinely hoped the little dude was safe. He turned to the rest of their shrinking group and gave them the thumbs up sign that it was all clear.

They fell into step with Ben and gravitated towards the Diamond to stand in front of the war memorial.

Chapter 20

Dearbhla mentally gave herself a shake. She had gotten such a punch in the gut when Susie had vanished off with the scrolls. This day was not going well. Surely, as the Gatekeeper, she should have remained in charge of the precious clues. She felt angry at herself for giving them to a teenager. In her defence, she had trusted Susie but that was another thing. Why didn't she have any feelings or reluctance to hand them to the young girl? She had honestly thought Susie was dependable. Not once had she picked up any bad vibes or ulterior motives. She kicked the kerb and berated herself again. Give her ten more statues after her rather than even one betrayal. That, she found very hard to accept.

Surveying the faces of the team that were left, she chewed on the inside of her cheek. Ben was flicking Mark's ear and generally being annoying. His friend was attempting to shuck him off and reassure Leanne at the same time. Orla was …well…being Orla. She had taken a compact out of her pocket and was applying a fresh cover of lip gloss. As you do! Caught in a crisis? Beautify yourself and all will be well. If only it was as simple as that. Dearbhla sighed, enough commiserating. She had to lead, not discourage, and not hide. In a way, this was a war. Shifting her position, she faced the memorial. A bronze soldier, poised and ready for battle holding a rifle and bayonet, stood on one side. The other side had a bronze sailor who was preparing to go on deck. His face showed the true emotion of war. Fear but the resolution to be victorious no matter what the circumstances. Her mind eased from tension and she resolved to do the same or die trying.

She felt movement to her left and turned to see Ben standing beside her. He leaned back to take in a view of the entire monument. In the centre was a stone pillar of almost forty feet high. It was a stage for a winged figure. She stood poised in grace and triumph, holding a laurel wreath. Slanting a glimpse at Dearbhla, he cleared his throat and said, "How old is that centaur, do you reckon?"

Dearbhla's shoulders started to shake and Leanne glanced worriedly at Mark, who had also overheard Ben's question. Strangely, Mark was laughing. As Leanne regarded their leader once again, she realised that she had dissolved into a fit of giggles. Leanne was glad to have some light relief, although unsure as to what had caused such amusement, and joined in.

Feeling decidedly left out and miffed at having missed some sort of joke, Orla marched up to Dearbhla and demanded, "What's so funny?" This just seemed to make it worse and the laughter grew louder. Orla switched her question to Ben who looked as perplexed as she.

"I dunno. All I asked was the age of that centaur and she went loopy." He inclined his head at the older woman who was now bent over double trying to drag in a calming breath. Orla snorted in disgust.

"Nobody cares, loser. Can we all stop laughing like hyenas and get to the walls," said an exasperated Orla. Then she walked over to Leanne and blocked her view of Mark. "Zip it, Giggles. You're snorting like a pig. It's embarrassing." Then satisfied she'd shut her up, she moved away.

Ben was agitated and shoved Mark. "Tell me?"

Mark put his friend out of his misery. "You called that a centaur."

Ben screwed up his face. "Aye, so what..?"

"A centaur's half man, half horse, you dimwit." Mark slapped Ben on the back. "You mean it's a *cenotaph*." He watched Ben think about it for a minute and then gave a short laugh.

"Whatever. I knew what I meant."

"Well someone has to, cos the rest of the time you need an interpreter."

"You're just jealous, Mark that I'm the brainy one of this group while you're the dopey one!"

Orla roared out a laugh. "Worse than dopey, Mopey Mark was going all mushy over Susie the Sneak!"

Another howl of laughter indicated Ben agreed with her while Mark narrowed his eyes and fixed her with a stare.

"You're one to talk. You've got the brains of a goldfish!" Mark sneered at the annoying girl.

Ben high fived his friend and decided this was more fun than insulting Mark. He strode up to Orla and started to pinch her shoulders. She slapped his hands away. He nodded his head as if confirming something.

"Thought so; you wear shoulder pads. They protect your floppy head from damaging your tiny brain cells." He acted out by bending his head from side to side with his ears bouncing off his shoulders.

Mark did his own roar of laughter and pointed his finger at Orla, "Sickened!"

Orla tutted and stalked over to Dearbhla. Dearbhla had been secretly enjoying the trade of insults but braced herself for Orla's onslaught. It surprisingly never came. "Are we going or not?"

Maybe the girl knew when she'd been beaten. Or maybe she would just bide her time. That was more likely. Dearbhla concurred and signalled to the boys and Leanne to follow. She called out over her shoulder, "Go to Butcher's Gate. There are steps up on to the walls."

They crossed the road, weaving in and out between deserted cars and vans. The city was a ghost town. It felt eerie and unnatural. The only sound was their footsteps. Each of them was lost in their own thoughts as they progressed along Butcher Street. They passed by a popular hotel on the right. The Tower Hotel was the only hotel built within the city walls. Ben ran over and pressed his face up against the window.

"How about a quick snack?" he asked hopefully. He turned pleading eyes on to Dearbhla who was considering it. Then she thought of Takuma and shook her head.

"No. Let's try and find Takuma and then we can take a well-deserved break. Until then we carry on." There was a collective groan but no-one refused.

Ben sighed and patted his stomach, "You're going to have to wait." He looked up but the others had already moved on. He took off after them and slowed down when he reached Leanne.

"Stay close to me, Lee. I'll protect you." As she turned to look at him, he waggled his eyebrows theatrically. She thumped his arm good naturedly and they continued on in silence.

Dearbhla led the group to the left, just before they reached Butcher's Gate. She spotted the steps and was the first to climb them. At the top, she gazed around but saw no sign of anyone. Ben was the last to reach the top and made a show of being out of breath. Everyone ignored him. They needed to concentrate and be on full alert. Dearbhla shot a meaningful look at Ben, who swiftly got the message and went quiet.

"Which way?" asked Mark. He was edgy and could tell that Dearbhla was too. Her gaze kept flitting about as if she was expecting something to swoop down on them any second.

Dearbhla focused on Mark and tried to stem the rising panic. Before she could reply, a ball of heat ignited in her stomach. Her face expressed her fear and Mark reacted. He stood in front of her and reached for her hand.

"Don't worry, Dearbhla. We're here. Just go with it." He knew she was experiencing something. She was a Gatekeeper so it made sense that she would be at her most powerful on the walls, near the gates she was assigned to protect. He motioned for the others to gather in close which they did without fuss; even Orla. He returned his attention to Dearbhla and noticed her hand had grown warmer in his. Suddenly, her body straightened and her head fell back. A strong wind blew up and the air took on an almost electrical feel. She lowered her head and they could see that her eyes were actually glowing with the power that was infusing her body. The whole atmosphere around them was charged and Leanne bit back a gasp as she observed Dearbhla's transformation. She began to speak and in that very moment, her hand was burning hot and Mark had to drop the one he was holding.

"I am home upon my walls. To me the old ones call. They speak and I listen. They instruct and I obey. We will find the missing boy within a concrete womb. Hasten and we shall free him. Our trust was not misplaced. The girl awaits us and shivers in the dark. All is not as it seems."

Dearbhla's body arched back and then she pitched forward. Luckily Ben and Mark caught her before she fell. They led her over to a low section of the wall and sat her down. She was still unsteady so the boys sat down on either side supporting her. Dearbhla was shaky and drained. Wow. Every time that happened she felt like she was on a roller coaster ride. Her heart beat had accelerated and her mouth was so dry. She waited for her breathing rate to slow and the dizziness to pass.

Leanne crouched down in front of their leader and was concerned at how pale she had gone.

"Orla, do you still have that bottle of water you took your painkillers with?"

"No," she replied simply.

As Leanne swivelled to make eye contact with her, she said, "Can you go find some water? Try the hotel." Then she dismissed her by speaking directly to Dearbhla.

"You told us that Takuma is in a "concrete womb." We need to find him before he runs out of air." She patted the pale woman's hands and stood up.

Mark scrambled his thoughts together. "Lee's right. Takuma is trapped inside something concrete so let's start the search for things a person could fit into. Orla, hurry up and get that water."

He pinned the huffy girl with a no nonsense glare. She tutted and flounced off down the steps. Ben ran after her.

"Wait up. It's best if we don't split up."

Orla paused and a flash of alarm crossed her face.

"Just, to be on the safe side. We wouldn't want you to scare the life out of the Divider. He might resign from the all-powerful nasty wizard position and you'd get promoted!" He grinned widely and strolled on towards the hotel.

Orla stared after him, considering taking her shoes off and tossing them at the back of his big egotistical head. She restrained herself and trailed after him. Leanne was getting altogether too bossy for her liking. She'd have highlighted that to the group if it hadn't been for the very real possibility that someone might die; someone her age. Not even she had truly believed their lives were actually in danger. Now it seemed they were all under this massive threat and two of them were experiencing it alone.

Chapter 21

She shivered as she entered the hotel foyer. Ben disappeared around the corner off to the right. If the situation was reversed and it was her stuck in some spooky hole, she would hope the rest of them would be looking for her. If they didn't, she'd haunt them and make their lives such a misery, they'd wished they would have died with her. Heartened by that particular notion, she caught up to Ben. He had found the bar and was leaning into a fridge. He grabbed a couple of bottled waters and shouted out a celebratory "Yes!" when he found a few loose packets of crisps. She surveyed her surroundings and found the stillness was 'creeping' her out. All of a sudden, she wanted out of there.

"Ben. Move it."

Ben was too busy shoving as many crisps as possible into his mouth.

"Hey Spiderturd…Stop filling your fat gob and get over here."

He did and the broken crisps fell from his mouth. Wiping a hand across it, he closed one eye and regarded her with the other one.

"Why don't you kiss my fat hairy ar…? Orla! Run to me, *NOW!*"

Orla reacted immediately. She flew towards him and he dragged her over the top of the bar. They stood facing each other. She was panting and frightened. He still held both her upper arms. Afraid to look behind her, she whispered, "Is it him?"

Ben inclined his head, "Who?"

Her eyes widened. "The Divider," she whispered in terror.

He leaned in close to her. "Nah, I just wanted to tell you, your moustache needs a trim!" He pushed her away and strutted over to the exit.

Orla stood alone and felt the blood rushing to her cheeks. She glanced around ensuring no one had witnessed that rare humiliation. He was such a prat. Still, it was better than the Divider being after her so she moved quickly to the door. As she exited the front door, she saw Ben leaning against the wall with his foot resting on it. Choosing to snub him, she passed by and strode onwards to the steps. She heard his annoying humming right behind her but refused to be baited. Orla skipped up the last couple of steps to increase the distance from Ben but he matched her pace easily. He overtook her then and handed a bottle over to Dearbhla who looked much better now. Colour had returned to her face and she even seemed a bit more relaxed, if that was possible in the circumstances.

"Thanks." Dearbhla sipped the water and enjoyed the cool taste slipping down her throat. She had been parched. This was like a slice of heaven.

"What now?" Mark asked, anxious to get on with the search.

"We go put our team back together. Obviously Susie is being held against her will too so this has changed into a rescue mission. Takuma and Susie are our first priority." Her little team all agreed and oddly Orla was quiet but not wanting to tempt fate she didn't comment. Pushing herself up from the wall, she stretched and finished the last drop of water. She waited until the rest had each taken a drink of water they shared. Orla turned down a sip from Leanne who had also noticed Orla's unusual silence. She shrugged and decided to leave well enough alone. After all, Orla was more than capable of fending for herself.

Dearbhla scanned the area and evaluated that the best way to go was further along Upper Magazine Street. This was just the matter of staying on the walls and following the path ahead. Mark and Ben were leaning on the wall looking out over the area of the town called the Bogside. Long ago, when Derry~Londonderry had first been inhabited as a town, this part of it was bog land. As the town grew, so too did the need for more housing. The boys were morose as they saw the people standing down below, as in fact they were around the entire city, in a trance. No one stirred. It was quite frightening to witness. Unable to look at the vacant bodies, frozen in their enchantment, the boys joined the others in silence. In Victorian times, this part of the walkway was known as The Grand Parade. Ladies and gentlemen would have a leisurely stroll and soak up the tranquillity of a pleasant setting. Today, the Guardian of the Gates and the remaining Children of the Oak, wandered warily over the same promenade, not in peace but in the knowledge that danger surrounded them. It was waiting to pounce at any time and in any form.

They passed by buildings that were centuries old and have borne the sights of many events in the history of the city, both in good times and in bad. The anxious group drew near a stone platform on their right. It was situated in a widening of the path. The names of those lost during the siege from within the city walls, were remembered there. Dearbhla approached it with caution. She imagined it might be the concrete prison their friend was being held in. Ben and Mark flanked her every movement as she got closer to it. Inspecting it all over, they realised there was no way anyone was inside. Leanne and Orla were waiting patiently and saw their grim faces. Disappointed Leanne went to peer through the railings of St. Augustine's Church. She marvelled at the beautiful gardens and the mixture of colourful flowers that were more usual outside a cottage. It was a beautiful old church that had been there for hundreds of years. It was a neo gothic style building that caught your eye. Its feature was a circular window above the main entrance. It was divided into tiny panels of glass and reminded her of one such building she had seen in a fairy tale movie. The building was similar to the magnificent Notre Dame in Paris, although this was in no way a smaller scaled version. There was just a hint of it in the construction. It was nestled in between large, tangling trees which guarded the special place from intruders. As she pondered this, her breath hitched. Visions of the dark and sinister trees coming alive and trying to capture them filled her mind. Perhaps they could give this particular landmark a miss. Then she was struck by a thought. Scanning the small, deep rooted cemetery, she pursed her lips and knew where Takuma was being held. Turning to the others she said just that.

They all looked at Leanne and waited for her to elaborate.

"The graveyard...He's in the graveyard!" she was eagerly pointing over to the grounds of St. Augustine's.

Dearbhla moved closer to the railings and peered in. She smiled and turned to wink at the observant girl. "I think you could be right. Let's get in there and do a sweep of the graves." She watched Ben try the gate and hit it in frustration, "Locked!" Then he grabbed Mark and pushed him forward. Mark resisted at first but then realised what he needed. He edged in closer to the railings and supported himself. Ben climbed on to his back and using the rails to balance he stood up. Mark began to sway under his weight, so Dearbhla ran over to help give Ben a leg up. He heaved himself up and caught the top of the gate. As he swung his body over, he grunted with the effort. He began to lower himself by slithering down the gate. His arm muscles were protesting a lot but he never complained. Then he was able to let himself drop and landed lithely on the path.

He bowed and thanked no-one in particular. Ben caught the urgency in Dearbhla's face and ran off towards the church. He tried the door and was surprised when the latch clicked and it opened. He turned to the others and called out that he would look for the keys.

"No! Ben we don't have the time. Come back." Dearbhla cried out uselessly for he had already entered the church. She poked Mark. "Right, give me a leg up. I'm going in." She saw his startled look but he knew better than to argue. He was about to boost her when Ben came bursting out through the wooden door jangling a bunch of keys as if they were castanets.

"Got 'em," he beamed at the group and then attempted to match the key to the lock.

Dearbhla was grateful and thanked Ben for his quick-thinking.

"Ah sure, that's me, hero of the moment." As he fiddled with the many keys and tried to sort them out, he added, "Maybe I should leave this part to you. I mean you are the *Gate Master*. Does that not give you some kind of clout over keys and locks?" Then he waggled his fingers over the keys and muttered "Abracadabra". He grinned when Mark rolled his eyes until finally he found the right key. Pulling the gate open, they all filed past him.

"Any stone chest you can find, that's a tomb. The lids can be moved and it contains the coffin. Takuma could be just inside the stone part, or he could be in an actual coffin. We need to split up. Call out if you find him." Dearbhla nodded to Leanne and Orla. Mark and Ben started investigating the cemetery towards the rear.

Chapter 22

Leanne was not enjoying this. She glanced at Orla and saw that she was grimacing as she stepped around gravestones. She followed Dearbhla but remained alert to any grasping branches. She still didn't trust those trees. As they came to the first stone chest, Dearbhla kneeled beside it and listened for any sound.

"We can't take the chance that he's even conscious. Does this thing look like it has been shifted recently?"

Leanne and Orla checked around the top and the sides but it looked secure. A rustling of leaves began from the trees which were scattered inside the graveyard. Usually this sound was peaceful and relaxing but today in this setting it only created an ominous atmosphere. The girls moved on to check several other graves. None of them had been altered recently. Next they came across one nestled in the middle of three trees. It lay in front of the centre tree and the little group had to duck down to get near it. Branches hung over it almost caressing the top of the stone chamber. It had peculiar markings on its flat surface which didn't seem to fit in with the era it had been erected. Dearbhla ran her fingers lightly over them and then hissed in pain. Pulling her hand away, she said, "Orla get the boys. This is the one. He's in here."

Orla nodded and ran off to find Mark and Ben. Leanne moved in closer to Dearbhla.

"It's protected by some kind of force field." She circled the tomb and confided in Leanne.

"I don't know how we're supposed to open this. Brute force isn't going to do it. Neither is 'Abracadabra.'" Dearbhla said as an afterthought.

Leanne smiled but knew this was serious. Takuma was below them in that cold, dark tomb. She shivered in the knowledge he must be terrified. She heard voices and the other three came running up to see the tomb.

Ben and Mark looked horrified. Orla was standing a bit behind and seemed as frightened as Leanne had ever seen her.

"Let's get it off." Ben bent over and reached for the cover but Dearbhla extended her arm to prevent him. He started to argue but fell silent when he saw her expression.

"There's some kind of magic on it. It burns to touch it." Ben rocked back on his heels and considered this.

"Okay. We have to do something if Takuma's inside. Any suggestions..?" Mark asked as he perused the uncertain faces of his group.

Orla stepped forward. She sat down beside the tomb and folded her legs in a meditation like stance. Then she slowly raised her left arm and gently placed her hand on the tomb. The others gasped and watched intently, aware they were witnessing something remarkable. Orla started to shake and tremble. Smoke was rising from where her hand made contact with the stone. Then she turned her face up to the tree shielding them from the sky. The branches began to shift and extend. Dearbhla pulled Mark and Leanne back. Ben had already jumped clear and was torn as to whether he should body knock Orla out of the way. What he saw next, left him so stunned, he couldn't have reacted if his life had depended on it.

The leaf covered limbs spread out around Orla's body. They slid around her torso and lifted her tenderly up on to her feet. Her left hand remained on the stone throughout. Supporting her weight, they also began to smoothly encase the tomb. The heat produced by the spell blasted the branches and they burst in to flames that speedily changed them into black ash. The ash fell like dark snow and lay on the grey and weather beaten stone. It formed layer upon layer, soon concealing the tomb from view. Orla remained motionless and was getting coated in the ash as well. The flames didn't touch her. It was as if they burned and hurt the tree that touched it but those that held lightly on to Orla, did not burn. They didn't even smoulder. They shielded her from the fire, or perhaps it was she that shielded them. The group had inched further away as the flames had licked at the branches. Suddenly there was a loud crack as if something had been smashed. They jerked back at the sound.

"What's that?" breathed Leanne.

The ash was beginning to move and rise. In fact it resembled a figure. Fascinated, they watched as the figure straightened and as the ash fell off, it was clear what it was. As Dearbhla glanced at Orla, she could see that the girl was no longer touching the stone but in fact holding a hand. *A human hand...*

The branches slowly receded from Orla and let her go. She stumbled but the hand holding hers tightened and helped steady her. She began to cough and splutter. Her mouth felt as if she had eaten about a tonne of the dust. In that moment she was glad she didn't smoke cigarettes. There was no way she could bear walking around stinking of smoke and feeling like an ashtray. Yuck, so gross. She dropped the hand she had been clinging to and shook herself from the layers of black powder.

She heard similar coughing from beside her and thought she had better come to his aid again. She turned to Takuma and began quickly brushing off the ashes from his head and shoulders.

Dearbhla closed her mouth, which had fallen open from the shock of what she'd just seen. This day just got more bizarre as it went on. She surveyed the lumps of stone that lay strewn on the grass. They had been split apart by…well…Orla, or the tree or the ash. She wasn't quite sure which.

Leanne stood looking up at the incredible tree which had just helped both her friends. To think she had been so mistrustful of the same tree when she had first stepped in to the cemetery. She was familiar with trees being portrayed as evil and demonic in ghost stories and horror films. So naturally she had been convinced the trees would be on the Divider's team. Shaking her head, she smiled and approached Takuma.

He looked healthy enough for someone who'd been trapped inside a stone coffin for a couple of hours. That's if time even meant anything. Watches and clocks had all been brought to a standstill when the town had first come under the enchantment.

Takuma thanked Orla and tried to scrub his face clean but it was to no avail. He only succeeded in smearing the black dirt across his face. He breathed in gulps of air and closed his eyes in relief. He had lain terrified in the dark. He hadn't known where he even was. As he scanned the scene around him, he realised he had been in a graveyard; in a coffin. No wonder he couldn't move. There hadn't been one spare inch for him to do so. The whole time he had an itch in his neck and had been so tightly ensconced he couldn't lift either arm up. It had been a nightmare and he thought his life had been over. The scary thing was that he didn't know his location and supposed no-one else would either so his parents wouldn't even be able to properly mourn him. He suppressed a shiver.

Mark and Ben took turns giving him a bear hug and then there was a flurry of voices and activity. Takuma felt a bit overwhelmed. He had gone from lying immobile in complete darkness and silence into the bright daylight and enthusiastic but overpowering rescuers. Taking a step back he glanced pleadingly at Dearbhla. She picked up his wordless message.

She moved herself in between the boys and Takuma.

"Why don't you two run back and get some water and food ready in the hotel. We'll follow you over. Orla and Takuma need to get freshened up and I think we all need a chance to rest and replenish our energy reserves."

The boys nodded eagerly and raced each other out the church gate. Leanne walked over to Orla and asked her how she was.

Orla eyed her with a black smudged face and managed to croak, "Peachy. How are you?"

Leanne sighed and grasped the surly girl's arm.

"C'mon let's get you cleaned up. If you don't play nice, I'll find one of those nice tombs and plop *you* in it."

Orla grudgingly smiled but didn't reply. She allowed Leanne to steer her out the gate, thankful that she had survived that last incident in one piece. At one point she had believed she would go up in flames but an inner peace had filled her and she knew she would be unharmed...so weird.

Chapter 23

Takuma and Dearbhla stood in the empty graveyard. The teenager quietly walked over to what had been his stone prison. He kneeled down and grabbed a handful of ash. Squeezing it hard, he opened his hand and blew the loose particles watching them float down to the broken fragments of stone. Then he looked up at Dearbhla and she could see the tears in his eyes.

"I thought I was going to die," he stated simply.

Dearbhla hunkered down and put her arms around him. She was so pleased he was alive and unhurt but knew this was a hugely emotional ordeal as well. Wanting him to feel safe, she hugged him tightly.

"It's over. I promise I won't let anything happen to you. I'm so sorry. It was my fault. I should have taken better care of you."

She pulled back and looked him in the eye.

"I mean it. You are all my responsibility. We found you. I swear we'll find Susie too and then I will fight to keep you all safe." She squeezed his arms and then let go.

Takuma believed the older woman. She had an aura about her of barely contained power. He could almost feel it bubbling beneath her skin. Heaving himself up off the ground, he was overcome with a desire to put as much distance between himself and this deceptively peaceful place as possible. Dusting his clothes off once more, he turned to Dearbhla and said, "Let's catch up with the others so I can get cleaned up. Then we can formulate a plan of action."

Dearbhla smiled and led the way across the many undisturbed resting places of the dead. At least it would be peaceful again. The thought of a live human being buried there must have unsettled any spirits roaming the beautiful little graveyard. She shivered at the thought of Takuma lying there in the darkness, unable to move. Glancing up at him, she reached out and looped her arm through his, trying to reassure herself as much as him. He squeezed her tightly and then relaxed and they carried on towards the Tower Hotel. The voices of the others could be heard distantly. Ben's rang out louder than the rest. "When hunger strikes, feed the beast, eh Orla?" A roar of laughter filled the silence and it was almost possible to believe everything would be alright...*almost.*

***

Susie gripped the spire tightly and tried to wedge her body in as close as she could. It didn't help. She just slipped down even more. One minute she was standing in Austins, the next she was whisked away to a dark room. When the Divider taunted her telling her she made a good minion, she had ran at him with her fists ready to wipe the smug smile off his leery face. That's when there was a flash and she ended up on top of St. Columb's Cathedral clinging for her life to a long thin spire. That was the first problem. The second was that she didn't have long until the Divider figured out her secret. She was definitely in big trouble with Dearbhla and the others.

First thing's first. She had to get herself down from this spire before she fell to her death and didn't give Mark a chance to kill her himself. Mark's expression as he had realised her intent flashed through her mind. She shut her eyes and groaned. He had been concerned and then panicked; there had also been a moment of disappointment. After she was gone, no doubt that had switched to anger. She couldn't blame him but if only she had a chance to explain. It hadn't really been her as such. The Divider had used her, had sent one of his Shadows to invade her. Nobody had noticed. She had felt its presence immediately, coldness had crept over her bones and tiny pinpricks of pain had broken out all over her scalp. It had happened so quickly that she hadn't had time to warn her team.

She wanted to scream but had already wasted time and energy doing so for the first ten minutes she'd landed on the spire. No, no one could hear her, see her or help her. It was up to her to get out of this mess; there was no way she was going to be the one to let everybody down and be responsible for the end of life as she knew it. She opened her eyes and braced herself against the sudden breeze. It was almost as if the Divider had sensed her renewed bravery and was trying to squelch it. Well that wasn't going to happen. She was going to get off of this or die trying. Susie looked all the way down to the ground below and gulped; preferably not though! She shifted her weight to the left and manoeuvred her legs so that she could turn her full body towards the spire. Then she inched over towards the hanging part and reached out as far as she dared. Her fingertips brushed the surface but she couldn't get a grip on it. Sighing, she pushed herself forward, letting go of the spire at the same time and tried to grab hold. The sudden movement knocked her off balance and she dropped too far forward landing on her knees with her hands stretched out in front of her. Yelping she desperately scrabbled for something to cling to but there was nothing. She kept sliding forward and pitched onto her hands and knees continuing to slide down the slope of the roof.

Susie couldn't even scream. She was so shocked and terrified of what was about to happen, she just slid with her mouth hanging open waiting to reach the edge of the roof and fall to a really messy death. It seemed to be happening in slow motion and she waited for her 'life flashing before her eyes' moment. It never came. Figures, she thought. As she neared the edge and could see the sickening drop below, she uttered a silent prayer and thought of her friends. Sorry guys. Her hands reached the edge and as her weight pulled her over, she made one last attempt at holding on. It was too late. She plummeted downwards. Closing her eyes she waited for the pain.

As she fell, her feet caught on to something and brought her to a standstill. She peered down and saw her saviour was a musket lip around the base of the spire. Susie sighed in relief. Thank goodness for snipers! If the old standing ground for snipers during the famous siege hadn't been there, she would have been taty bread. Very flat mushy taty bread.

Finding her balance, she carefully jumped into the parapet and promptly fell on to her knees on legs that felt like jelly. That was too close for comfort. Susie slowed her breathing and closed her eyes. Right, enough was enough! Where was that big, oversized bully? She was ready to do battle that would make Orla proud. Preferably on his sneering face. Grabbing the edge of the wall, she pulled herself up, squinting to see any sign of friendly life. Not one person was near her. She looked over at the amazing view.

"Wow." That one word didn't even begin to express the amazing scene around the city. Life had simply been paused. Nothing stirred. People dotted out around as if statues. A flashback of every zombie movie or programme she'd ever seen filled her mind. Susie shook her head to chase them away. What chance would they have if that happened? Oh creepy. On the plus side, it really was a fantastic view. Pity no one would ever experience it, well, not without falling to their death. Now, if she could just manage to get down, preferably in one piece, she'd be more than satisfied.

Chapter 24

When Dearbhla and Takuma entered the lobby of the Tower Hotel, they were met with a cheer. Leanne handed them both a fresh bottle of water and ushered them in to sit down. A feast of sandwiches, crisps and nuts were presented on tables hastily pulled together. Dearbhla smiled and took a seat. A sense of normalcy was important. Seeing the boys bickering over who was getting the largest sandwich, achieved that and she felt herself begin to relax. She looked at Takuma and was delighted when he snatched the coveted sandwich from Ben's clutches and took a huge bite from it. Mark laughingly slapped him on the back.

"I think you deserve that Takuma. Enjoy!" He lifted a smaller one and began devouring it.

Ben was still standing in mock shock but the ever disappearing pile of sandwiches spurred him into action. He plucked two up and halfway through eating the first, admitted,

"Yeah, Tomb Boy earned it. But for one time only. Next time it'll be a battle."

Leanne giggled and Orla rolled her eyes.

"Whatever, Spiderturd, Tomb Boy didn't do a thing. He just lay there like a dead man. I did all the hard work. What do I get for my bother?" She looked disgusted. "Look at me! I'm covered in ash. Not a good trend!"

Leanne smothered a laugh while Ben eyed her and waggled his eyebrows.

"Hmm. Kind of like it myself. Makes you look...earthy...human almost!" He ducked from the flying missile she sent his way.

"Ben, why don't you take a hike? Go play with your two best friends, the heavy metal brothers. You've got the same mentality as them – thick!"

Dearbhla stood up and put a stop to their banter.

"Let's finish up and head back on to the walls. We have to find Susie and the clues. The Divider won't stop until he has everything and destroyed us all in the process."

Ben straightened to his full height, "No pressure then."

Leanne and Takuma finished their water and made their way over to Dearbhla. Mark hung back and watched the group gather at the door.

"I think we should try looking for Susie before we do anything else. She's in danger. I mean, Takuma was stuck in a tomb! She must be terrified. We have to help her." He watched the expressions of fear, anger and hopelessness flit across their faces. Mark stared back and hoped he looked as firm and confident as he wanted to because he needed to do this. Susie was out there somewhere alone. He had to...no, *they* had to help her and soon. He didn't understand why he was pushing this but there was no way in hell he was giving up on her. They were a team. Even the Spellbinder had told them to stay together.

Of course, Orla was the first to respond, "I say we leave her sorry ass."

Leanne gasped and Ben choked back laughter. Mark's jaw clenched and he waited.

"Well, she was the traitor – stole the clues and disappeared in a puff of black smoke to be with her very own bad boy. I mean, I'm not judging, he has a few hundred years on her and a face that could curdle milk, but hey, whatever floats her boat!"

Mark felt the anger coursing through him and tightened his fists. "That's crap, Orla, and you know it. She didn't have a choice. He had her possessed or something. That wasn't Susie. She would never betray us."

Leanne nodded in agreement, "He's right Orla. Of all of us, she's the bravest and would never let the Divider get his claws on the clues."

Orla snorted in disbelief and opened her mouth but Ben cut her off. "I hate to say it Mark, but the Goblin has a point. How do we know she wasn't a plant from the start?" He held out his hands to placate Mark but it wasn't working.

"For God's sake, that's rubbish. She's one of us or the Spellbinder would rat her out to us." He ran a hand through his hair, a frustrated gesture that wasn't lost on the others. Mark marched up to Takuma and Dearbhla. He glared at them in turn and asked, "What do you believe? Traitor or stitched up by Bird Boy?"

Ben snickered but earned a dirty look from his friend.

"Man, where's the love?"

Mark ignored him. "Well, which is it?"

Takuma looked him straight in the eye.

"Mark, Ben's right. We don't know her and can't be sure if her being part of the group was a set up."

Ben and Orla murmured their approval. Leanne worriedly looked at Mark; certain he was going to punch something or someone. She silently voted for Orla. She was just too selfish and catty.

Mark lowered his head in defeat. "But if you had made the same decision for me, I would be dead. So, I have to agree with you Mark, we go find Susie, we can't leave her to the Divider's fate."

Mark's head snapped up and he blew out a breath of relief. He patted Takuma on the shoulder. "Thanks Takuma", he turned to Dearbhla. She eyed them each and pinned Orla with a glare, "We don't leave anyone. We'll go find Susie. She needs us. We're all she has. Let's return to the walls and do a quick search of them. Keep alert and if you notice anything strange at all, let the group know."

Orla dragged her feet and heaved out a loud sigh. "That's the great plan? We'll never find her. She doesn't want to be found. She's cuddling up to her Lord of Darkness and laughing at our stupidity."

Mark whirled round and towered over her, "I tell you what, Orla, next time someone gets taken, we'll dump their ass. Happy?"

Orla had held her breath when he faced her. He was pretty intimidating in a bad mood. Ben grabbed her arm and pushed her towards the door.

"Yeah, we might get lucky next time and he'll kidnap you."

He turned and winked at Mark who closed his eyes and settled his temper. Then he joined the others outside. They walked up the steps at Butcher's Gate and decided to go down towards Castle Gate, the opposite direction to St. Augustine's, where they saved Takuma. It was still a bit raw for him to return to the site of his entrapment.

Takuma eased to the back of the group and surveyed his surroundings. They passed Castle Gate and neared Gunner's Bastion. Takuma stopped. His whole body seemed to become shivery. He looked at the rest of the team. They too had ground to a halt. Something was wrong. Takuma slowly rotated his body in a full circle but couldn't see anything out of the ordinary.

"This place gives me the creeps, let's keep going," Orla muttered and tried to move but found that her whole body was trembling violently.

"What's happening?" Leanne worriedly asked. "I can't m- m- m- move," her teeth chattered.

Ben turned and quietly addressed the group. "I just saw a thing... someone, I'm not sure but I know it's not good. Time to go..."

Dearbhla had paled and glanced over at the corner. This part of the walls was nicknamed Hangman's Bastion because during its construction, one of the workers got caught up in ropes and fell over the walls hanging until he gasped his last breath. It had always seemed a bit colder, a bit darker, and a bit creepier. Now, it was positively frightening. There was a coldness seeping through their bones and it was paralysing them to the spot.

Leanne shrieked out, "Did you see that? Did anyone see that?"

"What?" shouted Ben, "I don't see nada!"

"I swore I saw a f-f-figure," stammered Leanne.

"It's nothing, just keep moving," said Mark.

The trouble was they couldn't. They were frozen to the spot. The hair was rising at the back of their necks with a feeling of dread. Hearts were racing and mouths went dry.

"What the hell?" Ben jumped. "Someone just whispered in my ear."

Leanne whimpered and closed her eyes.

"Leave here," a voice boomed out, "Never pass this way again. This is my home. *Go!*"

The paralysis seemed to leave them all at once. As soon as they moved they ran forwards and got as far away from there as possible. Even when they reached Magazine Gate, they carried on and stopped at the row of cannon. They hunched over to catch their breath. Mark walked over to the cannon and smacked one with his palm. "This is useless. We're running around clueless. She could be anywhere. Where's the Spellbinder? I thought we would get help?"

The group remained quiet unsure of what they could do. Dearbhla felt the weight of the day on her shoulders. She was not a good leader. She didn't know what to do next.

Fresh out of ideas and exhausted by the stress and worry, she sat down and put her head in her hands.

"Ah, what just happened? Did we just get our behinds frozen by a ghost?" Ben asked.

Orla rolled her eyes, "Of course, genius. We disturbed the loser and he kicked us out of his sad little house."

Ben smiled. "Okay, just checking. This day is *crazzzy*."

Leanne sat down feeling deflated. It was hopeless. They were fighting all sorts of entities, pointless. Takuma sat beside her and squeezed her hand. Leanne could barely smile because he was being nice but really he felt the same. This was a lost cause.

Ben looked over at his friend who was staring out over the walls at the people in the Guildhall Square. He slowly went to him and swallowed. Somebody had to be honest. Susie was gone. They had to focus on finding the first object. After all, it was bigger than all of them. This was a fight for survival of their city.

"Mark, my wee mucker, this is harsh but Susie's AWOL and we're wasting time."

Mark flinched but didn't reply. Ben squeezed his friend's shoulder and started to turn away. Mark knew what had to be done. Then he caught a shape moving in the distance in front. He squinted and tried to decide whether it was friend or foe, ghost or god – 'cos this day was seriously messed up. What he saw made a huge grin spread over his face.

"Hey joker," called Orla. "What's tickled your funny bone?"

Ben shook his head and pointed at the approaching figure. Orla, Takuma, Leanne and Dearbhla started to stand as they saw the figure unsure of what was in store for them. Then as they too identified their visitor, they beamed and laughed. Except Orla, she smirked.

Ben held Mark by the shoulders and turned him around. "Look bud, someone's coming to say hi."

Mark looked over and couldn't believe his eyes. "*Susie?*" he whispered.

Chapter 25

Susie stopped in front of the group and shyly made eye contact with each of them. "I'm really sorry. I didn't – it wasn't... I ..." she hung her head and simply repeated, "I'm sorry."

Dearbhla gently hugged her and whispered, "Okay, we know it wasn't you. We're just glad you're safe."

Orla marched up to stand directly in front of her. She drew back her arm and slapped her face. Susie's head jerked to the right and tears filled her eyes. The others shouted in protest and Dearbhla pushed Orla away.

"Why did you do that?" she shouted at Orla. Orla walked away and leaned on the cannon.

"That was for always looking down her nose at me when all along she was the little witch that sold us down the river." She folded her arms in defiance.

Susie put her hand over her stinging cheek and rubbed it. She looked at the group pleadingly. "I swear I didn't willingly betray you. It's like I was watching myself do it and had no control over my body. I was screaming to stop but whatever was doing it was much stronger. I couldn't fight it. But I swear it wasn't me. I'd never endanger our mission."

Orla harrumphed loudly but the others ignored it. Mark stood rooted to the spot. First he felt incredulous that Susie had just casually walked up to them when he was beginning to think she was a goner. Then he was getting ready to welcome her back when Orla belted her one. He just stood there like a waste of space. Now he couldn't say a word. He felt uncomfortable. What was up with him? He eyed Ben uncertainly as he strode up to Susie and smiled charmingly, well with as much charm as Ben could manage. He noticed Susie shrinking back, wary of his intentions. Mark straightened. No way would Ben touch her. If he did, it would be the last thing he ever did. Ben mirrored Orla's stance and closeness to Susie, however, when he raised his arm, Mark lunged forward his heart in his mouth. Leanne shrieked but Ben just gently set his palm on the red handprint marring Susie's cheek. He leaned into her face and quietly said, "Don't listen to that clueless bitch. She's just jealous you got to go on an adventure without us. We all know it wasn't your fault." He winked and drew back. "So come on…spill. Where did he take you?"

Mark let out a breath of relief while Susie allowed Leanne to hug her. When Takuma did the same, she squeezed him tightly. "Takuma, I'm so glad you're okay," she smiled up at him.

"Thanks. These guys found me in a tomb in a graveyard. I know Orla was out of order with that slap but honestly she saved my life."

Susie frowned and glanced over at the surly girl who was still glaring at her. It must be just her she has a problem with. Thank goodness she hadn't been in the tomb; Orla would have danced on it.

"Ben's right. What happened you Susie?" Dearbhla asked.

Susie peered over at Mark who she was sure had made a move towards her but then hung back again. He was the only one who hadn't spoken to her. Maybe he agreed with Orla. She shrugged off his disapproval and addressed the group, "I'm not sure but one minute I was with you in Austins and the next I was clinging, for my life, to the spire of St. Columb's Cathedral."

She saw their disbelieving expressions and sighed. "I know it sounds mad but I was."

Orla snorted. "Oh, yeah, course you were. And you got down sprouting your little angelic wings and flying back to us. How sweet…"

"Shut up, Orla. Let her speak," Leanne spoke angrily.

"Exactly, I mean, if you can get all jiggy with a tree and break a stone tomb, then, maybe Susie *flew* down." Ben laughed over at Orla.

She narrowed her eyes at him and he could tell the tree remark had riled her. Good. It was still his purpose in life to bring that girl down a peg or two. She was way too opinionated. After all that was his job and there was no room for another.

"What tree?" asked Susie, confused by the banter.

The others laughed while Orla shot her a cold stare.

"Okay, never mind. I was slipping down the spire and my feet caught in a musket lip. It helped me to stop and climb into the parapet. I was stranded because I was still too high up and had no way of climbing down." She took a breath and braced herself for their reactions to this. "I was admiring the view..."

"Oh come on!" snarled Orla, "You're stuck up a cathedral and you admire the view, what a loser."

"Ignore her Susie. Go on," encouraged Dearbhla.

"Well I noticed something white in the sky. It was moving and I got really scared. I was convinced I was going to get knocked down."

"What was it?" asked a curious Leanne.

Susie smiled. "Doves," she replied.

Takuma's eyes widened in surprise, "Doves," he repeated.

Susie nodded. Orla rolled her eyes in disgust.

"God, you're even loopier than I thought. So the wee birdies came and carried you down? Aw, how very *Disney*...!"

Ben choked and coughed to cover up a laugh. Mark frowned over at Susie. He wasn't sure what to believe. It did sound a bit farfetched.

"Susie, what did the doves do?" asked Dearbhla.

Susie quickly glanced uncomfortably at Orla.

"Am…well, they sort of did what Orla said."

Orla's eyebrows lifted.

"They gathered round me. Some were under my feet and they kind of formed a spiral round my body, under my arms."

Ben couldn't hold back his laugh any longer while Orla smiled smugly.

"I knew it. *Snow White* was off playing with birds while we were saving Takuma."

Susie chose to let that remark slide and continued,

"The doves lifted me up off the parapet and flew me down to the ground. They were so gentle. It felt like I was floating. I promise you I was as amazed as you, but it happened. I knew they were sent to me to help. You know, by the Spellbinder."

Leanne had her hands clasped throughout the incredible story. Now she walked over to Susie and hugged her tight.

"Wow, that's the most amazing thing I've ever heard. But I believe you. And of course it was the Spellbinder." She turned and looked at the others. "He has our backs. He's not going to abandon us. If he can help, he will. Isn't that right, Dearbhla?"

"Yes, Leanne. It's so incredible that it must be the Spellbinder. He seems to be as equally as dramatic as the Divider. Thank goodness he's on our side."

Mark acknowledged this and said to Orla, "If we told anyone what happened between you and that tree, we'd be locked up. So why is it so hard to believe that doves would help Susie?"

He made eye contact with Susie and nodded. Susie nervously smiled at him, relieved to know he didn't doubt her. Then she quietly asked Ben, who had agreed with Mark, "What's with the tree again?"

Ben took her arm and patted it. "Never mind that, let's just accept that Orla has a thing for trees and the feelings are mutual. Go figure. I always knew she acted like she had a stick up her butt so…" he trailed off as Leanne giggled and he winked at Orla.

"Yeah, you just help *Snow White* to find her next flock of birds. I hope they peck out your eyes," she said nastily.

"Maybe but if they sense your tree like qualities, they'll land on you and we all know what birds do when they're relaxed and perched." He waggled his eyebrows at Orla.

"Eww, you're disgusting!"

"Relax, Orla. It's a natural thing. Pooping is essential for the existence of life."

"BEN! No bird will be pooping on me or I'll break its little dove neck!" said Orla, furious that everyone was defending Susie. Why couldn't they see she was playing them all? Little-Miss-Innocent…Yeah, right! Orla pushed off the cannon and sashayed past Susie. However, Susie wasn't as vulnerable as when she had first arrived back. Now she had the support of the group, Orla couldn't intimidate her any longer. Susie matched her stare for stare, curled lip for curled lip.

Ben elbowed Mark. "The showdown has begun." He nodded over to the two girls locked in a battle of wills. Mark shook his head. "Susie. Do you know where the scrolls are?"

That got Susie's attention. "Of course, *I have them*," she stated proudly. Then Susie glanced around guiltily, as if expecting the Divider had finally discovered her secret and was ready to pounce.

Chapter 26

The group watched in astonishment as she opened her jacket and lifted out four pieces of paper rolled up but flattened. Dearbhla started to laugh, relieved and delighted that they still had a chance at beating the Divider. Takuma and Ben whooped and high fived each other. Leanne hugged Mark and then Susie, who was laughing at their excitement.

Mark walked up to her and looked down into her happy eyes. "How did you get them? We saw you, or the demonic you, take the bag."

Susie grinned up at him. "You did. But what you didn't see was that just seconds before, I had stuffed them into my jacket."

Dearbhla was confused. "But, why..?"

"I know it was reckless but I had a bad feeling just before that thing took over my body. I wasn't planning on keeping you in the dark or stealing them. I felt it was the right thing to do. So I did!" She watched as Dearbhla chuckled and said,

"Your gut instinct was preparing you. That's a lesson to us all. Follow your instinct. More times than not it's right." She put her hand on Susie's shoulder and gave it a squeeze.

"Well done, Susie. We're all indebted to you for saving the scrolls."

Mark smiled at her and winked. "Let's go to work."

Susie handed the first scroll to Dearbhla, who promptly reread it aloud.

"**Deep within the bastion of those that fought before you in centuries gone by, find Meg. Free her from the wolf spitting cleansing fire and use the silver sun to feed the spectre of twisted wood.**"

They all stood in silence, each digesting the clue.

"I think we should try all of the bastions and see if we can find this 'Meg'. Maybe she's a statue or something."

Susie nodded her agreement and added, "I definitely know the name Meg. I just can't place what or where along the walls."

"Okay. Let's go back round to Gunner's Bastion. That's the closest."

A collective groan went round the group.

"What's wrong?" asked a confused Susie.

Orla smiled at her. "Nothing, Snowy, I'm sure *Ghostie* will just LOVE you." She smirked at her and walked off.

"What she means is that that particular part of the walls was uncomfortable. We were ordered away from it and none of us fancy irritating it further," explained Mark.

"Oh. Well it's too far to go the other way. We might as well take the chance. I mean, as long as it's not the Divider, there's not much a ghostly voice can do," Susie reasoned.

"Pah. You must be joking? It sounded like Mr. Stewart before he's had his morning coffee. And this bloke's been without caffeine for a helluva long time, so I'm betting it wouldn't end well. For us!" said Ben.

Takuma waded in. "We don't have a choice. At some stage we'll have to check out that bastion so let's do it now and get it over with." He looked questioningly at the others.

Ben folded first. "Alright, alright, let's go." He clapped Mark on the back, "C'mon mucker, time to face Jasper." They both laughed and led the way. Mark glanced back and saw the others follow. Orla was huffing and puffing and trailing at the back.

"I vote that Snowy and Spiderturd go first. If Ghostie gets pissed, he can eat them or whatever, and meanwhile we can scoot past without fuss."

Leanne hung back and waited for her to catch up. She walked in silence beside her, better never to turn your back on Orla. You might miss the dagger she throws your way.

"Hey, tree girl! *Jasper* might fancy you but he whispered to me he thought your personality was a bit wooden," Ben shouted out and then creased up laughing. Mark smiled as did Takuma. Dearbhla was too nervous about a showdown with Jasper to even listen to the banter. Leanne shot Orla a glance and caught her sticking her tongue out at Ben's back. Things were bad if Orla had run out of smart remarks. Geez, maybe she should be more worried than she was.

As they neared the dark and foreboding bastion, Mark and Ben slowed to a stop. They waited for the rest of their group to catch up and stood anxiously to see what would happen next. Dearbhla made her way to the top and focused her gaze on the small seemingly innocuous piece of pathway that was the Gunner's Bastion. A cold shiver passed through her body and she half expected to be pushed away by their earlier acquaintance. She held her breath but seconds turned into minutes and still nothing presented a threat to their presence.

Ben stood looking over at the street running parallel to the wall.

"I was always told about the 'White Lady' who haunted Magazine Street but nobody ever mentioned a seriously hacked off dude roaming around." He turned to Mark. "Do you remember my Aunt Marnie talking about her?"

Mark thought of the kind woman who had raised Ben as if he was her own son when his own mother had died while he was only a child of four. Ben was too young to remember the younger sister of his aunt, who had been her universe. Mark recalled how Mrs Cooke had recounted many local ghost stories including the 'White Lady', who was often spotted wandering the walls late at night, seemingly forlorn and lost looking for something or somebody. Nobody knew for sure. Perhaps searching for her love killed in battle or for a child cruelly ripped away from her mother's protection. Mark offered his version of the tale and everyone stood enraptured.

"Well if it's true, we'll not see her 'cos it's bright daylight. If she only comes at night, that's one less ghost to worry about," declared Takuma.

"If she helped us that would be great…maybe she's like a protective mother," said Leanne.

"We don't have time to waste over her. Let's just keep walking and get through this bastion and move to the next one," Dearbhla announced.

They all agreed and tentatively made their way past the heavy atmosphere of where they stood. Just as they made it to the other side, a cold wind blew up from nowhere. Their eyes darted from the cloudless sky to the leaves and debris shuffling about their feet. Before Dearbhla could turn and shout a warning, she was lifted bodily off the ground and flung backwards into the bastion. She landed heavily and grimaced as her right leg and shoulder had taken the brunt of the fall.

As Mark ran back to help her, he was knocked to the side. He swung around to catch his balance and was pushed back into the wall where he was lifted and pinned there with a vice like grip around his throat. He kicked out at thin air. Grasping at his own throat to try to remove the deathly grip he found nothing. Coughing and gasping for air, he struggled frantically. Ben shouted and ran towards him but was thrust forward by a huge force and fell flat on his face.

Takuma and Susie sidestepped his body and rushed over to Mark. They each held a leg and tried to support him as his struggles weakened and he tried to drag breaths into his burning lungs. Orla was helping Ben up and they both went to Dearbhla, who still hadn't gotten up from where she'd been thrown. A trickle of blood dripped down the side of her head and Orla gasped when she saw the sickly pallor of their leader. She felt a pang in her belly. Once again, they'd been faced with danger and this time it seemed no one was exempt. Her fear reached new levels and she looked at Ben for some reassurance but he looked as worried as she felt. He put his arm around Dearbhla's shoulders and his other at her waist. Orla did the same and they gently lifted her up to a sitting position.

"Orla, stay with her. I need to help Mark." He hurried off to his friend, who was making horrible gasping sounds. Orla kneeled beside Dearbhla and took a tissue from her pocket. She wiped the trail of thin blood oozing down the right side of her face. Dearbhla was dazed and felt nauseous. She tried to move her leg and grimaced at the pain. Orla stilled her with the palm of her hand.

"Take it easy Dearbhla…chill. You need to keep still. That was a really crazy fall you had."

Dearbhla looked at the young girl and felt a smile breaking through. She winced in pain.

"A fall…? Orla, I was kicked into touch by Jasper the freaking unfriendly ghost!"

Orla smirked, "Told ya. We should have gone the other way but sure no one ever listens to me!"

Dearbhla rolled her eyes but winced again. Even that simple movement hurt. She groaned and leaned forward.

"Oh crap, you're not going to hurl all over me are you?" Orla stretched away from her even though she still supported her.

Dearbhla didn't answer. She gritted her teeth and turned slowly to see how Mark was getting on.

Ben was screaming at the phantom that clearly had the upper hand. Mark was beginning to lose consciousness, his eyes were drooping closed and his head was rolling forward.

"Come on you big chicken! Face us like a man!" Ben shouted desperately. He couldn't punch anyone or pummel the coward that was using brute force but was invisible to fight. Ben cursed under his breath. He looked down at Takuma and Susie who were frantically trying to support Mark's weight but it wasn't giving him any relief. As he turned a complete sweep of his surroundings, he began pleading.

"Okay big guy. We get it. We really pissed you off. Sorry. Do you hear me? *SORRY*," he yelled out the last apology at the top of his lungs. Mark's eyes widened and then fluttered closed. Ben lost it. "C'mon, Jasper..! Sorry. Sorry. Sorry!" He spun around, punctuating each word with his fist.

"Show.Your.Ass.Now…!"

Finally a breeze blew up and Ben got his wish. He was thrust backwards and slid down the wall beside where Dearbhla lay.

Chapter 27

A tall figure walked forward and stopped just before Leanne, who was shaking from head to foot. He was dressed in clothes that were tattered and worn with age. His shoulder length hair was straggly and tangled; his brown beard was unkempt and overgrown; his eyes were a stormy grey and he glared down at the frightened girl. Leanne backed away from him and gulped. Feeling the fury coming off him in waves, she met his stare. He was one seriously mad ghost.

As she watched fascinated, his image shimmered once, twice and then settled into a transparent form. It flickered again and to her surprise became solid. She muttered a quick "Sorry, we're so sorry," and closed her eyes as he leaned over her. He lightly pushed her and her body swayed with the movement. Then he gripped her upper arm. She tensed waiting to end up sprawled beside Ben and Dearbhla. Her eyes shot open when she was lifted gently and seemed to float over to Mark. She was set beside him. She looked up into his angry face and saw his lips move but she didn't catch what he said.

"Wh-wh-what did you say?" she stuttered.

His eyes flashed but he repeated, "I accept your apology but only because you are family. I guard the many souls within these walls lost as we laid brick and stone. Our bodies lay hidden in darkness, part of the very walls themselves. We worked here, died here and were buried here. This is our home. You should leave now before some of the restless catch up to you and are not as merciful as I."

He stared at Leanne one more time. Then he snapped out of focus and disappeared completely. Mark's lifeless body dropped to the ground. Leanne stood in shock and was still reeling from the comment that the ghost thought she was his family. Confused she looked over as Takuma and Susie tried to wake up Mark. Takuma leaned into Mark's face and could hear his light but raspy breathing. Purple marks stood out around his neck. Susie took off her jumper and folding it into a pillow she slid it under his head. She rocked back on her heels and sighed with relief as his eyes opened warily. He looked up as Ben made his way to him and hunkered down.

"Hey, big lad...thought we'd lost you there. You okay?"

Mark tried to talk but could only manage a croak. He lifted a hand to the tenderness around his throat and tried to clear it with a cough. Wincing at the sharp pain that shot through his throat, he gave up and winked at Ben. That was enough to satisfy his friend that he was okay. He raised himself onto his elbow and acknowledged Takuma and Susie with a nod and a grateful smile. Then with a bit of help from Ben, he stood up on shaky legs. He still felt a bit lightheaded. After all, he'd nearly been choked to death. That was definitely a first. Not one he'd care to repeat any time soon. He leaned against the wall and closed his eyes as a wave of dizziness hit him.

Leanne had walked back to Orla and helped her lift Dearbhla, who seemed to be able to move without as much pain. She still held her leg but the cut on her head was cleaned and thankfully it hadn't been deep. Orla broke the silence.

"So, turns out you're Jasper's, like, great, great, great, great granddaughter. I always knew you were a lightweight but go figure. Ghost blood in your veins; that's pretty messed up. I bet you can 'see the dead', you know, freaky stuff!"

Leanne ignored her and spoke to the others. "I never saw that man before. He doesn't even look like anybody in my family. Why would he say that I'm his family?"

"Maybe he's a really distant ancestor but being…er…dead he can sense family. Don't be worried. Being his family saved Mark. In fact, it saved all of us so let's be grateful," said Susie.

"Yeah, I think we should get going before we overstay our welcome," added Takuma.

They all murmured in agreement. Orla looked Leanne up and down and put her finger on her bottom lip.

"I disagree. I reckon you're very like him Leanne. Same ratty hair and terrible fashion sense! Plus, you're not great at making friends. And let's face it; your da's da has a bit of trouble in that department." She sniggered and flipped her blonde hair over her shoulders. Leanne was saved from responding as Ben commented.

"*Your da's da..?* What the hell, Orla?! You're so thick. That would means it's her granda. Do you even know how old these walls are?"

Orla looked at him blankly. Ben tutted and grabbed her arm impatiently.

"Look at them, Orla. He said he helped build them. They're four hundred years old!!"

She tugged her arm back. "Whatever. You're so pathetic. Who cares? Just silly details… I don't want a history lesson. Anyway, it still doesn't change the fact that she's a, you know…" she nodded over at Leanne.

Ben raised his eyebrows. "What …Orla? Enlighten us."

"She's a septic…okay?"

Ben burst out laughing. "You are clueless." He walked on to catch up with Leanne and helped her with Dearbhla who was still limping.

"What?" screeched an exasperated Orla.

Susie brushed past her. "I think you mean she's a psychic."

Orla screwed her face up. "You know what I mean. She's got a fifth sense, the freak."

"Sixth sense you idiot," shouted Ben over his shoulder. "Now shut it before I force feed a dictionary down your throat, 'cos you need it!"

He grinned when he heard her snort and mutter under her breath. He could just make out 'Spiderturd' among whatever it was she was spouting.

"Quit your muttering and get a move on, Woodworm!"

That shut her up. Satisfied, he looked down at Dearbhla.

"Where to, boss?"

She smiled up at him. "Let's just make it to the next bastion. I think it's past Butcher's Gate and on past St. Augustine's."

The determined group moved on past Castle Gate without incident although they were a great deal warier and sensitive to their surroundings. Leanne was still shocked that one of her ancestors was haunting the walls. She sighed as she thought about Orla's snarky comments. Orla wouldn't let this one go. She'd feed off it forever to keep putting her down. Despair washed over her. Everyone she knew would be informed of her ancestor's less than friendly introduction. Then she remembered how Ben had retorted to every comment she threw out. A grin spread over her face and she felt a bit lighter. She'd just have to come up with a few tree nicknames of her own. She caught up with Dearbhla who was limping slightly from where she'd been thrown. Glancing down at her leg, she took a deep breath, "Dearbhla...I-I'm...."

"Don't Leanne!" Dearbhla cut in. "It's not your fault, I'm okay. Stop taking the blame for everything. You're just making it easier for people like Madam over there to get their digs in." She smiled but hoped Leanne would take her advice on board. The young girl needed to be a bit tougher and not allow herself to be walked on by people who'd more than happily dance a jig on her head while they were at it. Only she could put a stop to it and the sooner she realised that the better.

Leanne nodded and fell into step beside her.

Chapter 28

Takuma and Susie were flanking Mark, who was still a bit unsteady on his feet. Susie kept flicking anxious looks up at him until he relented, "What's wrong, Susie?" He didn't look at her, just kept walking.

"Nothing...but how are you? You nearly... you know…"

Takuma glanced at the two and decided to leave them to it. He quickened his pace to match Leanne and Dearbhla's.

Mark shrugged it off. "No big deal. I'm fine so don't worry."

She looked unconvinced but decided not to push it. "Okay. Just tell us if you're feeling tired."

Mark continued staring ahead and then muttered, "Okay, will do. Er…thanks for helping."

Susie smiled and they walked along in affable silence.

Ben and Orla were walking right behind. Ben was rolling his eyes at Orla as she feigned being sick. Ben went to the other side of Mark and threw an arm around his shoulders. "Well, my wee mucker, what was it like?"

Mark frowned down at his friend who was only an inch shorter than his six foot height. "What do you mean?"

Ben sighed dramatically, "I mean, nearly getting strangled to death by Jasper."

Mark shot him a dirty look. "He was no *Jasper*. His grip was like iron. I couldn't budge him. Jasper! Pah."

"Aw sick man. Sorry. I know he was bigger and *badder* than his friendly bro. He was, after all, a Derry ghost! What did you expect…chocolate and roses?" Ben laughed at his own joke and hung on to Mark, who was trying to shrug him off.

"Get off!" Mark was getting more aggravated by his friend.

Ben chuckled and gave him a last squeeze before letting go. They passed by the Tower Hotel on their left and looked longingly at it. If only they could rest again but there was no time. Every minute they wasted was another chance for the Divider and his minions to be a step ahead. As they reached the Grand Parade, the stillness was more powerful than any noise. The group slowed down fearful of what was about to happen. As they shot quick glances around, the silence became palpable. Tension filled the vacuum and it was hard to move.

"Ahem. Does anybody feel that?" asked a nervous Leanne.

"Yip, you can bet we're not going to like it so get ready my boyos." Ben shuffled his feet and looked pointedly at each of his friends. They all nodded. When it came to Dearbhla, she leaned a hand on Leanne's shoulder as she was still a bit sore. Then she added, "Keep together. We're stronger together."

"Okay boss, bring it on!" encouraged Ben.

They waited until the air was buzzing with static. As they watched, the most amazing scene unfolded before them. Looking straight in front of them the pathway widened. Trees lined the left side, thirteen to be exact; thirteen oak trees, to represent the thirteen Apprentice Boys, who had locked the gates at the beginning of the siege of Derry. On the right were the walls and a plinth which used to hold a statue of Rev. George Walker who died in the Battle of the Boyne. This was the broadest part of the walls and so called 'The Sabbath Walk' or 'The Parade Walk'. Unbelievably, the group were being treated to a rare view of what took place here in the 17th century. Ladies strolled at a leisurely pace with their beautifully detailed dresses and twirling their delicate parasols as they conversed with each other. Occasionally they stopped to speak with an acquaintance and then they would continue on with their ladylike posing. Once they reached the end of the walk, they turned a dainty heel and strolled back again.

The group stood on fascinated by the spectacle that had been caught by time and woven in front of them. No-one uttered a word as they absorbed the little memory replayed by the trees or the walls that had first captured them hundreds of years before. It was precious, but like the ripples of water caused by a single stone they would soon begin to fade. At the side of the walkway were a cluster of four to five young children. Such a contrast to the 'high society' ladies, their clothes were drab and torn, worn from hard labour. They were dishevelled and dirty, bones jutting out from almost translucent skin. Skinny elbows and gangly legs. The ladies sent sidelong glares their way filled with distaste and disgust. Some were even so bold as to raise their fingers and hold them underneath their nose as if the children's very presence offended their senses. The children's voices grew louder so their spectators were able to hear the words.

"Go on youse oul cats," shouted a child about eight years old. He had freckles sprinkling his nose and cheeks. His curly red hair sprung around his angular face, giving him an almost angelic appearance, if it were not for the abuse he hurled at the strutting ladies.

"Ugly cows...ooh look at me!" He had his friends falling about laughing, as he mimicked the 'oul cats'. He jumped onto the 'catwalk' and swished his imaginary skirt around his legs. Then he puffed out his chest and stuck his nose in the air. He took long strides and marched up beside them with cockiness and stuck his finger over his nose.

"Yuck. Smell youse oul cats, covered in oils and potions. Like witches youse are. Go get your brooms."

As he kept his friends entertained and the ladies scattered away from his offensive body, a gentleman who'd been accompanying his wife, ran over to him, and clipped him on the side of the head.

"Away with you lad, before I have you thrown into the workhouse!"

The young boy smarted at the hit to his head, stuck his tongue out and ran off back to join his friends who were laughing uproariously and were slapping him on the back for his entertainment to their miserable existence; days working and trying to scavenge enough food to get them by. The image began to fade just as quickly as it had come. Suddenly all the group could see was the empty Grand Parade. Surprise was on each of their faces as they turned and gave each other 'did you just see that' looks. The tension dissipated from the air and they could move easily again. Ben was the first to break the shocked silence.

"That wee fella! Now, he must be my da's, da's, da's da 'cos he has *my* sense of humour."

Orla snorted. "Yeah he looked like you too except I think he has more brains. Now, those women; one of them was bound to be related to me; pure breeding and class."

Leanne groaned. Orla truly did love Orla.

Ben disagreed. He walked up to her shaking his head. "No, no, no, Miss High and Mighty. Yes, you may be descended from one of them but only because you're an oul cat too! Oh and what was the other thing my great, great, great, great granda said…" He looked round questioningly at the group.

Mark laughed back at him, "I believe it was ugly cow!"

Ben hooted out, "That was it! Sweet…aw Orla don't get mad. You couldn't help your animal '*breeding*,' " spluttered Ben in between laughing and emphasising the word breeding.

Orla scowled at both Ben and Mark, "You're such losers! Go and jump off the walls, Ben, and see if it improves your looks 'cos your face is seriously annoying me."

Ben tutted, "Now, now Orla don't get nasty. I'm only stating a fact. You however are taking it personally."

"Oh grow up!" shouted an exasperated Orla.

Ben continued laughing with Mark, "Meow! Go find your litter tray!" He managed to choke out. That sent Mark into another fit of laughing; more so, at Orla's expression, than the actual words.

Dearbhla stifled a smile and tried to diffuse the potentially childish tantrum that was about to ensue, "Okay guys I think we need to get back on track. I don't understand the relevance of seeing what we just witnessed but we need to figure out our next move."

Chapter 29

Takuma was still grinning at the exchange between Ben and Orla. Glancing at Orla's murderous glare, he decided to help out Dearbhla as Ben kept meowing at Orla and licking his 'paws' whilst batting his eyelashes at her.

"Er, yeah, I think we just stumbled upon a time relapse of that particular event but there were no clues. I'd say it was more a privilege bestowed on us by the walls themselves."

This sobered up Ben, who twisted around to look in amazement at the usually sensible boy.

"What the hell? Was that you or were you possessed by the Spellbinder or Septic Sue?" Ben asked cheekily.

Takuma shrugged, "I just mean that places have memories. Have you ever been in an old house and got a strange feeling, maybe a cold patch or a feeling that makes the hairs on the back of your neck stand up? That's an event – a recording of feelings of some kind of event that took place in it, usually unpleasant but I believe you can have happy houses as well."

Orla predictably rolled her eyes and groaned, "Oh geez another Jasper relation. Get a grip, Takuma."

Susie thought it actually made sense and asked a question.

"That's interesting Takuma. So do you think that the houses or places are not so much haunted as just holding on to bad memories or feelings?"

Takuma thought it over before answering, "Partly, although I'd say our experience at Gunner's Bastion would definitely bring authenticity to the existence of…well…ghosts. Maybe it's a case of whichever presence is the strongest is the one that breaks through."

Leanne was a bit confused. "So does that mean we saw a load of ghosts just now?" she asked.

Takuma shook his head.

"No. They had no awareness of us being there. I believe we shared a memory of this place but no more. These people had no clue we were there and didn't try to engage with us; either friendly or otherwise."

Leanne nodded with understanding. Takuma looked at the rest of the group who had fallen into contemplative silence. Mark winked at him to show he supported his theory. Well, at least one of them didn't think he was crazy. Seeing Orla's frank disbelieving look, he concluded that she had put him in a definitely 'crazy' category. Oh well, he wasn't pinning much hope on her anyway.

"That sounds like a strong theory, Takuma. So I think if it hasn't got any bearing on what we are doing, we should go straight to the Double Bastion now. That's our next step on this route." She looked round at all their sceptical faces and spread her hands out in front of her. "Come on guys. Are you ready?"

Leanne muttered an 'okay' while Susie pulled a face and gave an aura of 'maybe'. Mark looked undecided and Ben was still staring at Takuma as if he'd lost his mind. It was Orla who surprised them by letting out a loud sigh and walked over to Dearbhla. "Let's get this over with. Ghosts or not, we're still in this mess and we need to get out of it."

As they looked blankly at her she grumbled under her breath and losing patience shouted, "C'mon. Hurry up. Have you lost the power of movement?" She shoved Ben and strode off towards St. Augustine's.

Ben growled at her back and started after her. "Seems that you got rid of your hairball; such a rousing speech. *Not!*"

Mark followed as did the others. Dearbhla took up the rear to make sure there was nothing coming from behind them to cause any damage. She was stunned that out of everyone, it had been Orla to support her. They reached the end of the Grand Parade and passed the Walker's Plinth on their right side. Memories of their urgent search for Takuma came flooding back. They'd tried the Plinth first before seeing St. Augustine's graveyard.

As they passed by, Ben opened his mouth to comment on Orla being reunited with her wooden boyfriend, when she beat him to it.

"Any snide comments, Ben, and I swear in front of all these witnesses, that I'll flay your skin off and feed you to the Divider myself."

Ben held his hands defensively in front of his body. "Hey, I never said a word." He looked over at Mark. "She's one touchy feline."

Mark smiled but didn't trust Orla not to do him some bodily damage so he chose not to comment. Ben laughed at

Orla's dirty look and wiped the smug look off his face. Even he knew when to draw the line; most times.

Leanne glanced anxiously at Takuma who tried to suppress a shiver as they passed the tomb where they'd freed him from. As she peered through the fence, she could see the piles of grey ash and the remains of branches hanging limply from the imposing tree that had helped them, as incredible as that sounds. The broken halves of the stone tomb lay amidst the ash. Leanne reached out her hand and slipped it through into Takuma's hand. He squeezed her fingers lightly and managed a weak smile. He truly hated the reminder of lying in that dark hole in the ground, unable to move, unaware of where he even was. He was grateful for Leanne's warm hand in his; it pulled him from the terror he felt and the loneliness that had swept through him.

Dearbhla had sped up her tread when they drew parallel to the lovely old Gothic style church in order to reassure Takuma but slowed up when she saw Leanne tune into his discomfort and take his hand. She smiled. Maybe this group would do alright after all. They all started off as separate pieces but thankfully seemed to be fitting in nicely together. The more they bonded, the stronger they'd be as a united front for the Divider. She just had a feeling that if they could keep together and watch each other's backs, they could possibly be unstoppable.

For the first time since this had begun, she felt the first tendrils of hope uncurl in her chest. She watched as Orla, Ben and Mark arrived at the couple of steps leading up to the Double Bastion.

Chapter 30

This bastion was actually two originally separate ones that were then joined together and hence the name the Double Bastion. It is the largest of all the bastions and has a beautiful view out over the once boggy marshland of the original isle of Derry years back in the sixth century. Now called the Bogside, it is home to numerous murals on houses including a poignant one of a dove with wings represented as oak leaves. Rainbow coloured squares are the background to the dove and it all signifies a new day; an important peace mural.

On the Bastion itself, sit two cannon proudly angled to show them off to their best appearance. The group scattered and searched for anything that looked out of place or a stone that perhaps didn't quite fit where it was.

Dearbhla grasped Susie's arm and pulled her back from the stones she was poking and prodding at.

"No. We need the clue. Take it out and read it to us again."

She called to the others to listen to Susie. They all gathered close. Ben of course had chosen to sit spread legged on a cannon. Ben wiggled his eyebrows at Leanne, "Feels familiar."

"Ewww Ben!"

Orla snorted. "Hah. You wish. It's the biggest thing you'll ever…"

"Enough Orla," shouted a desperate Dearbhla, "Too much information, Ben."

Ben slid a glance to Mark who was choking back a laugh. Then he bowed to Dearbhla, "By all means, continue."

Dearbhla ignored him and encouraged Susie to read out loud. She cleared her throat.

 "**Deep within the bastion of those that fought before you in centuries gone by, find Meg. Free her from the wolf spitting cleansing fire and use the silver sun to feed the spectre of twisted wood.**"

"Okay, well there's no chick called Meg here so we need to move on," reasoned Ben.

"No, I don't think Meg is a person but I can't remember. It's in the back of my head but….ah, it's so frustrating," exclaimed Susie.

Mark frowned over at Dearbhla. "Susie's right. There's something about Meg and the walls but I'm not sure how they're connected."

Takuma agreed but was no help either. Orla wandered over to some signs that held historical information about the walls and quotes from famous poems and songs written about the city. She scanned down until she found exactly what she needed. Then she sauntered back over to the others.

 "Ahem. Don't fret freaks. The steam is just about pouring out of your ears from the amount of brain power you're using." She smirked cockily at them and settled herself against one of the cannon.

"I know who Meg is...or rather *WHAT* Meg is!" She paused and enjoyed the perplexed looks on their faces. Leaning forward she was thrilled with having all the attention on herself. Then she announced, "Meg is one of the cannon." She leaned back and folded her arms across her chest in a gesture of satisfaction. They exchanged the usual shocked responses of 'What?' 'No way' and, 'How do you know?' Feeling empowered, she inspected her fingernails to draw out the tension of the situation as well as basking in the feeling that she was the one with the knowledge. Oh, it felt so good. She finally looked up when Ben made a move to get up off the cannon. Knowing he was going to head to the signs she held up a hand to stop him. He stopped half way up and plonked down again.

"Well, go on, tell us how you know. What are you waitin' for, a brass band?!"

Orla narrowed her eyes at him, "Well, if any of you had bothered to read those things," she turned and pointed over at the signs, "Then you'd know."

"Okay, almighty and all powerful one tell us the craic," drawled Ben.

Orla smiled and put them out of their misery. "It says that one of the cannon is called 'Roaring Meg'. It was a gift from London in 1642 and was used in the 1689 siege."

Dearbhla laughed and looked at Orla with admiration.

"Well done, Orla! Now we need to figure out, which of these two beauties is Meg."

Leanne mused out loud, "I wonder why they called it Meg?"

Mark, Ben and Takuma shared amused looks with each other. Ben jumped down from the cannon, straightened his clothes and spoke to the other two boys. "Let me do the honours, lads." Clearing his throat, he donned a serious expression and rolled his shirt sleeves up. "Meg's a woman's name. They named it 'Roaring Meg' 'cos all women do is moan and groan-perfect name for a cannon; the ultimate mouth!"

Both Mark and Takuma laughed. Dearbhla scoffed and retorted, "No she was named after a woman because Meg, like us, is filled with fire and can bring a man to his knees!"

Leanne and Susie laughed and muttered agreements while Orla looked at Ben and said, "The cannon are a deadly weapon, just like some of us." She shot a disgusted look at Leanne who tutted at her pointed remark and stopped Ben with a glare. Ben stood back and grinned at her.

"You know Orla, some of us don't want to actually kill a man to get him, it's enough to use our charm and personalities – but then I suppose you have to get one whatever way you can so to take a phrase of yours, whatever floats your boat." Orla stood with her mouth hanging open at the usually weakest target of the group.

"Oh, that was sick, Leanne!" Ben slapped her on the back and theatrically laughed behind his hand as he neared Orla. She turned her head and shot him a murderous glare.

"Is that how you trap your boyfriends, Orla? You stun them with a glare and take them down when they can't move. Lethal! *Ouch!*" Ben hissed as Orla punched him full force in the stomach. He doubled over in pain and dragging in a ragged breath, he raised his head. "Uncalled for, I'm telling you now; I ain't going there with you so forget about it."

Orla shrieked in irritation and joined the others to search for some kind of hidden button or drawer in the cannon. Dearbhla paused in her search and considered the clue.

"Wait. We have to free Meg and 'use the silver sun to feed the spectre of twisted wood.'"

They all stopped and listened intently to their leader. Dearbhla snapped her fingers and shouted excitedly, "I've got it. All of the cannon have silver markings on them, like a stamp or something." She walked over to Meg as she looked for the symbol. She closed her eyes briefly in relief as she found a silver engraved sun.

"Here it is." She lightly ran her fingers over the symbol and waited for the others to gather around. The excitement was palpable. Ben was the first to break the sense of amazement.

"Am, not that I want to be the one to break the mood, but, ah," he looked around warily, "Should we not be watching our backs. If we've cracked it, then Bird Boy's going to be showing up to reveal to us his whole lot of nasty."

The others began to get more nervous and shifted their positions so they could also see anything that could make an attack. Curiosity won out and their gazes fixed on to the silver sun gleaming as if it held the treasures of the world.

Mark urged Dearbhla on, "Go on Dearbhla. See if it moves or presses in."

They all waited anxiously, almost holding a collective breath.

Chapter 31

Dearbhla wiped both of her slick hands on the legs of her trousers. She leaned over and carefully ran her fingers along the outer shape of the small symbol. Taking a deep breath, she tried to push it in but it didn't budge. Then she tried to get her fingernails under it to attempt to pry it out but nothing happened. Sighing, she leaned back and looked at the faces watching her expectantly. No one uttered a word of advice nor challenged her to try. In fact they looked a bit crestfallen. All this energy and hard effort, risking their very lives and they were going to fail at the first object.

It was within their grasp yet it never seemed further than at that moment. Dearbhla cleared her throat.

"Okay, here goes again. We have to remember this cannon is centuries old and it won't just come off in hands otherwise it would have been discovered years ago."

The group murmured in agreement and Ben still flicked anxious glances around because he wanted enough time to shout a warning if necessary. Dearbhla used both her hands for sheer strength but she couldn't see anything that would shift or lift in anyway. Frustrated she rocked back on her heels and groaned, "Ugh! I thought it would be hard but not impossible."

Takuma shifted in front of her, "Let me try. We can't give up. Like you said, it's really old. We need to have patience."

He twisted the sun, tried to jam his fingernails under it and then put his full weight on it to test if it would move even a fraction but to no avail.

"Wait. Remember, there are two cannon here. We're not even sure this one is Meg. Maybe it's the one on the right," Leanne pointed out sensibly.

They all hurried over to the next cannon and located the same symbol in its identical position to the other. This time, Mark stepped forward and began to poke and prod and pull at the silver shape. Once again, there wasn't any sign of movement and the disappointment spread through the group. Mark began looking around the bastion for something to use as a lever.

"Spread out. Find me something to lever underneath the sun so I can use more force."

They did as he asked and keenly collected any object or stone they could find to help him. None of them lingered too long as it was still unsafe and they recognised the need to do this as quickly as possible. They threw all the objects in a heap in front of the cannon and Mark began sifting through to find the most suitable one he could use.

"Jackpot!" he exclaimed. He grabbed a flat sided piece of wood and jammed it in as far as he could beneath the sun. Sheer brute strength helped him actually burrow under the edges. Some of the wood split and he felt splinters entering his skin but he ignored the sharp pain. He grunted with the effort but didn't give up. Leaning his weight down heavily he swore he saw a slight movement. Blood began to trickle down his fingers and over his hand but still he pushed down on his makeshift lever. The wood strained under the pressure and he knew he didn't have much time before it snapped completely. He tried to distribute his weight over the wood to give him a bit more time. Then unbelievably, he heard a sound that told him he was doing the right thing. He could hear the others laughing incredulously and egg him on. He knew the wood was going to split apart so he gave it one last push and shouted out. The wood cracked apart and stopped the laughter immediately.

"Aw crap. We're stuffed then," muttered a deflated Ben.

Mark was breathing heavily with the strain. He turned around and a huge grin broke out over his face. "You need more faith in your mucker, Ben." Spreading his bloodied hands, he displayed the sun. The group gasped as they saw that the silver sun has been pried upwards. Now, it stood out proudly, apart from the cannon into which it had been sunken.

"Wow. I can't believe you did it." Dearbhla grabbed him into a hug. "You did it Mark!"

Mark laughed and hugged her back. Ben eyed him wickedly and shouted, "High five, man," and swung his arm through the air towards Mark's outstretched hand. A look of horror passed over his face before Ben stopped just before making contact with his injured hand. Ben laughed loudly. "You should have seen your face!"

Mark laughed back at him but the throbbing had started in his hands and he really needed to get out all of the splinters. Dearbhla gently held both of his hands out and inspected them. She sighed, "Mark, we need to get those splinters out before they go any deeper. But I can't do it yet. I need some tweezers and some medical supplies so we can clean them up."

Mark nodded, "I can bear it for another while." He turned to Ben, "Next time you can do it."

Ben scoffed and pointed at himself, "What? And ruin these baby soft hands of mine. Oh, no. If there's any more heavy lifting its Takuma's job now you're out of action."

Ben looked at Susie, "Kind of macho isn't he?" He winked at her and watched the blush rise up her cheeks. Then he glanced cheekily at Orla and put on a woeful expression, "Ach Orla I'm wile sorry."

She looked at him perplexed. "What are you on about now, you eejit?"

Ben sauntered over beside her and wrapped his arm around her shoulders, "Aw c'mon. You can't hide it from me. I know you're raging Mark hurt your boyfriend but you have to move past it, Orla."

She pushed his arm away and shoved him back, "Get lost Spiderturd or I'll make sure some of those splinters end up somewhere on your body that'll have you picking them out for months afterwards."

"Oooh touchy aren't we! Never mind, Orla we'll find you another tree soon. It'll ease your pain."

Ben ducked to miss the punch she swiped at his head. Leanne had distanced herself from the banter as she knew Orla would be out for her blood if she so much as cracked a smile. She stood beside Dearbhla and Takuma as they studied the amazing sight of the silver sun standing up from Meg. It was held up by a cylinder of steel that disappeared into the body of the cannon. It was clear that it was an old mechanism built into it during the time of its manufacture hundreds of years ago.

Takuma glanced up at Dearbhla, "I think there's more to it."

Dearbhla nodded and peered into the cylinder, "It looks like it can be turned."

Takuma leaned in as well, "Yes, you're right. Try it," he encouraged.

Dearbhla reached over and very carefully began to twist the sun in a clockwise direction. As it completed one full rotation it locked in place and she couldn't turn it any further. She looked at Takuma who shrugged in defeat. "Maybe it needs to go anticlockwise," she thought to herself. She began to twist it carefully in the opposite direction and as it reached back to where it had started she hoped it wouldn't lock again. It didn't. Feeling no resistance she continued to turn it. When it reached one full rotation, a click sounded. Dearbhla smiled up at Takuma who had an excited glint in his eyes.

"Keep going," he urged.

The rest of the group gathered around again and she could sense their excitement. She felt it as well. Finally, they were getting somewhere. Hopefully, if they got this first object, solving the remaining two clues would be much easier.

A tight band of exhilaration gripped her, her senses prickled alive and she could almost hear her own heartbeat as excitement increased her pulse rate. Her breathing came in short gasps, as she turned it again. She could feel the resistance increasing in the cylinder and knew they were closer to unveiling the object. As it clicked out loudly she inhaled a deep breath. She jiggled the cylinder to see if it would turn any further but at her touch, it locked into place and a louder clicking sound echoed around them. It appeared that something had been loosened and popped out of place. She searched over the top of the cannon but couldn't see anything.

"I found it. Oh my God. It's here. It's here," cried out Leanne. They watched as she hunkered down at the underbelly of the cannon, where a small hidden compartment had been uncovered. A flap had been removed and the contents it had sheathed for hundreds of years lay in wait. Leanne looked to the group for silent permission. They nodded encouragingly at her and she gingerly kneeled down beside it.

Chapter 32

Reaching in with her left hand, she leaned on the cannon with her right. She felt around and her fingertips brushed against something smooth and cold. It felt about the size of a medallion and she enclosed it into the palm of her hand to lift it out. She transferred it to her left hand and checked that the compartment was empty but there was nothing left but the straw it had been resting on. She stood up and held her hand flat out, palm upwards with the object for everyone to see.

"That's it? A freaking stone! We're risking death for a stone from the bloody beach!" Orla walked off in a huff.

Takuma asked Leanne if there were any inscriptions on it or any such markings. Leanne turned the stone carefully around in her palm and ran her fingers softly over the surface. She raised her head and answered, "No...nothing. What do we do now?"

She passed it over to Dearbhla, who double checked there were no markings. Then she remembered that there was more to the clue so she asked Susie to read it again. Susie took the scroll out and quickly scanned the clue. "You're right. 'Use the silver sun to feed the spectre of twisted wood.' What does that mean?"

"I know what it means," said a relaxed Ben.

Dearbhla surged forward in anticipation, "What? Tell us, Ben."

He sighed, "Feed it to the spectre of twisted wood. It's obvious. Shove it down Orla's gob!"

He doubled up laughing while Dearbhla sighed and looked imploringly at Mark. Orla looked murderous and slowly walked up to Ben.

She poked him in the chest with every word she uttered, "You listen to me, shut-the-hell-up-or-I'll-sink-your-ass-the-first-chance-I-get!"

Ben grabbed her finger "You promise?" and knocked it away. He rubbed his chest where her bony finger had threatened to poke a hole. "Stop being so sensitive, I'm only takin' a hand "

She turned an icy glare his way to which Ben held up his hands defensively. "Alright, truce. Geez..!"

Orla ignored him and went over to sit on the steps of the bastion.

"Ben. Wise up. We don't have time for messing around," warned Mark. Ben shot him an innocent look, folded his arms and smirked. Dearbhla rubbed the smooth stone over and over between her fingers, as if hoping it would give up its secrets.

"Ben does have a point," suggested Takuma. Ben choked and Orla began spluttering. The others stared open mouthed at the normally quiet young man. Takuma sighed and explained himself. "I don't mean that. I believe the 'twisted wood' could be a tree." He watched the dubious expressions cross their faces.

"Why not, it's plausible."

Dearbhla was the first to respond, "Okay, I can see that. Let's come from that angle then. We're looking for a tree that looks...er...like a spectre so it must be scary looking; a tree that stands out."

Leanne and Takuma stood up and Susie looked questioningly at Dearbhla.

"Should we split up and check out all the trees near here?"

"Absolutely not," said Dearbhla firmly. "We can check them together. Remember, we're..."

"Stronger together," the rest chorused as one.

Dearbhla chuckled. "Okay, I get it. I'm harping on about it but guys it's so important."

The laughter turned into groans as their leader emphasised her point on sticking together. She understood their mild irritation but she was ultimately responsible for their lives and she wasn't taking any chances - the more she drilled it into them, the more it would become second nature. The Divider, by his very name, would salivate at the idea of getting any of them alone. Divide and conquer was probably his daily mantra for goodness sake.

Takuma interrupted her serious thoughts. "If we're looking for trees, we should backtrack to the oak trees on the Grand Parade. Maybe it's one of them."

They decided this was a good plan so began to head back to where they had encountered a snapshot of history.

"So what are we looking for exactly?" asked Ben.

It was Susie who answered, "Well, 'twisted wood' suggest it's a really old, gnarled tree so look for a tree that belongs in a scary movie."

Ben turned to Orla and waggled his eyebrows. Before he could open his mouth and before Orla physically assaulted him, Mark stood right in front of his friend and murmured, "Know when to stop, Ben. You always push it too far."

Ben grinned up at him, "She deserves it and anyway I always know you have my back!" He eyed Orla as she moved away from him and made her way to Leanne. No doubt the other girl would be getting a touch of Orla's bitter tirade. He shook his head in disgust as he saw Leanne's eyes widen and then she bowed her head. He hated the way Orla bullied the docile girl; time to get stuck in. As he went to walk towards them Mark spun him around and redirected him to the line of trees.

"Keep out of it, Ben," he whispered. Before Ben could reply, Mark pinned him with a look. "She has to figure it out for herself. You can't keep interfering." Ben nodded reluctantly and shot one more glance over at the two girls. He was surprised to see Leanne straighten her spine and snarl something at Orla before turning her back to her completely. He smiled. Mark was right; Leanne would have to learn to defend herself. Seems she was getting the hang of it by the look of shock on Orla's face.

They inspected each of the trees for any sign of 'twisted' features but nothing stood out. They all looked like healthy oak trees; old yes, scary no. Takuma stood beside Leanne and noted how she looked quite proud of herself. He had seen Orla go over to her with meanness oozing out of her very pores. Obviously Leanne had held her own which was indeed progress.

"Everything okay, Leanne?" he asked tentatively. The quiet girl beamed a huge smile at him and he caught in a breath.

"Everything's just peachy Takuma. Orla was stepping on my toes, so I tramped a little extra harder back."

"No kidding!" He sniggered as Orla was shooting dirty looks their way. He winked at her and addressed the group.

"It doesn't look as if any of these trees fit the profile we're looking for so we should carry on."

"Yeah, but where to *Einstein?*" snapped Orla.

"Duh... You tell us. You're the tree whisperer!" Ben retorted.

Orla ignored him and stated what she thought was obvious. "The graveyard... We need to go back there." She flicked an apologetic look at Takuma who couldn't repress a shudder. "There are loads of trees there we need to check out."

"I don't know. Maybe we should check out the rest of the walls first." Dearbhla gave Takuma a concerned look. She didn't want to bring him back there yet. It was too soon. The poor boy had virtually gone white when Orla had suggested it.

Mark picked up on her reticence to go to St. Augustine's and pitched in, "Yeah, she's right. Let's go on past the Double Bastion and see if there's anything there." He looked at Susie who had also picked up the vibe and was nodding vigorously. Orla threw up her arms in surrender, "Why am I surprised? Nobody listens to me."

Dearbhla tried to placate her. "That's not true. You found out about Meg for us. I just think we should try this. If we need to come back, we will." She tried to quickly glance meaningfully at Takuma hoping Orla would pick up on it.

"I get it. I'm not dense. But we'll have to come back at some stage," she muttered begrudgingly.

Dearbhla mouthed a silent thank you to her and then followed Ben and Susie as they led the way.

Chapter 33

They all fell into step and quietly passed by the bastion that housed Roaring Meg. On their left, they saw The Verbal Arts Centre and approached Bishop's Gate, which is the highest gate of those around the walls. The group had to fall into single file as it is also the narrowest. Ben stopped and leaned on the wall. He surveyed Bishop Street and looked out towards The Fountain area. He caught sight of an old brown tower like construction. It was similar to what he imagined the tower prisoners of war would be kept in. He glanced over as Takuma rested beside him.

"You see that tower?" Takuma nodded at the building he had been gazing at. "That used to be a jail."

Ben said nothing, content to allow the clever boy enlighten him.

"They used to say it was easier to get out of, than, to get put into." Both of them shared a laugh at this. "In fact at one point, twenty eight men tunnelled out of it. Do you know when the guards caught on?"

Ben was picturing Derry's version of *'The Great Escape'* when he pulled his attention back to the question.

"An hour..? No wait, five minutes? I bet they got their dumb asses thrown back in jail. I mean twenty eight men escaping at the same time! They didn't think that one through."

Takuma smiled, "No…" he paused for effect, "Two days later they still hadn't realized."

Ben burst out laughing. "That's priceless, man. What a joke."

Takuma enjoyed feeling a bit more light hearted. He soaked up the laughter and disbelief as Ben shared it with the rest of them.

Dearbhla brought everyone back to focus again. "Let's go on before we get any reminders of who we're up against."

Leanne shivered. She didn't want to ever see the Divider again. He was the stuff from nightmares. He was inspiration for horror movies. Actually, it felt like she was starring in her very own horror flick. Unfortunately, she couldn't hide behind a cushion or turn it off if she got too frightened. She quickly scanned her surroundings and tried to stifle a feeling of panic. Those awful things that had happened Takuma and Susie, even Mark and Dearbhla had gotten hurt. She wouldn't be able to cope. It made sense that her time was coming. She just hoped that when it did, she'd be brave and wouldn't completely embarrass herself by collapsing in a terrified heap.

As if sensing her fear, Susie put her arm around Leanne's waist and gave it a small reassuring squeeze. Leanne gave her a half-hearted smile and took a deep breath to calm her racing heart. Susie was so much braver than she was. The girl had been possessed, whisked away by the Divider and stuck on the top of St. Columb's Cathedral. Did she crumple and cry enough tears to flood the River Foyle. Oh no. She got her feet on solid ground and walked by herself to find them. Now that was some serious 'heroine' stuff. She would probably have impaled herself on the spire or slipped from the helpful doves grasp and been smashed into really messy, unattractive lumps. Then Orla would have made some snarky comments about her being as much of an ugly mess in death as she was in life. She chuckled at the thought and earned a puzzled frown from Susie.

The group arrived at the next bastion called the Church Bastion. It was directly opposite the cathedral. Susie watched as Mark paused to look up at the spire. He turned his gaze to her and it seemed they just stood staring into each other's eyes for ages, when in reality it was but a few seconds. She could clearly see the concern in his eyes and it gave her a funny warm sensation in the pit of her stomach. Ben broke the special moment by calling Mark over to him. He took one last look and gave her a smile filled with warmth. Then he strode over to Ben. Susie flushed and felt a bit flustered. She turned away and bumped right into Orla who had been watching the silent communication between her and Mark. She raised her eyebrows as she noticed the flush on Susie's skin. Interesting...

"So this is where your little birdies came and flew you to safety Snowy?" she asked caustically.

Susie shook her head, "Orla, why do you have such a problem with me? Oh no, that's right, you have a problem with people, full stop." She left Orla standing there smirking.

"Over here!" Takuma's shout echoed across the silent walls. He was standing beside a tree that was situated at the mouth of Church Bastion. As he moved aside to let the others get a better view, a few of them gasped.

"That is one seriously twisted piece of wood," drawled Ben.

"For sure," breathed Susie.

Dearbhla got a really good feeling about the tree at the centre of their perusal. She could feel a bubble of excitement which seemed to match the expressions on the faces of the others. They drew closer to the tree. It was very old and seemed to be filled with character. It was gnarled and almost looked like it had fought in a few wars itself. Its branches twisted and twirled through each other, adding to the aura of intrigue it projected. If ever there was a tree that could be taken from any scary film or fairy tale it would be this very one. Dearbhla stepped closer to it and noticed that above her head, there was quite a noticeable indentation in the trunk. It seemed to be a knot or a bit of damage to the bark although this too increased its presence.

"What did the clue say about the wood?" she asked Susie.

Immediately, Susie unravelled the scroll and found the line they were interested in, "Use the silver sun to feed the spectre of twisted wood."

Takuma was reading it over Susie's shoulder.

"Okay, there must be some kind of hidden drawer or hole in the tree. If we place the stone in it, it must be like a trigger to release what we're looking for."

Ben was the first to respond. He nodded eagerly. "Sounds good…let's give it a go!" He clapped Takuma on the back.

They all watched each other with a mixture of nerves and excitement. This could be it, their first success.

Orla broke the buzz with a few words, "Put the stone where?" she asked with her arms outstretched. "It's a tree. How do you feed a tree a stone for its lunch?"

Ben tutted and refused to let her ruin the moment. "Well if a tree can choose you as a girlfriend it can sure as hell eat a stone."

He tried to dodge her thump but miscalculated and ended up taking it in the chest.

"Oomph, uncalled for!"

Orla's smug smile faltered when he lunged towards her and sent her flying backwards into the tree at the centre of their attention. He tried not to land heavily on her but failed and heard her head crack against the tree trunk.

Chapter 34

His stomach roiled violently as he worried that he'd hurt her very badly. In the background he heard the shrieks and shouts of fright as the others battled the black tornado that was the Divider. Ben gently lifted Orla's head into a more comfortable position and whispered her name. She was out cold. He felt the back of her head and pulling his hand away, he was relieved to see there was no blood although he had felt a sizeable lump forming. She was going to have a serious headache when she woke up. Then he was pretty sure she'd return the favour when she remembered him literally jumping on top of her. He grimaced at the thought of the tongue lashing he would get. Hearing an ear piercing scream, he swung around in time to see Leanne flying through the air. With a violent jerk the Divider caught her in his bony hands, laughing like a maniac.

Leanne was shaking with terror but couldn't seem to look away from his cold, empty eyes. He smiled cruelly and his thin lips pulled back to reveal uneven teeth. She was kind of surprised as she expected foul breath and rotten, missing teeth. Instead, he had pearly white gnashers but that's not what had her scrabbling to get out of his arms. He bent his head closer to hers.

"Come now, dearest Leanne. You should not fear me. I can help you. I can make you strong and brave. You will never again be treated with disrespect or suffer the cruelty of scorn from those not worthy of your company." He hissed low and every vibration sent a shockwave through her nerve endings. It was almost like he held her spellbound or in a trance for she couldn't move a muscle. He gave a throaty chuckle as her eyes widened and then he opened his mouth. This was what had first had her attempting to jump from his arms in mid-air. A black and yellow striped reptile began to slither out of his mouth where his tongue should have been. It hissed with every wriggle and its own tongue flicked up and down enjoying her reaction to its closeness. The Divider's eyes were as black as any cave and his pale skin stretched unnaturally over his features.

Leanne squeezed her eyes shut as the snake reached right in front of her. She could feel its breath on her skin and just when she thought she'd die of fright, felt the snake's tongue slide over her nose. Her eyes shot open and she squirmed in the hard grip she was being held. Her head was straining back as far as she could but the snake hissed in defiance and worked its way further out of the Divider's mouth. Horrified at what was happening, Leanne realised that she couldn't break free and whatever was going to happen to her would be truly dreadful.

Susie picked herself up from where she had landed when the Divider had flung all of his power at them in a grand entrance that only he could make. She grimaced as her ankle was sore but she quickly shook it out and turned round swiftly to check on the others. She saw Mark lying on his side groaning but was reassured that he was just winded; she hunched down and rushed over to Dearbhla. The older woman still hadn't moved and that worried Susie. She crouched down beside her and spoke urgently, "Dearbhla, Dearbhla. Wake up. Are you okay?" She lightly patted both her cheeks and breathed a sigh of relief when Dearbhla's eyes fluttered open. As she tried to sit up she let out a whimper. "Where does it hurt?" asked Susie concerned. Dearbhla met her eyes.

"Everywhere…it hurts everywhere!" Then she managed a half smile. "But I think I'll live. Nothing's broken. What about everyone else?"

Susie glanced quickly around. "Mark and Ben are okay. Takuma's fine. He's over with Ben trying to help Orla. She still looks knocked out."

As she finished, they heard a long heart rending wail and tried to find the source. Susie gasped and shook Dearbhla gently to get her attention. The other woman exhaled loudly when she saw Leanne in the deadly grip of the Divider who was hovering about twenty feet in the air. She shot bolt upright and then scrambled to her feet, using Susie to support herself. Screaming up at the Divider she demanded, "Let her go. Leave her alone!"

She glanced around frantically and found a few stones. Aiming at the Divider, she catapulted her arm back, then forward and released the first stone straight at his head. Then she sent a few more his way. This enraged him and he glared down at her snarling. Mark and Susie joined in and soon there was a barrage of stones sailing his way. Some of them caught his head again and succeeded in knocking off his hat. It floated to the ground and landed next to Dearbhla's feet with a soft thud. Dearbhla smirked up at him.

"I said, let her go. She doesn't have what you're looking for."

He scowled down at her and penetrated her bones with his dark eyes. Worse than that was the snake poking out of his mouth like something from your worst nightmares. *Medusa* didn't have a patch on this creature. As he snarled at her again, the snake sprung out from his mouth and stretched out fully until it suddenly halted before her face. She reared back, banging into Susie. The snake hissed and spat angrily. It flung its body from side to side and forwards but it couldn't get any closer to her. She sighed in relief but decided to distance herself from the furious serpent. As she backed away slowly she tried to formulate a plan to free Leanne from his dark clutches.

A sudden movement from her peripheral vision put her on guard. She swung round ready to attack, only to see Mark desperately hitting the snake's body. It swivelled its head round hissing and spitting violently at Mark but he had a grip on it squeezing it hard with one hand and beating it frantically with a branch in the other. He grunted with the effort. His injured hands were bleeding heavily and the splinters, he had got earlier, dug deeper into his skin. Dearbhla saw his discomfort and had enough of being on the side lines. Obviously Susie and Ben had similar thoughts. They all descended upon the snake, helping hit it, beat it, claw at it, and wound it in any way possible. Ben had ripped a couple of thin branches from the tree and threw one of them to Dearbhla. She used the sharper ends to try to pierce through the scaly skin. She was able to make slight scratches but she could see that Mark and Ben were creating gashes which were beginning to bleed heavily. In between, Susie was battling the snake's head away enraging it in its pain filled state. A loud roar reverberated in their ears but they refused to be diverted from their task.

They were all grunting from exertion. Susie cried out, "Watch out, he's going to drop her."

With a final bloodcurdling roar from the Divider and a loud hiss from the snake, he dropped Leanne to the ground. Mark and Ben rushed over to catch her, but the force of her hitting them, sent all three of them sprawling in a heap. The Divider whirled around in a cloak of darkness while the battered and torn snake curled up into itself and fled back into his master's mouth. With a snap of his long, bony fingers his hat disappeared from the ground and reappeared on top of his head. Then in a cloud of swirling darkness, he vanished.

Chapter 35

Susie and Dearbhla ran over to the three lying in a heap of tangled arms and legs. "Are you okay? Leanne. Did he hurt you?" asked an anxious Susie.

Slowly and painfully, Leanne managed to extricate herself from Ben and Mark's limbs. Embarrassed, she was certain she'd crushed both of them.

"I'm so sorry guys," she muttered apologetically.

Mark and Ben crawled away from each other and got on their feet more inelegantly than she had.

"No problem Leanne. You never hurt us. Sure Mark's head is big enough to bounce off and I'm so strong and manly that you were like a feather landing on me."

Mark laughed at his description of them both and reassured Leanne as well.

"Don't worry, Leanne. We're just glad we got to you in time."

Dearbhla and Susie wrapped their arms around the still shaking girl and hugged her tight. She wiped away tears and laughed shakily. "That was really scary. He's horrible. I looked into his eyes and saw pure evil."

Takuma called over to them, "Orla's coming round."

They all trudged over to the tree where Orla was leaning against it. She raised dazed eyes to them.

"Ben," she managed to squeak out though it seemed her mouth was so dry that her tongue had stuck to the roof of it. Ben moved closer to her and waited for her to speak. When he leaned close to her, her serene expression changed to one of fury.

"You lug head!" she whacked him across the face so that his head cracked to the side, "What the hell was that? You nearly broke my neck. Ooooh, my poor head." Orla broke off her angry words to clasp her head in both hands.

Ben, who had some lingering shock at being slapped for saving her life, stared at her gaping. Of all the spoilt bitches she seriously took the biscuit. As his shock was wearing off, he clenched his fists by his sides to stop himself from retaliating by grabbing the little witch by her hair and dragging her to offer a human sacrifice to the Divider. The muscles in his jaw twitched as he visualised doing just that. He was fairly sure the Divider would kill her after being in her company for five minutes because there was no person on this earth who would be able to tolerate the opinionated little wart.

Dearbhla rushed over to them and shook her head at Ben in silent warning. Usually he listened to their leader. He admired her courage but he strongly disagreed with her at this present moment in time. He stood upright and glared down at Orla. She glanced up at him still holding her head and just looking at her face was enough to set him off. He gritted his teeth but too late. He lost it. Pointing into her face he bent over and started shouting:

"I saved your pathetic life! You should be kissing my bloody feet in thanks. He was coming straight for you so I pushed you clear." He dragged in a deep breath and launched into her again. "I didn't think to saw down the bloody tree beforehand, I didn't aim for the tree, I just saw you in danger and reacted." Orla tried to comment but he stuck out a hand to stop her.

"Don't say a word you poisonous witch. I'm sick of you." He stood up again and included everyone with his arms, "We're all sick of you! You're a thorn in the ass."

Dearbhla rolled her eyes. She was tempted to agree but they didn't have much time before the Divider made a repeat performance. She gave Mark a pleading look and thankfully he moved beside his friend. He laid a bloodied hand on Ben's arm but he was still spitting mad. Mark flicked a glance at an astonished Orla who was half holding her head while staring wide eyed at Ben.

"Ben," he spoke quietly, "C'mon Ben forget it. You said what you needed to, now let it go."

"Let it go. Let it go? Are you kidding me? She's a total psycho. I can't work her out. So yeah, okay Mark, I'm done." He threw his hands up in defeat. He began to turn away but then turned suddenly.

"Next time, you're on your own so I hope you do a better job at not getting yourself hurt than I obviously did."

With that, he swivelled away and walked over to the fence at St. Columb's Cathedral. Holding onto the iron bar with both hands, he peeked into the grounds of the beautiful cathedral hoping it would help calm his temper. He dragged in a few steadying breaths and then closing his eyes, he leaned his head on the iron railings. The coolness of the metal helped soothe his heated flesh after his outburst. He heard someone approach him and knew before he opened his eyes.

"I'm okay Mark. She just winds me up no end."

"I know man. She definitely needs a few sessions of charm school."

Ben sighed and pushed off the fence. They walked back to the others although Ben kept at a distance from Orla and he avoided all eye contact. Not that he need have worried. Orla was stung from his verbal assault and she didn't want another from him any time soon. She didn't show this of course. She kept up her cocky demeanour to the rest of the group but Ben had definitely hurt her, a bit. She shrugged in annoyance at herself and listened in to what Dearbhla was saying.

"We don't have much time. I'm just going to do what Takuma said."

She took the smooth stone out from her pocket and set it into the hole that was in the trunk of the creepy tree. Turning it over and tucking it in, it fit snugly as if it was made for this exact defect in the tree. When nothing happened she blew out a breath. Then she gave it a little push and amazingly a loud click sounded, followed by a rolling swoosh. As she surveyed the trunk she caught a glimpse of something jutting out of the very middle of the trunk around the back to where she was facing.

Positioning herself next to it, she gasped and turned her head to motion the others over. She couldn't speak as emotion clogged her throat so she gestured down to the treasure.

Chapter 36

The others stood beside her on either side and stared down at the first object they had been challenged to find. They stayed like that for a few minutes, awestruck at the fact they'd succeeded. Exchanging glances, Dearbhla bent over slowly and very carefully she ran her fingers over a beautifully crafted silver oak leaf. Reverently, she lifted it out with both hands. Then she placed it flat on the palm of her left hand while lightly tracing the lines and markings ingrained in the silver; so realistic it was almost as if someone plucked a leaf from an oak tree and immersed it in silver so that every fine vein and feature was forever caught in time. The group crowded around her and each admired its beauty. Dearbhla's eyes glistened with tears as she looked at each of her young helpers' faces. Everyone was fascinated with the precious object. How fitting that the first object was a silver oak leaf, representing the city, home of the proud and glorious oak tree.

Susie felt the hum of excitement pulse through them and she laughed at the others, "I guess we're not so bad at this after all."

Orla rolled her eyes, and with every word dripping in sarcasm said, "Yeah, we're just regular adventurers!" She noticed Ben didn't even glance her way. Whatever, he's a loser anyway. He could huff all he wanted, she didn't care if he never spoke another word to her.

Takuma cleared his throat, "Erm, I... ah...can't believe we did it." He smiled at each of them, blocking out Orla's 'whatever' look. "Now we've done it, we're going to have one seriously peeved off Divider." He raised his eyebrows and watched the uneasy, anxious expression flit over their faces. "We've held our own so far. It's definitely harder for him to get at us when we keep together."

Leanne and Susie agreed while Orla stuck her hand in the air.

"*Excuse me!* So that's our great plan? STAY TOGETHER! Are you nuts? He nearly got me killed and his little serpent buddy just about French kissed Leanne!" She looked in disbelief at the group standing around, "Why don't we all sing and hold hands while we are at it?" Pausing for effect she then blurted out, "It's not over. We have two more objects to find." She started to pace up and down, "This is only the first flippin' one and look how much trouble we've had."

Dearbhla shot Susie a meaningful look. Luckily for her the young girl obliged her. She caught up to Orla and patted her on the shoulder awkwardly.

Orla turned to stare at her, "I-am-freaking-out-here!"

Taken aback, Susie wasn't sure what to say. As she opened her mouth to give some meaningless placations, a loud booming noise made her freeze. Suddenly the entire bastion they were standing on exploded and they were thrown into a fog of dust and debris. The tree that had lovingly protected the silver oak leaf for centuries was blown into pieces that would have made a wood chipper proud. Slabs of cement and pavement were blasted apart and a huge gaping hole in the centre of the bastion had smoke and dust pouring out from it.

Susie had landed away from the bastion because she had been over with Orla. Her eyes stung and she coughed and spluttered at the dust coating her lungs. She tried to sit up and saw that she was completely covered in a cloak of grey dust. Her ears were ringing badly from the sound of the explosion. Dazed and confused, she looked around for signs of the others. Her eyes were continually streaming and she found it difficult to see. She stumbled forward and got as close as she dared to the hole still pouring smoke out of it. She turned away and looked back. From the direction of the Royal Bastion, she saw a cannon pointing directly at them. The open mouth of the old fashioned weapon had smoke billowing out from it. Her mouth fell open in horror.

They'd been fired at by one of the cannon.

Bile surged up her throat as she recognised the significance of this. She fell on her knees and covered her mouth with dirty hands. Tears streamed down her face and heart wrenching sobs broke free. The fog of pulverised cement, trees and walls still hadn't cleared. It enveloped the once peaceful bastion in an eerie grey ash almost as if there was a fresh fall of snow but not as pure or cleansing. It sat thickly on Susie's skin and she cringed at the contact, as if her own flesh was so sensitive it felt like thousands of pinpricks. Shaking her head and rocking back and forth on her haunches, she whimpered in pain, "No, no, no. They can't be. They can't be dead." The nausea overwhelmed her and just as the fog began to dissipate she lurched to the side and threw up. Feeling weak and disorientated she wiped her mouth with the back of her hand and once again tried to catch a glimpse of other life.

Her vision was blurry from a mixture of tears and dirt. Just as she thought they had all been lost down the gaping wound in the ground, she saw a dark shape hunched over where the tree used to stand. Now, all that remained was a messy stump. She concentrated on the shape but it didn't move one inch. A sob lodged itself in her throat again and another wave of sickness claimed her. The fog continued to clear and revealed dark shapes of more figures lying strewn across what looked like a battlefield. She squeezed her eyes shut and cried uncontrollably. They were dead. All gone. He'd murdered them.

One minute they'd been thrilled at finding their first object, the next they were being blown apart by a cannon ball. Even as her eyesight righted itself, she could see blood splattered amongst the rubble. She threw her head back and screamed, "You killed them you evil….. *You killed my friends!*" Groaning she fell back against the scarred ground and buried her face in her hands. It was over. It was truly over. They had lost at the expense of six lives. She thought of each of her companions through the day from hell. They had been filled with such hope when they discovered the first object. Now it had been cruelly ripped away from them in an act of obscene destruction. She thought of the people outside the walls, trapped in their frozen state. They would all die. The Divider had won. Susie lay there in the rubble and wished that she could die too.

Chapter 37

As Susie lay sobbing in the rubble, that had been the Church Bastion, the dusty fog began to fade. Her ears were still ringing from the loud boom of the fired cannon. She raised her head slowly and through red rimmed and bleary eyes surveyed the destruction. Pulling herself up on shaky legs, she coughed up some dust and grimaced. Her eyes were drawn once again to the figures of her friends lying amongst the debris. They were so still. She choked back a sob and started towards the motionless bodies. Her stomach turned and twisted in dread whilst her heart beat wildly.

A sudden spluttering broke the eerie silence, and Susie swung round to find the source. She spotted Orla hunched over near the railings of St. Columb's. The girl was dragging in air but only succeeded in taking in more flakes of dust.

Susie limped over to her and thumped Orla's back to help clear her throat. After another coughing fit, Orla straightened and knocked Susie away from her.

"What the hell just happened?" she asked croakily.

Susie felt fresh tears filling her eyes but was too exhausted to hide them.

"They're dead. They're all dead. He…that MONSTER killed them!"

Orla blanched.

"He fired the cannon at us. That evil twisted creep, actually tried to blow us up," continued Susie. Her voice caught and she started to weep as her eyes were once again drawn to the catastrophic sight before her. Orla turned and took in the scene. She too saw the slumped bodies, trees blown apart concrete ripped into pieces. She shook her head as if she couldn't quite believe it. Then she wiped her bleary eyes with her dirty sleeve. She raised both hands in front of her and realized they were trembling. Another attack of coughing had her doubled over and this time she was grateful for Susie's help – even if she had been a bit too enthusiastic beating on her back.

Straightening, she cast a wan smile at the other girl who looked like an extra from a war film. Orla could see the gaping hole in the bastion where their lucky tree had once stood. When this was all over, the council were going to be seriously peeved, not to mention the tourist board; they were going to have to rework their walled city advert!

Orla addressed Susie who was silently weeping, "C'mon. We need to make sure they are…like…dead, dead."

Susie's eyes widened in horror, "No…No. I can't!"

She broke down and held her face in her hands. Her sobs echoed around the eerily still bastion. Orla sighed and put her arms around the heartbroken girl. She held her for a few minutes until she could feel Susie's sobs weaken. Then she drew back and tried again.

"Susie, I know this is horrible but we have to make sure. I mean, you never know – they all have pretty hard heads so they could be okay."

Susie smiled back weakly and nodded. They moved carefully towards the epicentre of the disaster.

Just as they approached one of the bodies covered in a layer of thick dust and debris, a sudden noise to their right made the girls jump and yelp.

To their shock, first one hand, then another, rose up from the ripped concrete. They gripped the broken sides and a dishevelled head appeared.

The two girls watched in complete astonishment.

"Ah…there's a sight I thought I'd never see. Orla's mouth wide open and no sound coming out. Am I in heaven?" Ben broke off coughing and struggling for breath.

Susie reacted first. She rushed towards him and grabbed underneath his right arm. Heaving him up as hard as she could, she wasn't strong enough to get him out. Ben was too weak to haul himself out.

"Orla, get over here. Quickly!" she snapped.

Orla blinked, closed her mouth and joined her. She took Ben's other arm and together they pulled him out until they collapsed in a heap of arms and legs.

"Ta very much girlies… *Orla...!*" Ben exclaimed with a horrified look.

Orla jumped. "What? Is he back? Where is he?" She struggled to look around and see the Divider.

Ben smirked as he lay with the two girls. "Nah, it's you. Stop pinching my butt."

Orla tutted and pushed him in annoyance, "You waster. I thought Bird Boy was back for round two."

"You may have saved my butt but you don't own it. I'm a man you know, not a piece of meat," Ben pretended to huff.

He jabbed her with his elbow and she was about to slap him when suddenly she grabbed him in a hug and planted a noisy kiss on his cheek.

Ben was so shocked he just lay with his mouth agape. Orla extricated herself roughly from the tangle of limbs and stood up. She caught Susie's astonished look.

"What's wrong with you? I'm just glad we have one more to help us fight this flying freak if he comes back."

Susie smothered her smile and squeezed Ben's arm, also extremely glad he was alive. "Are you okay, Ben?" she asked.

He shrugged, felt round his body and winked, "I am first class, baby...some cuts and bruises…"

Orla tutted at Ben;

"Wanna check me for yourself wee woman?" Ben shouted over to Orla.

She grunted and walked over to the huddled heap on the ground nearest her, ignoring his laugh. Clearing her throat, she kneeled down and gently began to clear the debris off the still body. She recognised Dearbhla and could see the huge gash on her forehead. It was bleeding heavily, caked in dirt and grit. Orla couldn't tell if she was breathing or not, so she placed two fingers on the older woman's neck. She held her breath waiting for a pulse. Closing her eyes she sagged and let out a breath.

"She's dead, isn't she?" stated a scared looking Ben.

She shook her head, "No, no. She's alive but her pulse is weak and she's unconscious."

Ben blew out a breath of relief and joined Orla, "Okay, what should we do?"

Orla watched him and was glad she had a layer of dust disguising her blush.

"Er…nothing…you go help Susie find the others. I'll stay with Dearbhla and make her as comfortable as I can."

Ben smiled a genuinely warm smile and winked at her, "Okay, doc," he saluted her quickly and caught up with Susie.

"Orla's giving Dearbhla some TLC so let's go get the team back together."

He squeezed Susie's shoulder to reassure her, even though his insides were quaking with fear. None of the others had appeared yet including his best friend, Mark. He kept a silent mantra going inside his head, "Please be okay, please be okay, please be okay….."

He caught sight of them the same instant Susie cried out, "There. Look. Someone's there."

They ran over and could see the dust covered bodies of Leanne and Takuma. Takuma was lying protectively over the girl. He had part of a large piece of wood protruding from this leg. Ben carefully eased the injured boy off Leanne. He checked Takuma's pulse whilst Susie checked for Leanne's. They both exchanged relieved glances and waited as they began to regain consciousness.

Takuma cried out in pain as he tried to move.

"What happened"? He surveyed the damage with his usual calm manner.

"We got blown sky high by Bird Boy himself," answered Ben.

Takuma saw that Leanne was coming round and relieved, turned his attention to Ben.

"How..?"

"With the cannon…the psycho blasted a cannonball at us," answered Susie angrily.

Takuma swallowed. He looked at Ben who seemed as shocked as he was.

"That guy has some serious issues," decided Ben.

"Are you alright, Leanne?" asked Susie who was too heartsick to even reply to Ben.

The frightened girl sat up slowly and tested her arms and legs. Then she smiled at Susie.

"Yeah, everything's working. I'm fine thanks. How is everyone else?" she enquired.

Susie told her about Dearbhla.

"We haven't found Mark yet," Ben added when Susie had finished.

Leanne squeezed Susie's hand.

"I'm sure he's fine. Mark wouldn't let a dusty old cannonball stop him!"

Susie smiled weakly. She wasn't so sure. Leanne hadn't seen the extent of the damage. It was a miracle they had all survived. She closed her eyes in dread. Maybe Mark was the one they would lose. Her stomach roiled in protest. This was a nightmare. She'd kill that Divider herself if Mark was dead. She'd die trying.

They all stood up. Ben had made a makeshift crutch for Takuma from a branch and he helped him on the other side. His leg had stopped bleeding but he was in agony. Ben didn't say but he thought he'd seen bone exposed which wasn't a good sign. Right now he admired how Takuma was gritting his teeth and carrying on.

They gathered back to Orla who was talking to a stunned but conscious Dearbhla. Now, if they could just get Mark back in one piece they'd have a full set again. Ben continued his quiet mantra and listened while Dearbhla exchanged words of relief that everyone was alive; so far. He carefully lowered Takuma to the ground and asked Susie and Leanne to help him search for Mark. They agreed eagerly.

He winked at Orla, "Doc, you're in charge of the injured."

Then he was off before she could respond.

Chapter 38

The search party fanned out and began combing through rubble and chaos towards New Gate. As they reached the narrow pathway they realised even the debris hadn't reached this far. No sign of Mark. Ben cleared his throat and tried to stem the rising panic.

"Okay. Don't freak out girlies."

He looked sternly at Leanne who was hiccupping with silent tears and Susie who just looked ill. They both nodded though didn't change their hopeless expressions. Ben leaned on the wall and looked out at the streets below. He felt a bit deflated. Where could Mark be? A thought suddenly struck him and he whirled round towards the startled girls. Grabbing their arms he propelled them along with him as he made his way back towards the Church Bastion.

"Keep an eye out. Susie, Leanne you check inside the walls while I check the ground outside."

Susie pulled her arm back from his grip.

"Hey! What for?" she asked.

"Duh! Mark! You know my best friend and your girlie crush."

As she continued to stare blankly, he sighed and ran a hand through his gritty scalp.

"He could have been blasted over the sides when the cannon hit. It's a possibility. How else do you explain his disappearance?"

Susie looked horrified and then calm.

"Okay, but if he's dead, I mean, hurt, I'm dealing with the Divider."

Leanne tried to murmur words of reassurance but Ben met Susie's determined glare. He gave her hand a quick squeeze.

"Trust me. If Mark's de…," he couldn't say it as bile threatened to slide up his throat. He tried again.

"If Mark's *hurt*, Bird Boy's gonnae get de-feathered and then de-winged. So get in line, Susie!"

Susie nodded with approval. They continued their perusal of the ground on either side of the walls. At first, the walls had looked inviting and harmless, but now seemed ominous that their friend could have been blown off them.

Once again, they met with disappointment. Mark was nowhere to be found. Just as they were beginning to think their friend had been taken prisoner by the Divider, Leanne noticed the railings surrounding the grounds of St. Columb's Cathedral were damaged. They had been bent backwards with the force of the explosion. She screamed excitedly and pointed at the railings.

"Look. Look. He could be in there. See how the railings are bent."

Ben and Susie caught on and moved quickly towards them. They were able to climb up and jump down to the other side. Ben went first and then helped the two girls. His heart was hammering in his chest.

As he was helping Leanne down, Susie cried out,

"There he is. Oh thank God. Mark! Mark! It's okay. We're here!"

She ran over to Mark who was lying at an awkward angle on the grass near some gravestones. Ben and Leanne followed closely and all three seemed to get carried away with the joy of finding their friend.

Ben's legs felt weak with relief as he saw his friend's dirty face. He was out cold but in one piece. No blood. Good sign. Susie leaned over Mark and could hardly speak she was so overcome with emotion. She had believed he was gone; either dead or abducted, whichever way, he could be beyond her reach. She smoothed a lock of his hair back from his forehead and waited for him to open his calming blue eyes so she could see the warmth in them whenever he looked at her. Leanne was on Mark's other side and was frowning.

"Something's wrong?" She leaned over his chest and looked up worriedly, "I don't think he's breathing."

Susie stared blankly at Mark's face. "No. No. He's just knocked out. Of course he's breathing."

Leanne hurriedly tried for a pulse on his carotid artery with shaky fingers. She felt sick. She wiped her hands and tried again. Slowly she met Susie's terrified gaze. Then she shook her head.

"I'm so sorry. He's…he's," her throat constricted, "gone. He's gone."

Ben pushed Leanne roughly aside and dropped to his knees. "Mark! Wake up you idiot! Stop messing. Get up!"

He kept shaking Mark's motionless body. Mark's eyes never flickered. It was too late. They had failed him. Ben sat back on his haunches and stared at his friend. He had known him for twelve years. He was like a brother and now he had left him. Just like everyone else had. It was pointless to care. They just left you anyway. He glanced at Susie who was lying over Mark weeping. He turned to see Leanne still lying where he'd pushed her, her shoulders heaving with sobs.

This couldn't be happening. It's not possible. How could he wake up from this nightmare? Someone wake me up please, he thought to himself. Then a feeling of such loss and emptiness hit him, that he hung his head and let the tears of grief trail down his face.

They sat in that position for the next ten minutes all wrestling with their emotions. Susie stirred first and carefully moved Mark's body until they could all clearly see the cause of Mark's death. His back had been broken. Susie glanced at the gravestones scattered about them. How odd that someone's comforting marker for their resting place had brought death to another. She wiped her stinging eyes dry.

"He didn't have a chance, Ben."

Susie watched Ben as he continued to bow his head in total despair.

"He must have landed on a gravestone when he was blown in here. It would have been quick and instant Ben. He wouldn't have known what happened."

She couldn't believe she was actually saying this. Her own heart was breaking. It was truly amazing she could even speak, never mind calmly explain what had happened. Leanne sat up and was unsure how to help the grief stricken boy. He looked completely destroyed. She tried to calm herself down. After all, she'd only known Mark since this had all started. Ben had lost his closest friend. She needed to be strong for Ben and support him but as she looked down at Mark's broken body she could feel the tears flowing again. It was no good. It was just so sad.

Susie gently placed Mark's head back on to the bed of grass. As she picked herself up from the ground, she took in the scene; there was devastation, and not of debris, but of hearts and lives. Shaking her head free of the overwhelming need to lie in the foetal position and sleep away the pain, she walked round to Ben and gently placed her hand on his shoulder.

"Ben, we need to tell the others."

Ben didn't move nor did he reply. He just let the words slide over him. It felt like he was in a bubble and everything, even sound, seemed so distant. Susie spoke to him again but he had no idea what she said. To be honest, neither did he care. He couldn't seem to think straight. Shifting closer to Mark, he nudged his shoulder. Then he reached out to his friend's hand and pulled back as if scorched. At Ben's gasp, Leanne sat up.

"What's wrong, Ben?" she asked.

He looked over at her with bloodshot eyes.

"Cold…so cold…" He broke off and closed his eyes. It was real. Already Mark's body was losing its warmth. Death had stolen his best friend just as it had robbed him of his own mother. Death sucked. The Divider did this. He *MURDERED* Mark. Ben's eyes flew open and Leanne could see his pain had been replaced by vengeance. Jumping up with renewed energy, Ben nodded at the two girls.

"Let's get this over with."

Leanne's tummy dropped. It was bad enough seeing Ben and Susie's reaction to the dreadful news. As they made their way towards the broken railings, Ben stopped.

"Wait. We can't leave him…you know…alone," he coughed uneasily "I don't want to leave my best friend alone," Ben declared and marched back to Mark.

The girls exchanged an uncomfortable look and then trudged back to help. They were able to lift Mark onto Ben's shoulder. Susie marvelled at his determination because Mark was tall and muscled yet Ben carried him with ease and gentleness that spoke volumes as to how precious his friendship with the other boy was. When they neared the railings for the second time, the two girls took turns in providing support on either side of Ben as he valiantly climbed with his valuable burden. How they managed to get across the twisted fence, Susie would never know, but between the three of them they did so. As they approached the rest of the group, applause broke out loudly in the stark silence.

"Well done. You found him!" exclaimed Dearbhla, who had been anxiously awaiting their return.

Leanne rushed forwards quickly waving her hands to stop the inappropriate applause.

"No. Stop. You don't understand. We ... We... Mark's not..." her voice quavered and she looked imploringly at Susie. Before Susie could say a word, Ben delivered the terrible news.

"Mark's dead."

Chapter 39

He avoided their shocked faces and with the girls' help, began to lay his friend gently down upon the ground.

"We didn't want to leave him all alone so ..." He couldn't finish.

The plan was to bring Mark back amidst much slagging and joking about, perhaps even playing dead. His stomach churned. It wasn't supposed to be like this.

He could hear Susie tearfully explaining what had happened. Then he heard the various reactions of shock, anguish and grief. Even Orla was stunned. He snorted. It should have been *her*. She was a pain in the ass and caused nothing but trouble. They wouldn't have missed *her*. Anger was building like a storm inside him. He clenched his fists beside him and was now shaking with rage. His best friend was dead and that useless, complaining twisted excuse for a human being was standing there without so much as a scrape on her.

"Well, I'm sorry it happened but at least he isn't lying there suffering. I mean that would be worse. What could we do with a cripple," said Orla speaking without engaging her brain as usual.

A shocked silence ensued. Something snapped in Ben. All the stress, fear, grief and anger exploded at once and he lunged towards Orla. He grabbed her around the neck and squeezed. His face was contorted in rage and Orla couldn't even scream as he continued to strangle her. Ben was unaware of the flurry of panic and activity around him. Neither did he hear the shouts and screams for him to stop. So caught up in a hurricane of hate, he was oblivious to all things except strangling this foul mouthed girl until she lay broken and dead like his friend.

Susie, Dearbhla and Leanne couldn't budge Ben's fatal grip on Orla's throat. Takuma was struggling to get up but the pain in his damaged leg was too great. He shouted out, frustrated at his inability to help.

"Stop it. Don't listen to her. You'll kill her Ben."

"You don't know what you're doing!"

"You're upset. We're all upset."

"Don't do this! Ben. *No!*"

The three girls shouted uselessly at the enraged boy. They were in a blind panic that Ben was actually going to kill Orla and they weren't strong enough to stop him.

Orla was making choking and gargling noises. Her face was changing from a bright red colour to deep red with a bluish tinge. Lights were beginning to dance about before her eyes. Her bulging eyes pleaded with Ben to stop but he was beyond reasoning. He was now a killer and she was going to be toast in another second.

Perhaps she should have been more sensitive, but hey, she didn't mean anything by it. Maybe it just came out wrong. She was glad Mark wasn't suffering. That would have been worse. She should know. She had to watch her own sister trapped inside a body that wouldn't work. She had died long before her actual death. She had been in a living hell for three years after the car accident that changed all their lives. As the lights danced furiously over Ben's face, her hearing and sight dimmed. She tried to let Ben know she forgave him.

The next thing she knew his steel grip was wrenched away and she was floating through the air.

Oh, she thought, this is it. I'll get to be with Claire. Her eyes flickered open and she floated past the forms of her ex-teammates. Funny, Ben looks like he's a frozen statue. Ha, serves him right for killing me. They all looked so shocked.

Yes losers, mourn me. I'm off to heaven to chillax, while you lot battle Bird Boy and Psycho Spiderturd over there.

"You're not dead, Orla," said Dearbhla drily.

Hmm…did I say that out loud? Oops! Orla thought. Wait, did she just tell me I'm not dead? Orla felt around her neck and winced.

"Ouch," she croaked. No, Ben had definitely tried to kill her. So why was she floating away?

She turned her head slowly and saw what everyone was staring at. The Spellbinder was back. The group sat and waited for him to speak. He was still surveying the grim scene all around them. His gaze was fleeting until it rested upon Mark's body. Sadness suffused his expression. Then he returned his attention to the remaining team, including a dazed Ben and a now seated Orla.

Ben sneaked a glance at the girl he'd tried to strangle only minutes before. She glared at him and he grimaced. This was going to be tricky. Just as she was about to open her mouth to spurt the usual insults, the Spellbinder held up his hand. Immediately she closed it. Ben straightened. Sick! Now if he could have done that he wouldn't have had to choke her! Then he felt bad for thinking that, as his hands were still shaking from the surge of rage and adrenaline that had overtaken his common sense and rationality. Though to be fair, he didn't have very much of either on a normal day. Just ask his Aunt Marnie.

Dearbhla stepped up to the imposing presence of the older man.

"Help him. He's only a kid. We didn't sign up for this; for death. Bring him back."

The Spellbinder looked at his Gatekeeper and shook his head.

"I'm sorry. Young Mark was brave but I cannot bring him back."

He looked down at Mark's body and then at each of them. As his gaze met Susie's, she shouted out,

"No. You can't let him die. Save him please. Don't abandon him…us. Please …" she broke off and wept.

Leanne enfolded her in a hug and cried as well. The Spellbinder however made his way over to Takuma, who still lay awkwardly on rubble and was suffering in silence. His leg was torn and still bleeding even though Orla had tied a belt to stop the flow. He placed his left hand on the wound and his right hand gently on to the piercing wood. Takuma gave a sharp intake of breath and closed his eyes.

"Takuma, look at me," instructed the Spellbinder.

Takuma reluctantly did as he was told and tried to prepare himself for the agony he believed would follow the removal of the shard of wood. Nevertheless his eyes met the Spellbinder's violet gaze. As he stared, he could feel himself relax. The Spellbinder's irises seemed to swirl and change colour, first deepen and then lighten until they were a lilac colour. Still he stared and felt like he was floating; almost as if he was sleeping with his eyes open. The Spellbinder had not moved either of his hands. Takuma fought to keep his head from rolling back as it felt so heavy with tiredness. As he began to see the Spellbinder's eyes return to their normal violet colour, his head snapped forward. When he lifted it, the Spellbinder removed his hands from his leg and stood up effortlessly. Takuma was puzzled and looked down to see his leg. Perhaps it was too deep to remove. He gasped when he saw that his leg was not only free of the wood but that the wound had also disappeared. It was as if he had never been hurt. Only the rip in his trousers and the bloodstains on his clothes proved that it had actually happened. Takuma murmured a quiet, "Thank you," as he felt torn between gratefulness that he had no pain but guilt that he was okay and their friend Mark was still dead.

Dearbhla smiled reassuringly at Takuma, as if she knew what was going through his head. He stood up and tested his weight onto the cured leg and couldn't believe it. Not even a twinge. Ben looked at Takuma.

"Cool, man. Glad you're okay."

"Thanks Ben. I-I'm really sorry about Mark," said Takuma.

Ben couldn't even reply. He was gutted that the Spellbinder couldn't save Mark. He watched the seemingly graceful movements of their guide, as he walked to Orla.

"Stand," he ordered simply.

Orla looked as if she was going to protest but instead sighed and got up. She looked unsure.

The Spellbinder lifted his hands and placed them lightly on each side of her bruised throat. To Orla, they felt like the flutter of a butterfly's wings, they were so soft. She stared into his eyes and noticed as they changed colour and swirled making her lightheaded.

"Aw c'mon...wise up! You're helping her but you can't do diddly squat for Mark?"

Ben was disgusted. He went to step forward but Takuma was beside him in an instant.

"Leave it, Ben. Don't mess with him. He's too powerful."

Ben shook off Takuma's arm.

"Yeah..? Well, he's not that powerful or Mark would be sitting here breathing."

Ben felt so angry he wanted to punch something...or someone. He would really love the Divider to make an appearance about now. He cracked his knuckles just thinking about how he could greet him in a *Legenderry* way...involving pain, *lots* of pain.

Meanwhile the Spellbinder stepped back from Orla and she could feel the ache in her throat had gone. She pressed against it but the tender spots had vanished. She cleared her throat and thanked the Spellbinder. Then she looked over to Ben who was cracking his knuckles like a Neanderthal; probably winding himself up for another attack on her. Well, tough. She would be ready the next time. As Leanne and Susie flanked her, asking if she was okay, she couldn't resist sticking her tongue out at Ben. Ha! Ben lifted an eyebrow and looked disdainfully at her. Then he caught the Spellbinder watching him. He groaned and rolled his eyes.

"Okay, okay," he muttered. "Orla, I'm sorry I *didn't* strangle you," he apologised most sincerely.

Takuma stifled a laugh. Orla was smiling smugly when Ben started to speak but her expression changed to a glare after his comment.

"Ben," warned Dearbhla as she felt Orla stiffen beside her. Leanne looked pleadingly at Ben, terrified that things would escalate and the Spellbinder would lose his temper. Who knew what damage he could do?

Ben held up his hands, "Okay. Orla I'm sorry. I shouldn't have hurt you."

He lost the joking air and even Orla could see the lost and vulnerable look he failed to hide.

"Losing Mark…he's…he *was*…like a brother." His throat clogged up and he stopped speaking.

Orla mumbled something but everyone took it as an acceptance of his apology. The Spellbinder rested his hand on Ben's shoulder. Instantly Ben felt calmer, as if the white noise that had started in his head, the minute he realised Mark was gone, had been muted.

"You share many of Mark's admirable qualities. Do not hide them. Use them. Be proud of yourself and know that Mark will be proud of you."

Ben nodded. He felt too emotional to talk, afraid that if he started to crumble now, he'd just fall apart.

The Spellbinder addressed the team.

"Remember your weaknesses, insecurities, they feed the Divider. Now more than ever you must stand strong, shoulder to shoulder. Do not separate or the darkness will invade and the shadows will settle into place."

No one commented. They were still too shocked at the events. It seemed wrong to be carrying on with the mission and yet, if they didn't, then Mark would have died for nothing. They owed it to Mark to at least try.

"Find the next object together. Remain strong and safe."

With that, he began to walk away. A flurry of oak leaves danced about him and became denser, blocking him from view. As he reached the steps at Bishop's Gate, the leaves fell like silent weights and the Spellbinder was gone.

Chapter 40

When the team looked around, they were surprised to see the entire blitzed area was back to normal, as if the explosion had never even happened. Ben panicked and his eyes darted about to find Mark. He breathed a sigh of relief that the Spellbinder hadn't made Mark disappear.

"We can't just leave him like this," he stated.

Takuma and Leanne murmured in agreement. Orla was still feeling around her neck for possible cracked broken bones from Spiderturd's attack. It was Dearbhla who turned proactive. Shaking her head, she walked towards Mark's body.

"No. I'm not standing for this."

Ben looked at her puzzled. "It's done. Even the Spellbinder can't help him."

"He didn't even *try*, Ben!" she retorted.

Ben sighed in exasperation.

"Look around you, boss. He set everything else to rights. It's like he pressed a reset button. Even Orla's not talking like a frog anymore. Do you get it? He *couldn't* bring Mark back."

Ben shouted the last part, becoming more agitated that it really was over.

"No!" shouted Dearbhla. "I can't accept that."

Leanne and Takuma looked worried but wisely kept quiet. Orla fiddled with her hair and felt at a loss how to argue with their leader who seemed to be working up into a temper. Susie was still sitting beside Mark. She looked up at Dearbhla and said tearfully,

"Ben's right. It's over. He'd want us to complete the mission. We have to do this for him."

Dearbhla glared at the young girl.

"You're giving up on him? I didn't expect that from you! What's the point in me being some kind of gate keeper and standing on walls containing four hundred years of magic and beyond?"

"That's not fair. I *do* care! I'm just being realistic. If the Spellbinder can't do anything, what can you do? No offense."

"Susie's right. The Spellbinder is the protector of the city while the Divider is the destructor. Unless you're telling us you're the good daughter of the Divider then we're still pretty much stuffed!" said Ben sadly.

Dearbhla was getting even more frustrated.

"Let me try," she begged. "I can do this. I feel it with every fibre of my being. Please!"

She looked at each of them in turn. Susie nodded first, then Takuma and Leanne. Orla snorted which Dearbhla took as a form of assent. Finally, she turned to Ben who had seen everyone cave in.

"Ugh! Whatever…just do it …but can you hurry up so we can accept Mark is gone and put him somewhere safe. The Divider's not going to wait forever."

Dearbhla smiled briefly and stood above Mark.

"Susie, move away," she asked quietly.

The girl stood beside Ben who was watching in fascination as their leader began to take on a relaxed stance and seemed to be almost asleep. Dearbhla focused all her rage, anguish and grief as it coursed through her body. She stared at Mark and knew what to do. The heat began in her core and spread out through her veins and arteries. It was like fire licking at her blood but she didn't break her concentration. The outside world faded into oblivion. Around her colours meshed into one as if being melted. The heavy atmosphere pressed down onto the group. The rest stood close together, even Orla, so aware were they of something imminent. They sought comfort from each other.

Dearbhla leaned forward and held Mark's head to face hers. As she watched his lifeless body and felt his ice cold flesh, her control broke and power flooded every system in her body. A groan ripped from her as it redirected itself out of her eyes in white and yellow light. Her eyeballs felt like two orbs of heat yet it only stung for a moment.

The others watched mesmerised as the light streamed out from Dearbhla's eyes and into Mark's closed ones. A continuous spectrum of light poured into his sockets and they each gripped one another in hope, fear and with the realisation that they had never seen anything so incredible before. Every molecule of air vibrated with the level of power that was emanating from Dearbhla. Her hair lifted in the static and her eyes shone white and unearthly. A bright glow surrounded her body and the electric charge reached the group. They could feel the hair on their arms lift and when they pointed their fingers into the air tiny blue sparks crackled like thousands of mini lightning bolts. Ben and Takuma exchanged looks of amazement, enjoying the spectacle before them.

Just as they thought they'd seen the best, Dearbhla shot upright and hovered two feet above the ground. She stretched out her arms in front. Mark was suffused in a melody of faint humming whether from the very air vibrating or what, no one knew. Light ran through his skin, almost as if he was transparent and there was a torch shining from inside him. His body shot upright and hovered a few feet opposite Dearbhla.

Suddenly Mark opened his eyes and a cry seemed to rip out from his very soul. His head whipped back and as he cried out, a myriad of colours exploded from his mouth. With the connection broken from Dearbhla, Mark fell to the ground in a heap. Ben and Susie yelled out and ran to him. Dearbhla lowered to the ground and the light around her dimmed and then disappeared. She sank wearily to the ground. Takuma and Leanne ran to check on her. Orla stood with her mouth agape.

"That didn't just happen?" She thought to herself. She couldn't even move with the amazing show she had witnessed.

Ben lifted Mark up to support him into a sitting position. His own heart was hammering so loud it could wake the dead. What had happened; could Mark actually be alive?

Susie met Ben's gaze.

"Mark. Can you hear me?" she asked.

Susie held her breath and was filled with such hope she could barely think. What happened next was enough to stop all their hearts.

Mark opened his eyes, squinted at the light, coughed and said,

"Ben you're not going to kiss me, are you?"

Susie laughed and felt her heart almost burst with happiness. Ben closed his eyes and let out his breath, unable to speak quite yet. He squeezed Mark's arm in acknowledgement but couldn't trust his voice.

Takuma and Leanne helped Dearbhla sit up.

"Is he....okay?" Dearbhla asked in a small frightened voice.

Takuma smiled at her, "You did it. He's cracking jokes already."

Dearbhla looked quickly at Leanne who reassured her, "He's back. You did it. You saved Mark."

Dearbhla closed her eyes in relief and felt that her entire body was drained and weak. She smiled and thought, "But it was worth it!"

They each took turns to check on Mark for themselves. It was nothing short of a miracle what had happened. Mark himself felt completely rejuvenated, as if he had been asleep for a week. His body thrummed with energy and his mind was the clearest and calmest it had been in a long time. He laughed again when Leanne leaned towards him to hug and tiny sparks of leftover static crackled between them. Every time someone touched him or even came close, there were sparks of electricity popping up.

"Maybe, you're like some super hero whose power is electric!" exclaimed Ben.

Mark chuckled and watched his friend excitedly poke him in the arm and chest. As he was going in towards his stomach, Mark caught his finger and squeezed.

"Enough. It hurts," he warned.

Ben looked at him curiously.

"*Seriously..?* You've been dead for the past hour and I'm hurting you!"

Mark glowered at him. "I'm getting electric shocks every time anyone gets close to me. So yes, it hurts. Back off Ben..."

Ben held up his hands and moved away. "Sorry!" The ordeal his friend had survived did not mean he was incapable of losing his temper. If he did have new super human electric powers, he didn't want to be the first victim. Ben grinned as he turned to look at Orla. Perhaps she'll open her mouth and wind up Mark. Now that would be interesting. Super fried Orla!

The girl in question stared back at him and then scowled. His face told her it wasn't good things he was thinking about. Idiot.

When Dearbhla reached Mark, he tried to jump up quickly. Takuma moved to help him but Mark brushed him off with a shake of his head and a smile.

"I'm fine Takuma. Like, I'm really buzzing!"

Takuma stepped back, glad he seemed to be in good form. He still couldn't believe what had occurred. This day seemed to get stranger and more dangerous, the longer they were caught in the time warp. No-one else mattered, not because he didn't care about them. After all, they were the reason they were plunged into these life threatening situations. They were trying to save all their lives. No, it wasn't that they didn't matter but they were frozen in time. They had no control over their future. It rested entirely on this little group of people standing here. They were fighting evil to secure their safety. It was monumental what they were involved in and though he wasn't sure if it was appropriate, he felt pride and excitement puff out his chest.

He smiled as he watched Mark embrace Dearbhla.

"Oh yeah...you can't give a bro some love but you're all over the Boss Lady!" remarked Ben as he saw the affectionate display.

They both ignored the sulky comments and continued to cling to each other. Mark pulled away first and made direct eye contact with Dearbhla.

"Thank you. You saved me. I can't explain where I was but I felt peaceful and I wasn't scared." He swallowed and took a deep breath, "But I kept hearing your voice calling me back. I knew you were fighting for me

Dearbhla. Thanks for not giving up." He kissed her on the cheek.

Ben caught Susie's attention and waggled his eyebrows.

"Looks like you have competition for Mark's body!" he said cheekily.

Susie blushed and looked away, annoyed at her body for reacting like that. Why did she get embarrassed? She knew he was just showing their leader some gratitude but a small part of her wished it had been her who had fought for him. Susie envied the older girl her powers. She wished she could have saved him, but she couldn't, so she had to suck it up and let him kiss who he wanted. Anyway it wasn't exactly a full snog on the lips.

Mark looked closely at Dearbhla and thought her eye colour had grown a bit dimmer.

"Dearbhla, do you feel okay?" he asked in concern. She must have used so much power and energy to bring him back; he hoped she didn't get ill because of doing so.

Their leader smiled and reassured him. "I'm great now that we're all back together again. Let's take a look at the second clue."

Everyone agreed and they gathered around as Susie took the parchment out and handed it to Takuma.

As they waited, Mark inspected his hands. It was amazing. Even the splinters had been removed. Every cut he had before Dearbhla saved him was healed. Mark shook his head in wonder. He saw Ben winking at him and mentally shaking himself he drew his attention back to the mission.

Chapter 41

Dearbhla felt a bit wobbly but she kept quiet. She didn't want them worrying about her. There were too many other things to worry about. She dreaded to think what was in store for them during this part of the mission. She noticed Susie watching her intently as if she had picked up on her weakness. Offering the young girl a bright smile and a wink, she hoped it would put her mind at rest. Susie smiled back and refocused her attention on Takuma. He had unrolled the second clue and was waiting to read it.

"Should I read now?" he asked. They all nodded.

Orla rolled her eyes in her usual impatient manner. "Get on with it. Are you waiting on a brass band intro?"

"Only if I get to beat the drum with your head!" added Ben.

"*Oh really..?* Well I know where I'll be sticking the flute," retorted Orla.

"Enough," scolded Mark, "We don't have time for you two playing tit for tat," glaring at the two guilty parties for emphasis.

More quietly he addressed Takuma, "Go ahead. There won't be any more interruptions." Again, he pinned Ben and Orla with a glare.

Takuma cleared his throat and began,

> **Walk along the broken paths**
>
> **Of bastions from the distant past;**
>
> **Pass the stones that lie upon**
>
> **A thousand hearts.**
>
> **See the guard, who at the gate,**
>
> **Defends the key to seal your fate."**

He read it again at their request. Leanne spoke first.

"Well, we know what the bastions are so what are the stones?"

Orla snorted, "Ah duh! Look around Brainiac. We're surrounded by stones."

Leanne shot her a dirty look but inwardly cringed that she had asked such a stupid question.

"I think Leanne means could there be a significant stone APART from those that are holding the walls up?" Susie added, always ready to defend Leanne from the viper's tongue of Orla.

The 'viper' sneered at Susie, fully aware that she'd argue black was white, if it backed up the loser formerly known as Leanne.

Ben stepped in between the girls who were doing a battle of the glowering stares.

"Okay, girlies," he placated while holding out his hands, "Let's dial down the bitchometer and figure out who the guard is. Huh?" He tapped the side of his head and nodded, "Am I the King of Puzzles or what?"

Orla stepped up to him and folded her arms. "You're definitely the King of...," she broke off and started sniffing the air, "Does anyone else smell sh-?"

"Orla..! Pack it in!" shouted Mark interrupting her. Orla raised her eyebrows at Ben, smirked and walked away.

Ben didn't get a chance to respond as Dearbhla picked up on the point he'd made.

"You know, Ben's on to something."

They all ignored Orla's loud jeer.

"We need to figure out who the guard is and where he is."

She could feel the excitement building as they were on the cusp of another adventure. Hopefully this would go more smoothly now they had seen what the Divider was capable of. Forewarned was forearmed. At least that's what she was putting her faith in. They couldn't afford any more surprises.

"Maybe the guard is you," shouted Leanne eagerly at Dearbhla.

"Brainiac strikes again," muttered Orla loud enough for everyone to hear.

"Why don't you go find the Divider and ask for flying lessons?" said Ben as he brushed past Orla and stood beside Leanne. Leanne smiled at his support and then she addressed the group.

"Dearbhla, you're a Guardian of the Gates so maybe the clue is referring to you… well not specifically but you are the one who is here today so… well… it makes sense," she explained.

"It does make sense," agreed Mark who smiled warmly at Leanne.

Susie hated the fluttering sensation in her tummy when she witnessed the warm way that Mark had smiled at the other girl. What was wrong with her? This was so annoying! She let out a frustrated groan and then blushed when everyone turned to look at her.

"Sorry!" she mumbled, "Just thinking."

She ignored Ben's knowing smile and cleared her throat.

"If it is Dearbhla, it means the object could be on her."

Dearbhla threw a startled look at Susie.

"Oh. That's weird. It would be really ironic that I've had the second object on me the whole time!"

Mark, Ben and Susie stood beside her.

"Yeah, but imagine if you did have it. This would have to go into the Guinness Book of Records for the quickest mission EVER! *Indiana Jones* wouldn't have a look in!" said Ben, eager to get this over with. Losing Mark had been epic. His nerves couldn't take any more drama.

Dearbhla blinked and paused to get her wits together. Even her thought processes seemed much slower since the 'Mark' incident. She really hoped her energy would return soon or the team would be one member down because she wouldn't have the strength to fight her own shadow, never mind the Divider. She turned out her pockets as her bag had been stolen. Lipstick, hankies, chewing gum … bingo!

"The medallion!" she shouted.

Everyone gathered around her and watched as she carefully removed the forgotten medallion from a side pocket in her coat.

"Whoa! That was fast!" said Ben.

Dearbhla laughed. "I know. I can't believe I forgot about it. It was with the scrolls."

"Oh goodie..! Well, what now?" Orla commented drily.

"Can I see it again?" asked Takuma who had inspected it earlier that day.

Dearbhla handed him the disc shaped medallion. He felt around and held it up to his eye to look through the hole in its centre.

"What's written on it?" asked Susie.

Before Takuma could answer Ben snatched it. Peering at it and turning it slowly, he sighed in disappointment.

"Nothing new…"

At their puzzled looks, he explained, "It just repeats a line from the clue. 'Pass the stones that lie upon a thousand hearts.'"

He flipped it back to Takuma who was smiling in enlightenment.

"Dearbhla this is part of the clue. It's not the object but it'll help us get the object. I swear there was nothing written on it before. It must have appeared when we found the first object."

Dearbhla smiled back. "Thank goodness I brought it then."

Mark spoke up as he looked about in agitation, "Can we move on from here?"

Susie understood his discomfort. This is the place he'd died and then been brought back. Anyone would be freaked out.

"Let's head over to the next bastion," offered Leanne.

They all accepted it was time to make tracks and walked over New Gate but didn't stay. They wanted to put as much distance between themselves and any cannon as possible. When they reached Ferryquay Gate they stopped and looked out towards Carlisle Road. People and cars were motionless, held fast by a pause in time. Seeing people caught up in that manner, reminded each of them what this mission was about. These were the people they were fighting evil for; their right to exist in peace and to live their unique lives in light. It was overwhelming to watch still bodies and be fully aware of how much they depended on the inexperienced team. If they knew who was defending their very existence against the Divider, the bodies would surely tremble.

Ben broke the contemplative silence. Leaning on the wall, he had turned to look in the opposite direction, in towards Ferryquay Street.

"Orla, I wonder if your Stoner boyfriends are still waiting on you to kiss them, so they can change into real BOYS."

"Ha! I heard they were more interested in you Ben, but they blew you out 'cos you were too *stoopid*."

"Nah…they dumped you 'cos instead of a princess they realised you were the Wicked Witch of the Walls!"

Orla huffed at the sniggers she heard from the others who were trying not to get involved. She zeroed in on her victim.

"Glad you think it's so funny, Leanne. The only boyfriend you've ever had was the 2D version on your bedroom wall – poor bloke can't run away like the rest do!"

Satisfied at Leanne's blush, she swaggered past the group towards Artillery Bastion. The rest followed slowly. Ben nudged Leanne on the elbow.

"C'mon. I'll let you practice on me if you want?" He waggled his eyebrows and licked his lips with loud slurping noises. Leanne giggled and linked her arm through his.

"You wish!" she joked letting the embarrassment disappear. She refused to let the 'Wicked Witch of the Walls', so aptly named by Ben, make her uncomfortable.

"Listen to this," whispered Ben as he squeezed her arm.

"Hey Orla..! If you called your flying monkey friends we could get there quicker!"

Leanne suppressed a laugh as he began to whistle a tune from a well-known movie about a witch. Orla made a rude hand gesture which made Ben roar even louder in laughter. Leanne smiled and turned her head to see Takuma staring at her. As if caught doing something he shouldn't, he quickly looked away. Hmmm, she thought, that was weird. Maybe he disapproved of her encouraging Ben's digs at Orla. Guiltily, she took her arm out of Ben's and frowned at Takuma's back.

Chapter 42

They arrived at New Gate Bastion. It overlooked Orchard Street on the outside and Market Street on the inside of the walls. Ben whistled in appreciation as he looked over those imposing walls.

"What is it? See a statue you fancy?" Orla asked snidely.

Ben looked confused and held his hand to his ear.

"Eh? Sorry. I don't speak wicked witch language. Go. Find. A. Flying. Monkey," he enunciated slowly.

Orla strode up to him ready to let fly but he sidestepped her as he threw his hand up in front of her face.

"Talk to the hand, W.W.W.!"

She spun round to him with murder in her eyes.

"Wait a minute." He made a show of thinking and then clicked his fingers. "I've got it. W.W.W. you're the original worldwide witch. We all know about YOU and your witchy attitude!"

Orla gritted her teeth and wished she had a blunt instrument to hit him with. He was infuriating.

"Before I was rudely interrupted by…," he stopped as he got slightly nervous at the bloodlust in Orla's eyes, "*Orla*, I was looking at the shopping centre and thinking, imagine we were stuck in there. Free food courts anyone?"

The entire group groaned with hunger. The shopping centre was so close yet they couldn't even enter it as it stood just across from the walls.

Mark had an idea.

"Yeah, but the other centre is *inside* the Walls!"

They all cheered except for their leader.

"We don't have time for food guys. The Divider could strike at any time and with our luck it would be in the middle of us slacking and filling our faces," said a serious Dearbhla.

Ben complained, "Aww! And that's why you're the Boss. But you don't have manly muscles that need, no, DEMAND energy!"

Mark actually agreed with Ben. He was starving. Especially after his return…or whatever you could call it.

"I have to agree with Ben. If I don't eat soon I won't be useful for anything," he explained.

"Me, too," agreed Leanne.

"Me, three," added Susie.

Takuma nodded and Orla shrugged.

"Anything to shut him up for a minute," she said tossing a disgusted look in the general direction of Ben.

Ben blew her a kiss which she dodged dramatically.

"Yuck. Keep your filthy germs to yourself."

He grinned and put a hand to his heart. "Such adoration…You complete me!" he continued to joke.

"Grrrrr…Someone stick food in his gob to stop sound escaping," said Orla clearly irritated by his constant jibes.

"You two are getting on my nerves," said Takuma. "If you carry on I'm going to actually chuck you in the Divider's path and let him deal with your never ending sniping!"

Everyone paused in shock at the usually quiet and relaxed boy. Ben slapped him on the back and apologised, as only he could.

"Sorry, my wee mucker, she's like a red rag to my stallion!"

"Bull!" Orla scoffed.

"What? I'm saying sorry to my friend. It's not bull," said an offended Ben.

Orla tutted, "No, you dumbass…the saying is 'a red rag to a bull.'"

Ben closed his mouth as he caught Takuma's expression and smiled innocently. When Takuma turned away, Ben caught Orla's attention and held up his index fingers with both thumbs meeting to make a "W" letter. He pulled a face and pushed it towards her three times mouthing the words World Wide Witch. Then he smirked in satisfaction and leaned back happily on the wall. Orla rolled her eyes but thankfully remained silent.

Susie sighed; a truce for the next minute at least. She peered at Takuma who was looking out over Orchard Street. It was unlike him to get so irritated with those two. He seemed troubled. Susie joined him and watched the shoppers who were oblivious to their life and death situation. Takuma knew Susie's purpose before she even opened her mouth.

"I'm okay. Those two act like annoying parrots bickering over the silliest things."

Susie thought the analogy was spot on.

"I know. Believe me, if they keep it up it's not the Divider they'll have to worry about."

Leanne had also joined them on Takuma's other side.

"Yeah like pick a number and get in line!" She pursed her lips and mimicked Orla's eye roll.

It had the desired effect and they all laughed.

Mark and Dearbhla had been discussing food source options but at the laughter, Mark stopped and watched the trio laugh over something Leanne had said. He smiled at the sight of their fleeting happiness. As his eyes found Susie, she looked up and met his stare. His stomach dipped as her laughter cut off and she gained a more sombre expression. Geez, he looked at her and felt warmth and something he couldn't explain; whereas, she looked at him as if he had ruined her birthday party. Embarrassed, he dropped his gaze and tried to focus on what Dearbhla was saying. At Mark's blank expression, Dearbhla sighed.

"You didn't hear one word I said, did you?"

"Yes. No. Sorry. No," he fumbled.

"I was saying I think we should send a few on a food gathering trip and the rest wait here."

Mark wasn't convinced. "I think we should stay together. We're stronger opposition then….well... apart from when I got killed but otherwise..."

Dearbhla tried again, "I know, but we only need snacks to stave off the hunger; a few bags of crisps, chocolate, water. That's it, then back here. Snatch and go. In, out."

Mark reluctantly caved, "Okay, but any sign of trouble and we regroup."

Dearbhla smiled triumphantly, "I'll tell the others," she said.

Before she could move off, Mark grabbed her arm and pulled her back.

"You're not going," he stated

"No way, I can't come up with the idea and then not go. I have to go," she explained.

"Then, we don't do it," he said adamantly.

"Mark, I'm quite capable of grabbing a few bags of crisps. Are you questioning me as a leader?" she asked, hoping that was not the case or things could get complicated.

"I'd never doubt you as our leader. It's just after you….you know…. brought me back, I can tell you're weaker. You try to hide it but I can see you walk more slowly."

He held up his hand to stop her protesting, "And you're short of breath. You gave me your energy so I'll go in your place."

Dearbhla was touched that Mark was sincerely worried about her. She blinked back tears and knew he was right. She hadn't been the same since she'd infused him with her life source energy.

"Okay, thanks Mark. Hopefully I'll be as good as new soon," she managed to say and hurriedly wiped her eyes with her hands.

He smiled and called to the others. When he explained the plan, it was met with a mixture of excitement of being fed and the genuine reluctance of splitting up.

Ben was part of the 'excited to be fed' decision. "Yup, I'm there."

He lifted his shirt up and spoke gently to his stomach, "I'm gonnae get you something nice, precious," he said patting it.

Mark nodded. "Okay. We need one more person. Any volunteers..?"

Susie waited for him to look at her. He didn't. He looked at everyone else but had avoided eye contact with her. What was his problem? That was enough to propel herself into a potentially dangerous situation.

"I'll go," she spoke up.

Mark glanced at her, dismissed her and then conceded, "Right. We'll go now and be back in fifteen minutes."

Takuma reminded him that all their watches had stopped during the mass evacuation of the walled city.

"Use your own perception of time," instructed Susie who was getting angrier at Mark's behaviour towards her.

"Perceptawhat?" said Ben frowning.

"Never mind Ben, we're out of here. If we're too long, all of you come to find us. Nobody goes alone!" ordered Mark.

He stared pointedly at Dearbhla. She nodded but wasn't entirely happy that she wouldn't be with them.

Chapter 43

The trio began to go forward to get onto Market Street. This was the only break in the walls and allowed easy access on to the streets. They headed towards the steps.

"Wait. What if we get in trouble? How do we get your help?" shouted out a worried looking Leanne.

Ben answered, "That's easy. Just get the Wicked Witch of the Walls to come get us on her broomstick and we'll be back in two shakes of a flying monkey's tail."

He winked at Orla and shuffled off whistling. Leanne ignored that and watched Mark expectantly. He looked as if he hadn't thought of that.

"Shout. Scream. Loudly..!" He grimaced, aware that this wasn't the best of plans but unable to come up with anything better.

Leanne's shoulders drooped and she turned to Dearbhla, "I don't like this," she said as she watched her three friends disappear from view.

"I know, but we need food and we have to take the chance," said Dearbhla trying to sound confident.

Takuma took the nervous girl's hand and walked over to the wall.

"We'll keep an eye out for them. They'll be back before you know it!"

Leanne hoped he was right. Even Orla seemed pensive and hadn't responded to Ben's remarks.

"Spiderturd will miss me, so he'll be back," she muttered, as she too joined them in their look out.

Dearbhla sighed. Her tummy was knotted with nerves. Will this never end?

***

"Hey. Wait up!" shouted Ben.

Mark glanced back but kept up with Susie's fast stride. She was obviously annoyed at him but he had no idea why. Ben caught up but was panting heavily.

"How can someone so short move so fast?" He referred to Susie, who ignored him and continued to make her way along Ferryquay Street. As they drew level with the shop they had left the 'Hands Across The Divide' statues inside, Ben stopped.

"Are we not going in here?" he asked pointing.

Mark rolled his eyes and grabbed his shirt, "Let's go. We don't want round two with the bronze brothers."

Ben stumbled forward but kept sneaking confused glances at Susie. She hadn't uttered a word since they'd left the others. Uh oh, trouble in paradise. He nudged Mark and looked meaningfully towards Susie. His friend frowned and shook his head. Ben got in front of them and started to walk backwards.

"Why don't you have a wee chat and I'll go on ahead," he winked at Mark but Susie was disinterested. Ben shrugged and moved on.

"Ben don't!" said Mark nervously.

"I know bro. I'll stay close," he said and then sped away from them.

Appeased, Mark swung round and stopped Susie.

"What's wrong?" he demanded.

She refused to meet his eyes. "Nothing… we don't have time for this." Susie tried to get past him but he blocked her.

"Yes. There is time. Why are you so angry with me?" he asked, his voice rising.

"I'm *not*," she shouted.

He folded his arms and rocked back on his heels, "Tell me," he urged.

She faltered and looked up into his clear blue eyes. He looked genuinely concerned. She felt so confused.

"I…I…don't know. You make me crazy," she relented.

He scrunched his face up and cocked his head in confusion, "Why?"

Susie felt her cheeks flaming, "Forget it. I'm being silly."

She attempted to get past him, but once again he blocked her escape. Mark was at a total loss as to why she was being so jumpy. As she got more agitated and tried to sidestep him, her face reddened even more. He could see he wasn't getting anywhere.

"Well, if I said something to annoy you I'm sorry."

He unfolded his arms and moved to the side. Susie went to walk past him but suddenly she turned and hit him full force on the chest.

"*Ouch!* What the hell was that for?" he shouted.

Susie glared at him. "Don't you ever dare die on me again!" she shouted back.

Mark closed his mouth, swallowed and felt warmth spread inside him. He had forgotten how bad it must have been for them when they'd seen his broken body lying on the ground. Pulling her close, he kissed her on the nose.

"Susie, I'm okay, better than okay. I'm sorry you were so worried but I'm not going anywhere ever again. Okay..?"

"Okay!" replied Susie with a bright smile, ecstatic at the way he was looking at her.

Mark's heart clenched a little as he stared into her deep chestnut coloured eyes. They pulled him in and all he wanted to do was to protect her and to spend time with her – preferably without the death knell ringing above their heads.

"Get a room you two! Ugh!" Ben cried out.

Susie pulled away from Mark and tried to will Ben to shut up with her mind. It didn't work.

"I was gone for five seconds! What did you do, Mark? Lunge at her!"

"Shut up Ben," Mark growled, as he saw how uncomfortable Susie was getting.

"Did you find a shop?"

Ben nodded eagerly. "Yeah, c'mon, we can get stocked up and head back."

Mark waved his arm in a flourish to encourage Susie to go on before him. She smiled shyly and caught up to Ben. Mark strolled up with a huge grin on his face. It seemed she liked him after all. Result!

They entered the small shop and filled some carrier bags with food essentials and some extra bottles of water.

"Hurry up. We need to leave now," said Mark who was becoming more nervous.

It had gone so smoothly that he expected that to change any minute. They grabbed their bags of loot and headed out onto the street. Quickly scanning the area, they saw nothing threatening so urgently made their way back to New Gate Bastion.

Reunited with the others, they cheered and the trio enjoyed the praise and gratefulness of those left behind. Happily, they distributed the food and water. As they sat on the ground and munched away contentedly, it almost seemed like normal. They could have been seven friends enjoying a picnic on a fresh summer's day. Although they joked and laughed, there was still an air of alertness should trouble arise. The food was eaten quickly so that whatever else was thrown their way, they felt ready with their replenished energy. Dearbhla particularly needed this rest as she was becoming increasingly tired and weak. She felt like she was dragging herself about and that even the smallest of tasks was a huge undertaking.

Swallowing the last of the water, she had felt a sharp burst of energy. She stood up and was relieved she had her old self back. No sooner had she thought that, when she felt it all drain away and her body depleted of its energy. Her entire being sagged and when she tried to walk, it was as if she was treading on pieces of broken glass. The pain shot up from her feet to her legs and she bit back a cry. Wanting to collapse, it took all her strength to pull her heavy and sore body over to lean on the wall.

Mark was beside her in an instant.

"You're getting worse," he insisted.

Dearbhla could barely lift her head to speak, "I...I know," she admitted.

There was no point lying. They were too far into the mission to start messing it up by pretending all was well. Clearly she needed help and besides she was too exhausted to hide it anymore.

Mark ran a frustrated hand through his hair, "What can we do?"

Dearbhla shook her head, "I don't know. I think this is serious, Mark. I can barely move."

Mark blew out a breath. He had known she was keeping how bad she was from him, from all of them. He felt so guilty. It was his fault. If she hadn't brought him back, she'd be fine.

"Dearbhla, I need to let them know you're not well. Okay?"

He added the last question as if he was consulting her approval but whether she actually gave it or not, he was telling them.

Dearbhla gave a whispered yes.

"Hey, can everyone come here?" he called out.

The rest of the group gathered to him and their leader.

"Dearbhla is not well. We need to help her. Any ideas..?"

He figured to get straight to the point. They hadn't time for anything else. The group looked worriedly at the older girl and noticed how pale she was. Her skin seemed sallow and her eyes were large and sunken into her face. No-one gave any options. They all knew deep down that nothing found in a chemist could fix what was ailing Dearbhla. Mark became annoyed at their lack of response.

"Really..? All of a sudden you've been struck mute? C'mon Ben, Orla. You always have plenty to say. What will we do?"

Susie stepped up bedside him and rested her hand on his arm.

"Mark. We can't help her; we can just get her to rest."

Dearbhla smiled weakly, "Sounds good to me. I could sleep for a week."

Mark stared back at Susie and let all his dejection show. He blamed himself, which was useless, but she understood. She would feel the same, if it had been her Dearbhla had saved.

Takuma silently moved beside their leader and put his arm around her. "No, Dearbhla, we stay together. We'll carry you if we have to. We can't do this without you. Where we go, you go."

He paused and met all of their surprised stares, apart from Mark, who was grinning.

"Takuma's right. We're a team. Nobody gets left behind."

Before Dearbhla could argue, Takuma continued, "We might find a way to help you as we go along, so c'mon Ben. You and I will have the first honour of helping."

Ben grinned, rubbed his hands together and shifted over to Dearbhla. "Right, boss. I'm at your service. Lucky you," he joked, while waggling his eyebrows.

Dearbhla still had enough energy to make a feeble swipe at him but leaned heavily on him when he took her arm for support. Takuma did the same on the other side. The two boys exchanged anxious looks.

"Stop fussing," Dearbhla ordered, aware of their concern. Takuma smiled to reassure her while Ben winked and chattered on to stop her from thinking too much or she'd change her mind.

"Wait. Where are we going?" Orla asked.

"Better we're on the move. We're easy targets in the one place," explained Takuma.

"Susie, can you read the clue again? I forget it," asked Leanne.

Susie read it as they walked on slowly, leaving New Gate Bastion.

"Walk along the broken paths

Of bastions from the distant past;

Pass the stones that lie upon

A thousand hearts.

See the guard, who at the gate,

Defends the key to seal your fate."

"Read the last two lines again, please," asked Takuma.

Susie did so and knew at once what he was thinking.

"You don't think Dearbhla was the guardian the clue refers to, do you?"

"No. I think it's something else. We need to go to the gates. That's where we'll meet the guardian."

Ben admired the other boy's deduction. It seemed Leanne did too, as she was beaming at him as if he'd just solved a chemistry equation: *IMPOSSIBLE*. Well, he found them impossible; Takuma probably did them for fun. Ben shivered at the thought.

"Good plan mucker. I was thinking the same thing myself."

Leanne looked at him dubiously and Mark just grunted.

"Where's the faith?" said an offended Ben. He glimpsed Orla rolling her eyes and smiled. You could always depend on Orla for a negative response.

Chapter 44

The group were making their way on to Market Street, when they heard a distant voice shouting.

"Ssh. Stop. Can you hear that?" asked Susie urgently.

Everyone listened to a distinct manly voice shouting. The group looked at each other in disbelief. There was someone else here.

"Be careful," warned Dearbhla, "It could be the Divider or one of his shadows."

They tried to detect where the voice was coming from. Mark ran down to the bottom of Market Street but the voice became much more distant so he quickly returned.

"It's definitely close. Try up there," he said.

Susie ran up to the top of Market Street and stopped still when she heard the loud booming voice.

"Yes! You, you little idiot…Come here at once!"

Susie's mouth dropped open and she stared in shock at the sight before her.

"What's wrong? Are you deaf? Get over here so I can get this over with," the impatient speaker ordered.

Susie could hear the others coming up behind her but she couldn't even turn to warn them.

"CAN.YOU.READ.MY.LIPS.GET.OVER.HERE, you little idiot," he mouthed slowly and rather rudely.

Susie's head jerked back in surprise. A talking head was being rude to her. In fact it sounded suspiciously like Orla. The team stood in a row beside her. No one spoke. They were equally as astonished as she.

"Oh. Here we go," he muttered sarcastically when he saw the rest of the group approach, "The backup singers have arrived. Go on then, give me a tune."

The head tipped forward giving the impression he was listening. The seven still never uttered a single word, in awe of the talking head. It cocked his head to the side and pursed his lips.

"Rubbish! Walk on by. Your presence offends me," he dismissed them. "I always thought people here could sing," he muttered to himself, "This is the city that gave the world a lot of famous singers," he bellowed.

"Oh no, but I'm stuck with boneless cretins. Pah! Leave me, you talentless creatures." The head closed his eyes and adopted a bored expression.

"This is some freaky show," whispered Ben, "Orla, is that your da?" He couldn't resist adding, "I think your da wants you to sing him to sleep."

The head's eyes sprung open and he growled.

"Are you still here? Okay, I'll try one more time." He sighed mightily as if sacrificing a great deal.

"Little Miss Idiot and your Backup Singers, COME HERE!!" he roared.

Startled, they shuffled towards the grumpy head who was glaring down at them from his lofty position above the arch of Ferryquay Gate. The carved stone head had long wavy hair and a long beard. The eyes were mesmerising. They were empty – no iris, no colour. His stone eyes were like being face to face with a crocodile; an increasingly irate and impatient crocodile.

"Hmm," the head gave a quick appraisal when they stood before him. "Now that I look upon you, I weep for mankind. Hoho!" he laughed in amusement, "You really must be the most sorry looking bunch of no hopers I think I've ever witnessed, and remember, I've seen *plenty!*" he emphasised.

Ben took a deep breath, ready to retaliate but Dearbhla had enough strength left to dig him with her elbow.

"Okay, okay," he muttered reluctantly as he felt he could give this piece of old masonry a run for his money.

The stone eyes rolled and he heaved a theatrical sigh.

"Go on. Ask me your question?" he encouraged gloomily.

After a moment's pause, Takuma took the lead.

"Are you the guardian who defends the key?"

The head never answered. He remained staring at the young boy. Just as the group thought he had gone away, he boomed out a loud, "Yay. Tis me, that holds that which you require."

Orla began to fidget. Grumpy head was getting on her nerves.

"How do we get the key?" Takuma asked.

"Why, you take it young master!" he said reasonably.

Takuma blinked in confusion. He still hadn't a clue where the key was. At a loss, he turned to the others for help. Orla had had enough.

"Listen. Head man!" she started agitated. This was not going to end well. "Enough of your games… where's the flippin' key?" Orla's voice was rising in temper.

The Head's beard fluttered at the huffing and puffing he was carrying out at Orla's tone.

"I will not tolerate this outrage," he bellowed at the team who each took a step back, apart from Orla.

"Tough! We didn't make it this far for a stupid talking head to play power games."

The head continued to bluster in rage.

"Impudent nincompoop..! Leave now."

"No. I will not, you big slab of concrete! I'll go up there and stuff a pigeon in your mouth 'cos you're talking bird–."

"Orla, stop..! We need him," cried Susie urgently.

The Head nodded quickly and pursed his lips.

"Ho! See. YOU NEED ME! You little ignoramus… Go play with the Divider. I'm sure he would just love to chop you up into pieces and feed your putrid body to the rats."

Orla was in a full temper now and was shouting back at the head pointing at him and mocking his 'big, bent nose' to which he yelled out in horror and seemed to be extremely offended. Ben was sniggering; glad not to be the brunt of Orla's bad temper. Dearbhla sank weakly into Ben and Takuma's supportive hold. They silently communicated a sit down and helped her onto the kerb. She smiled, thankful to be off her feet, her energy was draining fast and now she was beginning to feel quite ill. All this shouting didn't help, so she closed her eyes and let her head droop onto Ben's shoulder.

Leanne tried to pull Orla away from her newest enemy but the girl shoved her away and continued trading insults with her equal. Leanne shrugged helplessly at Susie, who shook her head in disgust. At this rate, the Head would never give them the key, even if his very existence depended upon it. Orla had a real knack of rubbing people, and inanimate objects, up the wrong way. It was a skill few were able to master. Orla was gifted with it as a natural talent. Susie sighed and wondered how they would beg for forgiveness or if it was even an option.

Mark saw Susie's face and knew she was feeling that Orla was ruining their chances. He hated to see her so hopeless. That spurred him into action.

"Hey. Enough!" he bellowed. It shocked both parties into silence. "Orla, go over and sit down," he ordered.

Before she could protest, he cocked his head to the side as if daring her to challenge him. She didn't. When she walked off to sit near Takuma, Mark faced the Head.

"I apologise for our…friend. She gets a bit overexcited." Mark ignored the low mumbling from Orla's direction.

The Head looked down haughtily, enjoying Mark's grovelling.

"Honestly. We're so glad you are the Guardian. No one could be worthier."

The group could actually see the Head preening with the praise.

"I appeal to your good nature and wisdom. Please give us the key," Mark held his breath, hoping that the Head did have a better nature than what he outwardly showed.

The Head did a slow perusal of the team. He huffed and closed his eyes when his eyes met the surly girl he had had words with. When he met Mark's wary gaze he let out a loud rumble of laughter.

"Ho! I tell you, you are not as hopeless as I thought."

Mark exhaled his nervous breath, and smiled up at the carved stone that held the knowledge of the second object.

The team relaxed at his announcement. Orla sat looking at her nails. She refused to even glance that block of stone's way. She couldn't care less if he gave them the key or not. He deserved a pickaxe being flung between his eyes; maybe it would chip a bit off his huge honker.

The Head enjoyed having the spotlight. He nodded Susie's way.

"Little Miss Idiot!" he called.

Susie rolled her eyes at the rude nickname but wasn't about to argue when Mark had smoothed things over.

"Yes?" She asked calmly.

"Ho! You were the first to see me. So I will give you the honour of touching my beloved face," he announced proudly.

"Lucky me..!" she said drily.

Mark grinned and then told Ben to help him. Ben eased himself away from Dearbhla and jumped up. They both lifted Susie up as far as they could. She reached the Head and patted its nose. It sighed in disappointment and then began to sneeze four times. Susie laughed, at which he glared sternly at her. She cleared her throat awkwardly and looked expectantly at him.

"Oh yes, the medallion... Do you have it?" he enquired.

Dearbhla tiredly fished it out of her pocket and Takuma threw it to Mark. He threw it up to Susie who unbalanced briefly but caught herself in time. Mark and Ben let their breaths whoosh out. Dropping Susie would not go down well. Their arms were under strain and beginning to tremble.

"Hurry up Susie," groaned Ben.

"I know. I am. Here it is," she held the medallion up to show the Head.

He narrowed his stone eyes and inspected it.

"Good. Now set it into my mouth."

Susie stared at him.

"Hurry..! There is not much time left. The evil draws near."

At that ominous statement, Susie shakily placed the disc into his mouth. She could feel a small raised cylinder. Fitting the complementary hole of the medallion onto it, she heard it click into place. Nothing happened. Her heart began to hammer. Why wasn't anything happening.

"What's wrong?" she asked the Head but there was no response. He was gone.

"Susie! What the hell? Hurry up," shouted Ben.

"We can't hold you much longer Susie," warned Mark desperately.

Sweat was rolling down both of their faces and they were frantically trying to keep still. Just as Susie was about to give up, she gave the medallion one last push down and it began to lower into a compartment below. Immediately another carved mouth replaced that one. It was identical in every way except that it didn't have a raised cylinder nor did it contain a medallion. As Susie leaned closer, she could see something glinting in the light. Reaching towards the mouth she took out an old iron key that was the same length as her index finger. It was so light and cold to the touch. Grinning, Susie held it tightly and shouted for Mark and Ben to set her down.

Relieved, they carefully lifted her down until Mark held her in both of his arms. She was smiling happily and showed him the key. He whooped loudly and swung her around. They each held the key and marvelled at their achievement. Two objects found and not a bad guy in sight. Leanne brought the key over to where Dearbhla sat. Gently, she placed it in Dearbhla's outstretched palm. The older girl stared down at the precious key. She couldn't believe they were winning. Her smile faded. If only she felt stronger. She didn't know if she could keep awake for much longer. Exhaustion was seeping into her very bones until her body was sending repeated signals to her brain. Lie down. Sleep. Soon she wouldn't be able to ignore them.

"What now boss?" Ben asked.

Everyone was eager to carry on. They seemed to be on a positive roll and hanging around in the one area left them exposed as targets for the Divider.

"Let's move on down towards the Millennium Forum. We can get a look at the last clue there".

No one disagreed which was a huge achievement in itself. Takuma and Ben helped Dearbhla up on to her feet and then supported her whilst walking. Mark and Susie had wanted to take over but the boys were content in their supportive role. The other two girls fell into step with the team and they happily chatted while strolling down Market Street.

Chapter 45

As they reached the end of the street, they took in the scene. This was the only part of the walls that was level with the road. The pathway of the walls dips down low until it becomes the footpath while a roadway cuts through where the walls should be. The road leads to Linenhall Street on the left and to Orchard Street on the right. Straight ahead of them stands the Millennium Forum, a popular theatre. As they made their way to the theatre, they also passed St. Columb's Hall.

Dearbhla looked at it fondly. It was an old building that had provided several happy memories. She had frequented the Orchard Cinema in it as a youngster. Even a few years ago she had attended salsa classes and shook her hips into a rhythm that a belly dancer would be proud of - well, perhaps not, as she was not very coordinated and had overheard someone describing her brave attempt as embarrassing and stilted. Needless to say, she had given up and practised at home where she could believe she was a strong rival to any dance queen.

"Go to the side entrance. It's not as open to attack," instructed Mark as he looked around, worried why the Divider was so quiet.

They did so and slowly descended the steps that led them back onto the walls. Leanne shivered at the thought of Mark's words. Having looked into the Divider's eyes, she knew what evil he was capable of. That's how she knew he was biding his time for an almighty showdown. She would feel more confident if she had a bazooka to blast him with. Realistically, the only weapon she had was Orla's nasty tongue; surely it was more poisonous than those snakes he'd conjured up. She caught Orla glowering and guessed she was still sore about the run in with Grumpy Head.

"What are you grinning like a maniac for?" Orla said snippily.

Leanne sighed. Looks like she'd be Orla's focus again.

"Nothing, Orla... Happy we're all alive," she explained.

"Pah! Don't get too comfy. Your boyfriend will be back, wanting a ssssizzling snog from you!"

She cackled at her joke and at Leanne's sick expression. Ben shifted beside Dearbhla.

"No, Ben. Focus. Orla's right."

Ben swung disbelieving eyes to their leader.

"I don't mean about that. But the Divider will be back."

Ben relaxed and nodded. Takuma however left Dearbhla's side and took his place beside one of the bravest and nicest girls he'd ever met. He wanted her to know that he didn't agree with Orla's behaviour. When Leanne sensed his presence, she gave him a heart stopping smile that left him speechless. He felt a bit lightheaded but smiled back with affection.

Susie took out the third clue and read it,

"Find the dove that cannot fly,

O'er the gem that does not shine.

A perfect leaf to hideaway

Such treasure of good,

To carry on the human line."

Susie's brow furrowed in concentration, lost in her own thoughts. Mark joined her and quietly read over the clue. At least they knew they were looking for a dove. That should be easy. Should be, but he knew from experience it would be anything but *easy*.

Ben dared not move as Dearbhla had fallen asleep. She was nestled into the crook of his arm. He caught Orla watching them with a softened gaze. As soon as she met his eyes, hers turned flinty and she rolled them at him. He smirked and hoped that she would stop fighting him over every single thing. Though he had to admit, it was a tad entertaining hurling insults at the feisty girl.

Mark and Susie were still poring over the clue. Dearbhla was sound asleep and Ben happily held her as he pretended not to stalk Orla's every move with his eyes. The restless girl was pacing up and down, muttering every now and again. She could feel the tension rise and it matched the dread gathering in the pit of her stomach. How Dearbhla could sleep was a sign of her level of weakness. Healthy Dearbhla would be preparing them for the inevitable onslaught, not off in lullaby land counting sheep. This was a disaster. Orla growled and threw her hands up in frustration. Then she continued pacing.

Leanne was fascinated at the girl's obvious restlessness. If Orla was disturbed, then she didn't fancy their chances. Uh oh, Leanne felt the panic building in her chest and fought to control her breathing. Takuma had left her a few minutes ago to join Susie and Mark. They were all intensely studying the clue. Everyone was so tired it felt harder to unravel this one. She bit her nails one by one and then wandered over to the wooden sculpture of a person with their arms stretched out like a plane's wings. The statue was a bit taller than her. It had no features, only eyes that had holes so you could look through them. The wood was smooth and clean. She traced the wooden head and arms. The front and back were the same. Then she stood and watched it. Hollow. It frightened her a little because of its emptiness though she figured it was a fun sculpture located at the theatre for that reason. Taking a breath, she decided to take the plunge. Standing on her tiptoes, she stretched out her arms and eased both hands into the woodman's ones. Leaning in, she rested her head on his. She positioned her eyes so she could look through his. Instantly, a buzzing noise started in her head. Frightened, she tried to pull away but couldn't. She was locked in place. It was as if she was held by a giant magnet. Not an inch of her could move. The buzzing grew louder and her terror spiked. Her voice wouldn't work so no-one even noticed her predicament.

The scene in front of her changed. Gone were her group of friends and the location they occupied. A hazy scene unfolded. As Leanne watched in silent terror, she was transported into the sky. Her friends were now below her and they carried on as if nothing was different. Her eyes widened as she flew higher still and could see the walls grow smaller below her. She soared into the clouds and up into the blue sky. Birds avoided her but didn't seem to think it strange that a human moulded against a wooden statue was flying amongst them. Leanne's breathing was quick and uneven, the only sign that not all of her body was being controlled. Butterflies were causing a riot in her tummy and tears streamed down her face whether caused by the breeze or fear she couldn't tell.

Suddenly, she stopped in mid-air. The clouds quickly changed to grey and black. The sky looked thunderous and lightning flashed in the distance. Leanne knew a moment of pure dread before they dropped heavily away from the clouds that only seconds ago they had soared past. Falling fast, Leanne clung to the piece of wood she was attached to. She was falling to her death, to be smashed into the very walls she had explored and made friends on. Her stomach seemed to be in her mouth and she silently prayed that she wouldn't feel any pain. A jerk halted her descent and she hung suspended in the air. She could see three statues and actually recognised them. They stood on top of St. Columb's Hall. She didn't know their names but right now that didn't really matter. As she wondered why she was hovering opposite them, a thick black jagged lightning bolt struck all three statues. They were encompassed in a black rain that caressed their bodies in rivulets before cascading down like mini waterfalls. In fascination, Leanne watched all three statues smoulder and then crack apart. The sound was like claps of thunder though sharper and more concise. What happened next made Leanne hold her breath and shut her eyes tightly. The middle statue turned its head as if working out a sore neck. Then it met her stare and let out a screech so menacing and spine chilling that Leanne wished she really had just smashed into the ground. Leanne scrunched her eyes so tightly that lights danced in the darkness. The terror rose up and seemed to open up her throat. She screamed and shrieked.

Surprisingly, the buzzing noise had stopped and she found she could actually hear her own voice. So loud was it that she didn't hear the rest of the group shouting out and running to her side. Nor did she hear them coaxing her to let go of the woodman. Finally, Takuma peeled her grip away from the statue. He held both her hands in his but still she screamed with tears rolling down her reddened cheeks.

"Stop it. Leanne. You're okay. We're here," shouted Takuma.

Eventually, his voice penetrated the fear and her screaming stopped. She snivelled but Takuma held her tightly in his arms. The others stood, silently in shock. Either Leanne had lost the plot or something very bad had happened. Even Orla knew it wasn't good news though she had suggested a quick slap might calm her down. That had brought a barrage of shouts and accusations directed her way. She'd only wanted to help, but whatever. Takuma patted Leanne's back and soothed her with words of comfort. Soon, the shaking girl drew back from his hold.

"I saw...so angry...they're coming!" she stammered.

"Who..?" Mark asked urgently.

Leanne brokenly tried to explain what had happened. The group all exchanged glances of apprehension.

"Leanne. You weren't flying," said Mark confused.

"What do you mean? I was up in the air. I thought I was going to die!" Leanne said angrily.

Mark shook his head.

"Leanne, I'm telling you. You were here the whole time. Then you started screaming blue murder and scared about ten years off my life!" he explained.

"No. I'm not lying. I was flying. I could feel the wind, I was terrified." Leanne was so confused.

Dearbhla leaned against Susie who had helped her over.

"Leanne you didn't move from here but you must have had a vision. What did you see?"

Leanne looked around at the sculpture. It must have shown her to help them. Feeling a bit more attuned to what was going on, she took a deep breath.

"I saw those statues come alive."

She pointed up to the roof of St. Columb's Hall. Amid gasps and groans, she continued,

"It's the Divider. He's using them to get to us. That's his plan." Leanne watched all of their faces show anxiety and the fear she herself had felt.

"And guys, they seem really pissed off."

"Great. Just great...How the heck do we fight three more statues," said an agitated Ben.

"*Flying* statues!" stated Leanne.

That caused uproar. Ben swung his arms around.

"The clunk brothers were bad enough, but how do we get the flying trio to slip around on oil?" He ran his hands through his hair and then kicked the wooden sculpture.

"Stop it Ben. He showed me. He was helping," Leanne jumped in front of the sculpture to defend it.

Ben opened his mouth in shock and then stomped off to kick the wall instead.

"Ow ow oww.." he howled, after being too enthusiastic in his assault.

The team were all separating out from each other and letting off steam in their own way. Dearbhla closed her eyes briefly. She needed to rein them in. If this was true, they were in for a tough battle.

"Calm down. We have to stick together. Here. Now..!" she shouted while pointing in front of her.

They all gathered and she saw their fear and uncertainty.

"The statues are Temperance, Erin and Vulcan. They may have weapons. They'll be much stronger than us. We don't have long. Ideas..?"

"Yeah... Go back to sleep and when we wake up it'll be over 'cos this is just one never-ending NIGHTMARE," said Orla, whose voice was getting louder as she spoke.

"Ouch," she shrieked when Ben flicked her ear.

"What?" He asked innocently, smirking when she narrowed her eyes.

Takuma noticed a shadow fall over them and looked up.

"Look at those clouds!" he breathed.

Leanne panicked. "This is it. They're coming."

Chapter 46

Everyone watched the dark clouds tumbling above getting ready to crash against each other. Before anyone could react, an ear splitting screeching echoed around them. The sound of things breaking apart soon followed with accompanying growls and roars.

"Run," ordered Dearbhla.

The team scarpered down towards the Water Bastion. Takuma and Ben had resumed their places beside Dearbhla. Their leader's feet barely touched the ground. The boys weren't taking any chances that she would be too slow. Lifting her, they ran with winged feet. Dearbhla didn't complain as she couldn't have escaped otherwise. Catching their breaths, they each turned to evaluate their situation.

Three dark figures rose high above St. Columb's Hall. They snapped and sneered at each other as if they were wild animals in blood frenzy. The seven humans stared in horror at the spectacle in the air. They felt like tiny inconsequential insects in comparison to the clashing titans above. One of the statues was in the act of striking at another when it turned its head and caught sight of the terrified ants below. Its eyes rolled back with the fervour of how it would crush these insignificant beings. Then it let out a high pitched bloodcurdling scream. Its mouth seemed to increase to three times its normal size.

The stupefied group sprang into action and grabbing at each other, they scrambled down the steps on to Bank Place. Nobody dared stop to see what the winged devils were doing or indeed where they were. Each second was too precious to put as much distance as possible between them. They reached Shipquay Gate and could see the hundreds of people standing as if they themselves were statues. There was no help among them so the team followed Mark who led them up Shipquay Street.

They cut across the road and Mark gestured towards the Craft Village. This was a hidden area that opened up into a group of shops and cafes. Mark had been here to a woollen shop with his Granny earlier that month. She had insisted on buying him an Aran cardigan which he only wore in her company. If Ben found out he owned one he'd never hear the end of it. Mark stood aside and waved them all in past. As Susie was the last to enter, he looked up in time to see the winged devils swoop down over the buildings opposite.

"Raaa…Arggg…" they snarled when they spotted Mark.

He had to stop himself from screaming in fear. They were so threatening and their murderous intent was mirrored in their movements. Their heads dipped and they cut through the air faster as they zeroed in on their first victim; this kick-started Mark to flee further into the Craft Village. He caught up with the others as they were having a quick rest. Grabbing Susie's elbow he continued past them.

"No time. They're right behind me," he explained breathlessly.

The other five rushed after him and Susie, terrified they were being chased by such evil voids. Behind them the snarling and clanging of biting jaws grew closer. Leanne cried out as a car door flew past her and smashed against a shop window. Orla gripped her hand and pulled her along. She herself was petrified. This was the most scared she had ever been since it had started today. If these guys caught them, they would pull them apart limb from limb.

Leanne was grateful for Orla's help because her legs were shaking so much she thought she would just fall in a heap and quiver like a lump of jelly. She swore she could almost feel their breath on the back of her neck. Shivering at the thought that they could be so close, she began pulling Orla who showed surprise, then grinned and tried to keep up.

When the car door had hit the window, Takuma and Ben had exchanged a quick look of "Oh crap, let's move faster!" They had lifted Dearbhla as high as they could and galloped through the deceivingly quiet village.

"This way," called Mark as the boys stumbled to a halt.

They turned in time to see Mark shoot out a side entrance and into the sunlight. Each of them followed though the terrible trio were hot on their heels. Running up Magazine Street, they knew their time was nearly up. A showdown was inevitable. The three statues came barrelling out of the Village and in their haste they lost their balance and tumbled into the walls. The force of it caused some stones to fall off and hit them on the head. It didn't even faze them. They just picked themselves up slowly, never taking their eyes off their prey. The group were nearly at Butcher's Gate. The terrible trio strode purposely past Castle Gate and gained ground upon the trembling humans.

Tired and out of breath, the group silently acknowledged the time had come to fight. They stood shoulder to shoulder and took on a stance of readiness for what was to come.

Temperance, Erin and Vulcan stood before them. They studied the humans that dared to face them.

"Puny humans, you have no chance against us. Give us the objects."

All three statues spoke the same words at the same time. Their voices had an almost mechanical sound to them that was completely unnatural.

"Go suck on some WD40! We aren't giving you zip!" shouted Ben. He was tired of being scared and bullied by scraps of metal, lumps of stone and the eejit with the stupid feathered hat!

There was a moment of silence followed by a chorus of robotic laughter. The seven humans watched the statues laughing in the most unamused manner they had ever seen. It was like programmed laughter, canned, no feeling or heartiness just bland and expressionless.

"The Divider seeks the key. Give it to us or we take it from you. We prefer the second option." They sneered in perfect timing with each other. Their entire countenance radiated violence and the pleasure they felt in perpetrating it.

"Come anywhere near us, and I'll show you where I'll put the key… Down your ugly tin throat..!" Orla grumbled as she was fed up with being intimidated by these jokers.

They laughed again but then each held out their right arm.

"Enough of this human talk..."

They stretched tall and lowered their chins. Glaring at the group, their intention was clear.

"Time to take it. ." they drawled menacingly.

Their first steps towards the group were met by a screaming figure in white who appeared from nowhere. The statues faltered, confused by the sudden interruption. The lady in white turned and her kind features urged the team to escape. She turned back and her face contorted into a mask of rage. These creatures would not harm her people. She floated above the ground and spread her arms out. Her white gown flurried about her body and added to the effect of a very angry ghost. The statues snapped out of their stupor and roared in three different tones. At that point, the group fled the scene, relieved that a saviour had arrived in the nick of time. They moved along Butcher Street quickly and came out on to the Diamond.

Gasping for breath, they rested, but were still on alert for the enemy. In the distance, they could hear the angry roars of the terrible trio but the mysterious lady was not to be outdone. Mightily she let out high pitched screams. Glass was shattering whether from the screaming or from things being flung about, the group were left wondering.

Mark approached a sweating Ben.

"Do you think that's the ghost your Aunt Marnie always tells us about?"

"I guess so. Wait until I tell her she saved our lives. She'll go nuts!" said an excited Ben. Then his smile faded as he considered he might not get the chance to share that with his Aunt if they failed this mission.

Dearbhla was leaning on Takuma but couldn't fight the energy drain any longer. Weakly she slid to the ground. Takuma called out and dropped down beside her. The others quickly joined him but they all knew their leader was unconscious. That she had lasted this long was a measure of her determination and will power. Before they could make a plan, a willowy figure appeared before them. It was the 'White Lady'. She spoke to them urgently, "I can't hold them. Get ready, my dear Children of the Oak."

Then she was gone.

"You heard her. Let's get Dearbhla to safety and deal with these three wannabes," said Mark.

They carried their leader over to the War Memorial and set her on the steps before it. Nobody could stay with her this time. They needed all hands on deck. If they had any chance against these enemies, all of them were required for this battle.

To put as much distance between them and Dearbhla, they ran behind the memorial on to Bishop Street. On their way they were stopped by the descent of the dreaded trio. They landed gracefully in front of them. One of the statues stood slightly closer to them. She was flanked by the other two who stood directly behind. They rolled their necks and fixed their prey with deadly intent. Then their battle cry pierced the tense air and the attack began.

They rammed into the humans with such power that their bodies were flung in all directions. The six scrambled up and tried to regroup but the trio wouldn't allow that strategy. They separated them out and continued to treat them like the pests they believed them to be. Some of the group attempted to jump on to the statues backs and punch and hit them but it was useless. They were indeed puny in comparison to the hard strength and might of these mammoths. The six humans were surrounded by fragility. Bones were fractured, blood was spilt and bruises formed. Still they fought on bravely. The statues seemed thrilled at the turmoil they were creating. Every now and then, simpers and whines could be heard from the injured but they picked themselves up and threw themselves at the titans. They kicked and clawed, punched and scratched but nothing weakened their attackers. The statues gloried in the blood sport and enjoyed the feeling of being unbeatable. This went beyond the Divider's mission now. They craved this win. In fact, they were so unstoppable as a trio, they didn't even need the puppet master that was the Divider. If they stole the objects for themselves then what could stop *them* from taking the magic of the walls. They could rule the world. Their thoughts were as one and they stopped their attack to agree on their new mission.

Confused by the break in the fury, that had been unleashed upon them, the six humans crawled and staggered to each other's side. They watched with wariness as the three statues silently communicated with each other. Once it was done, they straightened, lined up again and smiled menacingly at the six. The humans grimaced and did some silent communication of their own. They were in trouble with a capital T.

All six took steps to retreat, unsure of how they would survive this renewed onslaught. The trio screeched aloud and charged into the humans. In the ensuing commotion the key and the oak leaf were stolen and the enemy crowed out in victory. Immediately they dropped their attack and held the desired objects in their power crazed hands. The Children of the Oak lay battered and bruised. They watched in defeat as the trio decided upon their next step to outmanoeuvre the Divider. Lying helplessly, they tried to check that although hurt they were all in one piece and breathing.

"What do you think you are doing?" asked a barely controlled voice.

The six froze and then scurried together; the deadly trio *and* the Divider. They were too sore to run so they held on to each other and faced the evil. The statues turned and addressed their master.

"We have decided we do not need you. These belong to us," they announced while gesturing to the objects.

The Divider did not respond. He stood and surveyed the statues. Then he looked down at the group. Mark hoped he didn't notice that Dearbhla was missing. They had left her unprotected. He could capture her and all bets would be off. Suddenly, he raised his hands and a dark whirlwind developed behind the violent trio and in front of the six. They clutched at each other as it gathered momentum and the suction began to drag Leanne, Orla and Susie along the ground towards it. The statues did not move but the group could hear their dispassionate laughter.

Ben was sure that was as annoying for the Divider as it was to him. It was the one time he really hoped the Feather Hatted Demon would punish them in a suitable manner. The boys each clung to a girl, trying in vain to pull her back from the whirlwind's energy.

Above the girls' screaming and roar of the wind, the Divider finally reacted.

"You dare to double cross me? I made you. You are my lowly minions."

The monotonous laughter continued. Clearly the statues didn't realise these were their last few seconds of life. Mark's fingers desperately clung to Susie's as she slipped slowly from his grasp. Her eyes met his in terror.

"No," he shouted as the wind seemed to reach hurricane level and her body lifted up off the ground.

"Mark!" she screamed

"Hold on Susie," he shouted, "Don't let go!"

Mark was gripped by panic as she slipped another bit out of his grasp. Luckily, the other boys had been able to pull Leanne and Orla back to them and they lay huddled together. One of Susie's hands slipped free and they both shouted out as she was being sucked feet first higher up into the maelstrom. Mark grasped her right hand with both of his and grunted as he felt his muscles strain trying to keep her with him.

"You have been disloyal. I have no further use of you," the Divider stated simply and blasted the statues back into the dark and chaotic whirlwind. Then he disappeared with a swirl of his black cloak. As the last statue entered, it caught Susie's hair and tugged.

"*No!*" cried Mark as he lost his grip and Susie's body flew towards the statue. He watched in horror as she struggled and tried to loosen its grip. Her head disappeared into the angry twister followed by her arms. Mark dropped his head onto the ground and beat it with his fists. He'd lost her. Nausea filled him and he lay in shock. He couldn't watch her completely disappear; lost forever in a void created by evil. A scream had Mark's head snap up and with disbelieving eyes he saw Susie drop to the ground. Scrabbling up, he rushed over to her.

"Susie. Susie. Are you okay?"

She started to laugh, "Better than okay! Look what I've got," she declared and held out her right hand.

Mark saw the oak leaf and the key the statues had stolen. He smiled and gripped her face with both of his hands. Leaning in close he touched his lips to her soft ones. Pulling back slightly he looked into her brown eyes and silently marvelled at her bravery. She was in a deadly situation and not only did she escape, but managed to steal back the objects their very existence relied on. He had felt that feathery kiss the whole way to his toes. Deciding to go in for a second kiss, he was prevented by the arrival of the rest of the group.

"Ugh! Get a room," exclaimed Orla.

"That's what I said," joined in Ben.

"Leave them alone! Thank goodness you're okay Susie," said Leanne.

Susie had nearly recovered – not from the near death experience but the gentle kiss she had shared with Mark. Her stomach flipped again when she thought of the way he had looked as if she was the most precious thing on the planet. And the kiss...Wow! She smiled shyly at Leanne, a bit embarrassed their kiss had been witnessed by the others. Takuma voiced his relief that the objects were once again in their possession.

"We need to go check on Dearbhla," he said. He was concerned at what condition their leader was in. Perhaps they could contact the Spellbinder for help, although how, he didn't know.

Chapter 47

The six traced their steps back to the Diamond and gathered round Dearbhla. She was lying just as they had left her but her eyes were closed and her breathing shallow. Her face was pale and each person realised the seriousness of her condition. Susie and Mark crouched down beside her.

"Dearbhla," said Susie gently.

The older girl's eyes fluttered open. She smiled weakly.

"They're gone," she reassured their leader.

"Yeah, they're off visiting the windy city," said Ben.

Dearbhla laughed but began coughing. Mark helped her lean forward until it passed. It was clear to them all that Dearbhla would not be able to continue the mission. For her, it was over. The question now was where to keep her safe and if someone should stay with her.

Leanne was the first to offer but Orla objected.

"No way…! So you get to hide away while we are up to our necks in danger! Forget it. I'll stay with her."

The group argued for the next few minutes with Orla being stubborn about the issue.

"This is ridiculous!" said a frustrated Susie, "We're wasting time again. It shouldn't matter who stays with Dearbhla. It will still be dangerous, especially when the Divider figures out two of us are missing."

"Susie's right," agreed Takuma, "Leanne should do it as she was the first to offer."

"Oh yeah, nothing to do with the fact that you have the hots for her," said Orla nastily.

Takuma sighed and shook his head.

Ben noticed Leanne's painful blush and inwardly groaned. When would that wee girl learn to shut her mouth? he wondered as he glared at Orla.

"Jealous, Orla..?" Ben couldn't help taunting.

"Wise up, Spiderturd. I have better taste," she retorted, while directing the last comment to Leanne.

"I think you mean, *he* has better taste," said Leanne stepping towards the bitter girl.

Orla took a step towards her. "Nope...What he wants with a mousey, deluded little frump I don't get."

Orla smirked at the other girl's gasp and hurt look. Before she could glory in it, Leanne lunged forward and pushed her to the ground. Orla was too stunned to feel the pain of landing heavily on her back. The 'mousey' girl was clawing and hitting her. Orla turned from defending herself to fighting back. They were rolling around the ground pulling hair and screaming at each other.

"Do something," screeched Susie.

Up until that point, the boys had all been staring at the scene with their mouths agape. They couldn't believe Leanne had attacked Orla. Obviously enough snide comments had led to this act. Takuma was the first to enter the fray. He tried to hold Leanne's arms but they were flinging around with Orla's. He looked up desperately and this spurred Ben into action. He leapt forward and mumbled,

"I'm going to enjoy this."

Grabbing Orla roughly he dragged her away from Leanne. Her feet were still kicking out trying to make contact with the other girl who was being half carried in the opposite direction by Takuma. As they were dealing with the angry girls, Mark and Susie worriedly noticed Dearbhla's condition had deteriorated. They couldn't wake her up and she was barely breathing. Mark jumped up and shouted to the others.

"Pack it in. I think we're losing Dearbhla!"

Immediately there was quiet and they all rushed over to their brave leader.

"What can we do?" Ben asked, fearful of helplessly watching someone die.

"It's too late," whispered Susie, "She's gone." She bowed her head and wept.

Before another tear was spilled, a blinding flash of white dazed the grieving group. Each of them squeezed their eyes shut until they heard a familiar voice.

"Why are you crying?" asked Dearbhla, as she sat up and surveyed them. Speechless, no one responded. They watched as she stood up easily and stretched.

"Oh, that feels good. I feel great!" She laughed and did a little dance.

"Thank you!" Their leader spoke to someone behind them.

They all turned to see the Spellbinder.

"You are my Guardian of the Gates. You chose to save a life and proved your willingness to sacrifice and your ability to love others selflessly. Indeed, it is I who thank you."

The Spellbinder bowed his head simply but it was such a grand gesture that they all smiled to have witnessed it. He addressed the rest of the group.

"Children of the Oak, you honour our people with your courage. The final object awaits you. Carry on."

He faded from view and they stood feeling proud of what they had achieved. As the group hugged Dearbhla, Leanne approached Orla

"I'm sorry," she said and hoped they could put that awful event behind them.

Orla narrowed her eyes at the girl. Everyone held their breath, believing Leanne would receive a nasty earful.

"I'm sorry too. Let's just forget about it," said Orla and shook the surprised girl's hand.

Orla walked over to Dearbhla, glad she was in the land of the living again. She knew she had pushed Leanne too far and was a bit shocked she had turned violent. Though it was better they forgot it as she didn't want it getting around that she had been floored by 'mouse'. Embarrassing…

Leanne was relieved as she didn't want any awkwardness. She should never have pushed Orla. After hearing the Spellbinder praising them for their courage, she had felt so guilty. Apologising was the right thing to do. The group of seven were happy but knew that they still had a way to go before celebrating. The last object awaited them.

Infused with a sense of well-being, Dearbhla took control: "Okay, kids. Let's make it a hat trick!" She smiled, amidst grumbles at her reference to them being 'kids'.

She nudged Susie who was standing beside her.

"C'mon, wind your necks in. I'd rather be here with the six of you than anyone else."

Susie nudged her back, feeling that for the first time they were winning in their mission.

"Yes, same here, Dearbhla. You're not bad for an 'oul one!" she replied cheekily.

"Hey, I'm not that old!" said Dearbhla, though she acknowledged the age gap made it seem that way.

"Yeah, back off Susie. I've always wanted to date a cougar," said Ben. He sidled up to Dearbhla wagging his eyebrows and fixing his shirt.

"Whaddya say?"

Dearbhla patted him on the arm, "Forget it sunshine."

She ignored his disappointed look and asked Susie for the third parchment. She gave it over and was filled with excitement that this could be the last time they needed the clues. Dearbhla read it out loud for everyone to hear.

"Find the dove that cannot fly

O'er the gem that does not shine.

A perfect leaf to hide away

Such treasure of good,

To carry on the human line."

They mulled over the words trying to make sense of them. The group agreed that the object itself was in the shape of a dove but couldn't work out what the 'gem' was. Dearbhla was more animated than the others since she had just been revitalised. The rest of the group were still suffering the effects of being in battle with Temperance, Erin and Vulcan. They sat down on the steps of the War Memorial, watching the Gatekeeper pacing up and down trying to figure it out. She stopped and looked down Shipquay Street. From this hill, she could easily see the hundreds of people frozen in Guildhall Square.

Her tummy did a flip when she was reminded at the magnitude of their task. Failing wasn't an option. It would spell the end of this city and everything she had grown to love about it. Not only that, but the Divider wouldn't stop here. He would use the power from the walls to magnify his evil. Other cities would fall, giving him strength, power and worst of all the ability to be unstoppable. She shuddered at the thought. A dark cloud passed overhead and she felt a moment of panic until it breezed on by and the threat was dissipated. Shaking herself from her silent reverie, she turned around to face the memorial. Suddenly a smile tilted her face. How could she have missed it? Eagerly, she skipped over to her young friends. They were half lying, sitting with their chins on their knees or completely prostrate on the ground.

Kicking Ben's foot, she announced, "I know where it is!"

This woke them up and they snapped to attention.

"Well go on," encouraged Susie pleased they would soon be active. Sitting around gave them too much time to think and to get scared.

Orla rolled her eyes and started fixing her hair as if she couldn't care less. Inside she was queasy from the notion that finally this nightmare would be over.

Dearbhla rocked back on her heels enjoying her moment of inspiration. Carefully, she stretched out both her arms with her palms upwards.

"*This* is the 'gem that does not shine'. She smiled at their perplexed looks and waited to see if anyone caught on.

Takuma jumped up,

"She's right. It's the 'Diamond'.

Dearbhla laughed and enjoyed their confused expressions. One by one they began to understand. Ben was still having a problem with it. He turned to Mark and curled his lip.

"I don't get it!" he said, frustrated that he was the only one who seemed lost.

Mark sighed and put his arm around Ben's shoulders.

"The Diamond is a gem but it's not a real one so it doesn't *shine*."

Mark groaned when Ben just looked blankly at him.

"This Diamond is a place not a gem!!" Mark emphasised it by waving his arms around the Diamond area.

"*Awwww…!*" Ben cried, finally enlightened.

"Got it?" asked Mark.

"Aye always did. Just checking you did," he stated and walked around looking for the next part of the clue: a leaf.

Mark shook his head as he watched him go and then joined the search himself.

Chapter 48

Orla and Leanne were combining forces for the leaf search. Since the last incident between them, things weren't as strained or as unpleasant. It seemed that Orla had eventually accepted that Leanne wasn't going to let her treat her with such disrespect. In fact, Orla grudgingly admired the other girl. Instead of crumbling under her verbal attacks, she had stood up for herself. Fighting her had been a step too far, there was no excuse for that, but she had understood why it had led to that outcome. Hopefully, never again…

"What's that?" Orla pointed to a bronzed leaf on the footpath on the right hand corner of the Diamond. She hunkered down to get a closer look and Leanne followed her.

Orla met Leanne's excited look.

"I think this could be it," Leanne smiled and encouraged her to call the others.

Orla shouted so loudly that it made Leanne wince. The girl could be heard in Belfast. She moved back when the others ran over to their spot. They all exchanged excited glances and Dearbhla told Orla to check if it opened up.

Orla fiddled with the leaf. She pressed it down and tried to turn it but it remained stubbornly still.

Ben pushed her out of his way and said, "Let me try. It needs a bit of man power."

Orla snorted and moved aside. He put all his weight on the bronze leaf and tried to pry it up with his finger nails but nothing made an impact. Each of them tried but no amount of force could move it. The hopelessness was causing grumpiness within the group and they believed that this wasn't the leaf at all. As Ben and Orla began sniping at each other, Takuma caught sight of someone walking quietly down Butcher Street. He used his eyes to communicate a presence to the rest of the group. The 'White Lady' turned and murmured something. Then she continued walking towards Butcher's Gate.

The group watched her disappear and each of them thought that they would never quite get over their interactions with ghosts, statues and the dreaded Divider.

A minute of silence passed until Mark asked the question, "What did she say?"

He saw shrugs and mutters of "Dunno" and was getting ready to chase after the friendly ghost, when Dearbhla spoke:

"*'Perhaps only the Gatekeeper's hand can move the leaf.'*"

Astonished, they looked at their leader.

"But it didn't work," said Susie.

Dearbhla grinned at their downcast expressions. Then she shook her head, "I didn't try. I assumed it was the wrong one."

Orla blew out a breath, "Well, get on with it then." She wasn't being cheeky, only anxious to find the dove and put this all behind her.

Everyone moved away to let Dearbhla kneel beside the leaf. She hovered her hand over it and then made eye contact with each of them.

"This is it. We've been through so much together for this moment. At last we're a team."

Smiling, she gently placed the palm of her right hand on top of the leaf. A golden light exploded at the contact. Hearts were pumping wildly and breaths were held. Victory was theirs. Dearbhla moved the leaf, stem first, to face the Diamond, while the head faced the walls at Butcher's Gate. Then she pulled back quickly as the leaf was sucked underground. They heard something click into place and then silence. Dearbhla reached down into the hole in the ground. She instantly felt a velvet material and grinned.

Takuma and Ben bumped fists.

"This is so sick!" exclaimed Ben.

Dearbhla lifted a green velvet bag out and carefully opened it. Frowning she squeezed around and then desperately turned it upside down. It was empty. Ben wiped a hand down over his face.

"We've been stitched up!" he stated.

"No! Give me that," Orla snatched the bag from Dearbhla and turned it inside out. Angrily she threw it on the ground and groaned.

"What's going on?" she screeched out.

Leanne said nothing. She was so deflated.

Mark was running his hands through his hair, clearly agitated. Susie stood up and turned her back to them. Takuma asked her if she was okay but she started giggling. That spooky laughter sounded so empty of any feeling, that it set Mark's teeth on edge. Alarmed, he looked at the others and saw that they too had frozen. Susie slowly turned back to face them.

"Hee hee, I ruined your little moment of glory, hee hee."

No one responded. Takuma and Ben each moved closer to Mark to make sure he didn't do anything impulsive.

"*Aww..!* The poor gullible Children of the Oak….You thought you were so clever. Ha! You actually believed you could outsmart *me!*" Susie's eyes were coal black, and she continued to laugh manically.

"Get out of her." Mark said through gritted teeth.

Susie's head snapped towards him and glared at him through unseeing eyes. Baring her teeth at him she growled and then changed to a whiny voice:

"Oh Mark, help me. Hee hee. Make him stop. He's hurting me. Hee hee."

Ben and Takuma held Mark in a strong grip as he tried to step forward.

"No," whispered Takuma, "he's goading you. Find out what he wants."

Mark nodded but clenched his jaw in anger. He had better not harm a hair on Susie's head. Mission or not, he would hunt the Divider down and end him.

Bristling, he asked as calmly as possible, "What do you want?"

"Hee hee, I have the dove in a very safe place. Beat you to it. You didn't see me, hee hee."

"Stop your waffling. What do you want?" shouted an irate Orla. She was fed up with this thing playing games; plus the silly giggling was doing her head in. Susie's head tilted and she roared at Orla. The effect was like tiny pin pricks stabbing her all over her body. Orla screamed and grabbed hold of Leanne for protection who tried to soothe her reckless friend.

"This impertinent girl," Susie said while gesturing to her own body, "*stole* the objects from my grasp. I want them back or you will face my wrath; a fury that will have you begging for death."

Dearbhla stepped forward and knocked Takuma's halting hand away.

"Your statues stole them from us. They belong to us. So does Susie. Now get lost and leave us alone!"

Dearbhla lunged forward and gripped Susie's two arms. She stared into her black eyes and tried to ignore the mocking laughter emanating from the girl's mouth. Focusing all her energy, she let the power gather momentum inside her. Then she let it flow out of her eyes and into Susie's coal black ones. The laughter faltered and faded until it was gone. The white light fought black shadows in Susie's body until they were pushed entirely out of her.

Susie groaned and Dearbhla caught her as she stumbled. "It's okay Susie. You're safe now."

She turned and addressed the group.

"I saw inside his head. It's a mess of evil and darkness. He's going to throw everything at us to prevent us winning."

Susie shivered beside her and felt almost unclean. She was really sick of the Divider using her like a ventriloquist's dummy. Afterwards, she always had a craving for a shower to wash away any tracks of evil. It sounded silly but she couldn't help it. Mark and Leanne went to her side to check how she was.

"I'm okay. I just hate when he does it. I get this buzzing in my ears before it happens but it's not long enough for me to warn you."

Before Mark could reassure her, Ben piped up,

"No worries, nothing that a good exorcism couldn't fix."

Then he faced Takuma and grabbing his arm said in a serious tone, "Where can I get some holy water?"

Takuma stifled a laugh and then felt guilty when he saw Mark's angry face.

"Ben that's out of order," said an uptight Mark.

Ben held up his hands, "Sorry couldn't resist it. No offense Susie!"

Susie took it in the light hearted manner it was meant and laughed, "None taken." She patted Mark's arm, "It *was* funny!"

As she saw Mark relax and give a reluctant smile, she let the terrible aftermath of the Divider's visit fall away.

"Spoiler alert!" Orla announced, her voice dripping with sarcasm, "We're up the Foyle without a paddle!"

Ben screwed his face up at her, "What are you on about?"

Orla tutted but ignored him, "If the Divider has the last object, we can't complete the mission. So do we run around these walls forever or at least until the Divider gets lucky and kills us off one at a time?"

She pulled a face at Ben to emphasise her valid point, who responded by taking off an imaginary hat and bowing to her.

Dearbhla sighed because she knew Orla was right. They had no idea where to go from here and the Spellbinder hadn't made an appearance.

"I don't know, Orla. We hadn't considered the dove wouldn't be there. Any suggestions..?"

The stark silence that followed said it all. They were all out of ideas.

"I know!" said Ben snapping his fingers. All eyes swung to him.

"Let's trade Orla for the dove. One bird for another! Sound good?"

The group rolled their eyes at him even though they knew he was trying to diffuse the tension. Orla glared at him but didn't utter a word.

"No? Okay. How about we offer him Orla to be the new Mrs Divider? Two grumpy divas together; what could be more perfect? Even the *threat* of spending time with her, would be enough for him to give up the city."

"Shut up Ben," warned Mark as he saw Orla's face twitching with the need to retort. She was at least trying to hold it back which was a huge achievement for her. Would it last? Probably not, as she strode up to Ben flapping her arms about.

"*You!*" she growled at him while poking him in the chest. He laughed as he tried to avoid her bony finger.

"You're nothing but a loser that thinks everything's a joke."

Ben continued laughing as he knew it was winding her up.

"Well, you're the joke, Spiderturd," she said with relish.

She gestured to the group, "Everyone here has done something useful. *But you..?* What have *you* done? Not-a-single-thing," she punctuated each word with a poke to his chest.

That hit a nerve. Ben grabbed her offensive finger and squeezed it.

"Oww," she yelped until he let it drop.

"Don't preach to me you selfish little moan. You saved Takuma with your tree. Two planks together. *Big tickle!*" He glanced at Takuma, "No offense!"

Takuma wasn't getting involved. He shrugged his shoulders and pretended to be fascinated by the shop window nearest him. Ben pinned Orla with a look, challenging her to continue. She refused to back down.

"At least I saved him. You let your best friend *die*. Without Dearbhla, he wouldn't be here."

Ben reacted as if he'd been slapped in the face. That was a sore point. He still felt guilty that he hadn't protected his friend. Her remark had brought up the memory of his cold, lifeless body lying broken in the grass. He felt nauseous and looked at the girl in front of him with pain filled eyes. Orla shut her mouth and swallowed hard. She realised she had hurt him but he just kept pushing her buttons.

Ben lowered his gaze and mumbled, "You win," to her and walked away.

Mark joined him and spoke quietly assuring him it hadn't been his fault when he had been hurt. The others pretended nothing had happened and Orla felt lousy that she had gone too far. She braced herself and made her way to him. Mark read her intention and left them alone.

"I'm sorry, Ben. I didn't mean it. I was trying to hurt you. You just irritate me so much and then I talk rubbish."

Ben smiled weakly, "Its fine. We're a lot alike."

She looked puzzled. "How are we alike?" she asked.

He put his arm around her and they started back to the group.

"We both talk rubbish!" he stated and they laughed.

Chapter 49

They started throwing ideas together for a plan but knew they were tentative. There was nothing solid to work from so it all seemed too sketchy. Moving away from the Diamond they strolled casually along Ferryquay Street.

As they were passing the department store, Austins, a figure appeared at the entrance. Jittery, Leanne had screamed but as soon as they saw the familiar face, they relaxed and smiled at their friend. Amelia Earhart stood proudly at the door. She smiled winningly and winked at Leanne who had been the one to initially recognise her earlier in the day.

Amelia, or Meeley as she had asked them to call her, inclined her head for them to follow her inside. Eagerly, they did so; glad to be out from the open where the Divider had first appeared and snatched Takuma away. Amelia congratulated them on their achievements and told them she had been rooting for them all along. They basked in her praise as it meant so much coming from a woman who had accomplished so much in her short life.

"Now guys, I see you're in a bit of a pickle," she said, while gazing intently at each of them.

Dearbhla was about to fill her in but Amelia held up her hand.

"I know all about it. That's why I'm here. I can't bear to think of that creep winning the battle 'cos he cheated."

She grimaced. "If there's one thing I can't stomach it's a cheat." Then she grinned broadly and puffed out her chest.

"I can't tell you exactly where he hid the object."

She threw her eyes skyward, "The rules forbid it and *I'm no cheat.*"

The team waited in silence, terrified to interrupt her and lose the only hope they had.

"I'm no poet but I came up with this little ditty to clue you in. Okay?"

She watched as they nodded, then clearing her throat she said:

"Listen up folks:

See the cove of peace

Perched on golden string,

Around a neck, not human;

No body but a thing."

She stuck her head forward, laughed at their confused expressions and clapped her hands together.

"Ha. This is such a gas! The gals would get a kick out of hearing my poems!" she said, amused at the reaction to her own clue. Then she saluted them and told them it was time to go.

"No! Wait, wait!" shouted Leanne as she rushed to a counter and grabbed a pen and scrap of paper.

"Please, repeat it one last time, Meeley?" she asked.

"Sure kiddo, here goes ...."

Leanne scribbled it down as the older woman relayed it. When she finished, she slapped her thigh and laughed out loud.

"I just love watching your faces! All scrunched up in concentration. Ha! Anyway, good luck and *I know* you'll do it!"

She saluted them once again and before their very eyes she became translucent. Then with a final wink, she had completely disappeared. The group cheered and felt so relieved that they had been thrown a life line. Once again they were back on track. Victory was within their reach.

Leanne held out the clue from Amelia and they pored over it. She repeatedly read it out and the group milled about shouting out ideas of what it could mean.

Ben had wandered over to the make-up counter and noticed an arm and hand protruding from the glass counter. The slender fingers were adorned with various rings, different shapes, colours and gems. He frowned while looking at them. Reaching out, he started to trace the arm. There was something in his mind that was telling him this was important but he didn't understand why.

Orla had been watching him for the last few minutes and tried to catch Mark's attention. He looked over to his friend and saw him staring longingly at a plastic hand. Ben needed food. Before he could say anything, Orla sidled up beside him. Looking round to make sure everyone was watching, she nudged Ben, who jumped.

"Making friends?"

Ben ignored her and continued to stare at the hand.

Disappointed at his lack of reaction, she tried again, "You know Ben, I knew you had problems with girls, but I think even the plastic ones wouldn't touch you with a barge pole."

Sniggering, she began to move away when he shouted out,

"*That's it!*"

Orla nearly jumped out of her skin when he grabbed her and swirled her round. As her feet were planted back on the ground he leaned forward and smacked a loud kiss on her mouth. She was so shocked she didn't even wipe his germs off. He faced the team with a huge knowing grin.

"What is it Ben? Tell us," asked Dearbhla, beginning to get excited.

"The golden string is a necklace. The dove is on a necklace!" he proudly announced. They all heard his interpretation and knew he was right. Before they could say so, he held up a hand.

"Wait. I'm not finished. I know where the necklace is." Then he thought about it and half shrugged, "Well sort of know where it is."

"Where, Ben?" Takuma asked.

"What has a neck but isn't human and a body but is a thing?" He paused for effect and to see if anyone could work it out. They all stood dumbly looking back at him.

"Dummies!" he exclaimed and laughed at their faces.

Dearbhla sighed. She was losing patience and insults were not appreciated.

"Ben, can you get on with it," she said tiredly.

Ben furrowed his brow unsure of their reactions, "I just did. Dummies!"

"Ben, stop it. *Tell us*. We don't have time for your messing."

Ben was getting exasperated. At this stage they should all be telling him he's a genius and instead they were treating him like a time waster. What the hell?

He glared at them and tried again.

"Okay. *Bloody dummies!*" he roared.

Dearbhla was actually losing her temper. It was Takuma who caught on first. He started to laugh.

"No Dearbhla, he means the necklace is on a dummy; a mannequin!"

Dearbhla digested the information, closed her eyes and started to laugh. The rest of the team began congratulating Ben who was telling them it was about time.

"Pure genius," said Mark as he bumped fists with him.

Ben straightened his collar and brushed down his shirt, "I know. What can I say? I'm the man!"

Orla rolled her eyes but was glad they had something more substantial to work with. Leanne hugged Ben and he lapped it all up. He high fived Takuma and then stood in front of Dearbhla with a grim expression.

"Oh ye of little faith," he said while shaking his head.

"I know. I'm so sorry. Mark's right. **You're a genius!**" she shouted the last part and he picked her up and swirled her around.

Susie was laughing at their antics but was anxious to get on with the search.

"Should we split up? It may be faster!" she asked when the team quietened.

Dearbhla opened her mouth but was beaten to it by a chorus of,

"We're stronger together than apart."

She smiled but still believed it was the key to their success.

"Let's start with this floor and work our way up to look at all the mannequins," suggested Dearbhla.

They agreed and headed towards the window displays first. Ben waited until the team were all engaged in searching each of the dummies in all of the window displays. Then quietly he backed towards the staircase. He would have less chance of being discovered if he climbed the stairs rather than the escalator in the middle of the ground floor. He could be halfway up and someone could spot him. Likewise, he couldn't use the lift; too noisy. The game would be up. No. Better to use the stairs. The curve in it would prevent anyone seeing him escape.

He smiled to himself as his heels hit the first stair. Giving one last sweep, to make sure the gang was busy in their activity, he swiftly turned and ascended to the first floor. The creaks on some of the stairs were covered over by the noises coming from the team knocking over accessories and bumping into dummies. Ben grinned. Perfect!

As he reached the first floor, he carefully manoeuvred himself away from view and walked quickly to the first batch of the mannequins. He knew the others would be raging with him for leaving but he was still on a high from figuring out the clue from the American chick. He craved the victory of finding the last object. He needed it to redeem himself. Orla's words rang in his head, *"What have you done? You let your best friend die!"*

Those two accusations had hurt him and now it was his chance to save the day.

Chapter 50

There were only three dummies that Ben could see here and neither had any jewellery on. He frisked the pockets of the clothes they were wearing but there was nothing. Checking the storeroom he didn't find anything else, which seemed odd, as this was the clothing department. Moving stealthily towards the staircase, he detoured and peeked over the banister. Good. The team were still too preoccupied to have noticed his absence. They too had moved to the back of the ground floor. He didn't have long before they missed him so he went to the stairs and ran upwards to reach the second floor. This housed gifts and bedding.

Ben didn't expect to find any dummies here but he gave it a quick once over anyway. Looking at the Waterford Crystal he was tempted to see what it sounded like when it was smashed. Would it sound like a normal glass or would it tinkle more musically? He grinned at the thought and hurried onwards. He knew they must realise he was gone by now so he ran full speed up to the third floor which was the restaurant. Ignoring his hunger pangs, he found the storeroom and rummaged through it; nothing there but spare cutlery and dishes. Disappointed, he stood panting. Those stairs had exhausted him.

As he considered what to do next, he spun to the staircase and remembered he hadn't checked the storeroom in the last floor. Excited, he raced back to the second floor. He paused as he heard voices and knew they would be upon him soon. He tore into the storeroom and *bingo*. He was standing in mannequin metropolis. Some were clothed, others naked. He scanned them quickly. Some had limbs missing or no heads at all. None wore the necklace he wanted. Ben was all out of ideas. Kicking a lone leg in temper he watched it bounce off a mannequin's shoulder, knocking the arm off. Turning to leave, a sudden shuffle had him spinning round.

"Who's there?" he breathed. Frowning he looked at the mannequin he'd hit. Peering at its face, he swore it looked as if it was sneering at him. Closing his eyes tightly, he reopened them and focused on its face. Strange, it looked normal again.

"I know my problem. I'm suffering from an acute case of the munchies." Deciding he was going to visit the restaurant and grab a bite to eat he exited the creepy storeroom. The voices were louder now. They were directly below him. He sauntered back into the gift area and thought he had better wait for them. He'd have to face a tongue lashing but sure he'd take it and then eat.

Browsing the glass cases, he came to the corner of the store and froze. Pressing his face up against the glass, he gazed wide eyed at the sight. Slapping both hands on to the glass, he shouted out in delight. He'd done it! He'd found the third object. The glass steamed up from his breath. He quickly wiped it clean and marvelled at his discovery. The simple gold dove shaped pendant hung suspended on a fine gold chain around a neck. It was only part of a dummy, not the whole body. Ben grinned. He was on track for hero status.

He tried the door but it was locked. Glancing round he saw a heavy ornament. Running over to the linen and towels, he chose a thick towel and wrapped it around his hand and the ornament. Then he swung it full force at the glass pane and it crashed through easily. Throwing it down, he avoided shards of glass and reached in to take the necklace. As he held it in his left hand, he felt completely exonerated from being labelled 'useless' by Orla.

Hearing them come up the stairs, he couldn't wait to show them his treasure. Preparing himself to be hero worshipped, a noise behind him had the hairs on the back of his neck standing on end. A chill ran down his spine and his body stiffened in fear. Letting out a slow breath, he realised things were never this easy. Steeling himself, he turned to face whatever stalked him.

As his teammates arrived they watched in horror. Ben stood surrounded by a gang of mannequins. One of them stood slightly in front of the others. It sneered at Ben and pointed to its missing arm.

"Time for payback," it drawled and then before he could think, it fell on him. Ben cried out as he felt kicks and punches from more than one of the plastic freaks. He was trying desperately to hold on to the pendant so couldn't fight back. He curled himself up into a tight ball. His body jerked repeatedly at the beating he was taking.

"*Oomph...!*" He shouted as one hit him on the head. This spurred the team into action. They had initially been so shocked at the scene but now seeing their friend being beaten propelled them to defend. They launched themselves at the violent crew and tried to hold them back from attacking Ben. It was difficult to get a grip of them as they were so smooth and didn't mind if an arm or leg fell off. Even headless, they continued their frenzied aggression.

While Ben was on the floor, he spied another necklace. It gave him an idea. He needed a diversion. Lifting his head he saw an opening, thanks to the counter attack from his friends. He sprung up, pushing the lead dummy out of his way. Rushing over towards the bedding area he shouted to his friends. The disappearance of Ben had the dummies drop their fight with the group. They followed Ben and chased him as he jumped over the beds and shelves.

The group watched as he came full circle back towards them. He stopped and shouted, "Catch." He threw something at them which Mark caught clumsily. Then he winked made a show of swinging a necklace around his fingers and before their very eyes, he was flanked by two mean looking mannequins. As he met their stares, he disappeared in a black smoke that poured out of the mouths and eyes of the two that held him prisoner. The group were stunned and watched as the rest of their attackers collapsed in heaps. Mark held out his hand to see what he had caught. They all gasped when they saw the dove necklace.

"That idiot," exclaimed Mark, though he was so proud of his friend. It was a brave thing to do but he hadn't needed to prove that to any of them, despite what Orla had claimed. Dearbhla closed Mark's fingers over the necklace.

"The Divider still thinks Ben has this. We need to get out of here and find the Spellbinder before he returns."

Mark nodded and they began to descend the staircase.

"Wait. What about Ben?" Orla asked.

"We can't help him yet. We need to get the objects to safety and then we can focus on Ben."

Orla was not happy that they were abandoning Ben. He was with that evil thing who was probably torturing him. She was about to argue when Mark spoke.

"Dearbhla's right. I want to help Ben more than anybody but he knew the cost. He was giving us a bit more time, Orla. We can't throw it back in his face."

Orla nodded meekly but she still wasn't entirely convinced. Mark knew what she felt and looked more deeply at her.

"Believe me Orla, after this, we'll get him back. Okay?"

This seemed to reassure her as everyone knew Ben and Mark were best friends.

"Let's go then," she said and they all ran down the two flights of stairs. They headed out the front entrance of Austins and on to the street. Warily they looked around to see if there was any sign of their enemy. The Divider must know the truth by now. Poor Ben would be in trouble facing his nasty temper alone. A low rumbling that seemed to come from beneath them put the group on alert.

"What's that?" Leanne shouted, as she lost her balance.

The rumbling was like an earthquake and it grew louder until a crescendo of roaring forced everyone to cover their ears. They stuck close together, ready for the onslaught but nothing appeared. As they gained their footing and the noise dulled down, they silently watched every direction. Then distantly they heard a thud. Another followed. Seconds ticked by and brought with it a chorus of thuds which rose in volume until it completely echoed around them.

"Ahhh the dummies...!" Orla screamed.

The group swung round and in disbelief saw the mannequins in every shop window beating against the windows they dressed. The group huddled together all facing outwards. They jumped and shrieked at every pummel on the glass. Mannequins were relentless in their effort to escape their glass prisons.

"They're not alone," warned Takuma.

Susie saw what he meant. Every shape and size of mannequins filed out of shop doors. They came in a whole variety of formal attire, casual dress, underwear or just plain naked. There were those that had wigs and facial expressions, while others had no features, were baldy and the unlucky ones that were missing body parts. It was almost comical but for the ferocity which they had previously attacked Ben. This was on a much larger scale. It truly was an army this time and they were frightening in their intensity as they advanced upon the six. In contrast to the 'Hands Across The Divide' statues, their movements were more elegant and graceful than their clunky rigid ones. Somehow, this was more threatening.

"Plastic Fantastic is freaking me out!" muttered Orla.

"We have faced worse," said an unconvincing Dearbhla.

Mark glanced at her as if to say, "Yeah right."

Leanne was terrified. "How do we stop so many of them? We can't even hurt them."

Takuma squeezed her arm, "Leanne, we just fight any way we can. They can't fight if they've no head or arm. Start taking them apart."

"Good plan! You go first!" Mark teased and smiled at Takuma's choked laugh.

He had only been joking but as the glass around them began to crack and then shatter apart, Takuma threw himself bodily at the mannequin closest to him. The rest watched in fascination as he wrestled and grappled with a faceless dummy. Leanne giggled when its black long curly wig went flying off.

"Oops. Sorry. I'm nervous," she explained.

Orla rolled her eyes and said, "Toughen up and start ripping some arms off."

Shockingly, Orla was the next to attack a mannequin. The thought of saving Ben drove her onwards. Throughout this, the window dummies stepped through the broken glass and out onto the pavements. It was a truly spectacular sight. They moved as one, being so in time with each other as they were. That confirmed their suspicion that the Divider knew they had possession of the dove.

Mark was the next to launch into two baldy mannequins dressed in formal wear. One had on a beautiful midnight blue dress. Leanne really liked it. What was wrong with her noticing that when chaos surrounded her. She didn't get to appreciate the other mannequin's dress because a firm grip from behind pulled her up against a plastic body. She struggled and tried to wriggle out of the grasp but her clothes just tore. Frustrated she beat her fists against the dummy's chest but it didn't flinch or loosen its hold. Susie came to the side of the dummy and knocked off its head with an arm. Still, it held Leanne firmly. She tried again and started hitting one of its arms. It came off and Leanne easily pulled away during the confusion. She thanked Susie who muttered a quick,

"Look at Orla."

Leanne scanned the road until she saw Orla literally battering a mannequin with its own leg. Leanne was glad the dummy was on the receiving end. She had thought Orla would have liked to have done that to her a few times today. Then she felt panic at the hordes of mannequins marching their way.

"Oh crap," she sighed and did the only thing she could. She jumped on the back of one of the mannequins that was currently punching Takuma and ripped its head off. This gave him the chance to gain the upper hand. He grinned at her and began to 'de-limb' the rest of it. She grinned back and entered the battle.

Dearbhla was beginning to fear defeat. The dummies outnumbered them and were nearly impossible to hurt. They, on the other hand were bloodied, bruised and could get very hurt. A pair of hands grabbed her roughly and she was lifted off the ground. Then she was unceremoniously chucked into a heap of body parts. Thankfully plastic ones though it did give her a moment of worry.

Before she could sit up, Susie and Leanne went sailing through the air to land with loud thumps beside her. Their groans affirmed they were still alive. Next arrived Mark and Takuma who were dumped in a heap together. Dearbhla was concerned at their stillness but on hearing their weak groans, she relaxed. The last to be rounded up was Orla. Still gripping her weapon of choice, a plastic leg, she was dangled upside down by a male mannequin.

Mark, who had dragged himself painfully into a sitting position, decided to act on Ben's behalf. Turning his head to the side he asked seriously, "New boyfriend Orla?"

She swung her arms out and squealed, "This overgrown '*Ken*' doll better let me go. Or I'm going to melt him down into a litter tray for my cat!"

As if he understood her, the mannequin opened his hand and let her drop head first.

"Ow! You big oaf..."

Leanne watched the angry girl sit up and winced when she saw her head. Orla noticed.

"What is it?" she asked while touching her forehead with her fingers. Then she screeched out when she felt the bump growing to the size of an egg. Scowling she pinned the mannequin with her fiercest glare. It stared blankly back which aggravated her further.

Dearbhla was certain their enemy had a plan. She looked around and the dummy army encircled them. They were captured.

Chapter 51

One of the dummies with features stepped forward. It had long tresses of blonde hair and wore a slinky green cocktail dress. Her painted red lips began to move.

"Eeee. Uhhh. Ere uh?" it screeched.

The group all winced at the sound.

"Geez, go get some elocution lessons doll," said Orla drily. Leanne was too scared to giggle this time. If this thing was trying to communicate, it wasn't going to be good news.

The mannequin seemed to cough and clear its throat.

"Our master wants the objects. Hand them over now and you may see your friend again."

The group all exchanged glances. Mark shrugged and nodded to Dearbhla. Effectively they were giving her the decision. She was, after all, their leader. She smiled sadly. They trusted her and now she had to let them down. How unfair life was. Dearbhla stood up on shaky legs. She preferred to face this heap of plastic on an even keel. Behind her, she heard the rest of the group struggle to their feet; solidarity, right to the end.

Reaching inside her pocket she took out the coveted items. The mannequin's lips pulled back in a fake smile and then it held its hand out. Dearbhla dropped the oak leaf, key and dove into its palm and with a heavy heart realised they had failed.

Closing its hand into a fist it punched the air and the army of mannequins cheered in unison. It was a very unsettling thing to see. As she surveyed the masses of plastic figures, she knew it was their only option. What chance did they have of defeating this motley crew of overgrown dolls? The mannequin lowered its arm and turned to go.

"Wait!" shouted Dearbhla catching hold of its arm.

The dummy turned slowly and looked down at her hand. Dearbhla removed it instantly.

"Where's Ben? You promised we'd get him back."

The Queen of Plastic smiled that fake smile again and replied, "I made no such promise."

Then she turned and began to walk away. Dearbhla looked back desperately at her friends who all looked as devastated as she felt. Then a low rumbling started and they all stumbled as the ground shook.

"What now?" Mark groaned.

He had no fight left in him; especially since they'd lost Ben, as well as their only bargaining chips. Strangely, the dummies were also swaying with the tremors that shuddered through the earth. He'd thought they would be gone by now. Then a low humming noise seemed to emanate from the Diamond. Its pitch grew higher until the group urgently covered their ears.

The sound seemed to affect the mannequins equally as they too bent over as if in pain. The shaking of the ground got worse until every mannequin and every human was knocked off their feet. Just as they couldn't bear it any longer, it stopped and so did the movement. For some unknown reason every being found their eyes drawn to the war memorial to witness an amazing event.

The angel, that stood guarding the soldiers, glided down on to the ground. It waited, while the sailor straightened on his podium and jumped down to stand beside her. Soon after, the soldier swung his rifle over his arm, stood erect and jumped down to take his place on the other side of the angel.

"Whoa. That was cool!" exclaimed Mark.

"Amazing," breathed Takuma.

The girls were too wary of the implications yet to comment. Dearbhla reacted first. She jumped up off the ground whispering urgently to the others to do the same.

"Get up. Get up," she hissed.

They scrambled to a standing position preparing to face their next challenge. Interestingly, the mannequins were also picking themselves up from the ground. Perhaps the new visitors were the generals of this plastic army. If so, the group feared they would be the ones who would be taken apart limb from limb and used for litter trays. Dearbhla took stock of her friends' readiness, nodded in satisfaction and then waited for the gauntlet to be thrown. She didn't have long.

The Angel, Soldier and Sailor strode purposely towards the group of six. The group of humans seemed dwarfed by the force of the three approaching figures. Knees began shaking and hearts beat wildly. Leanne wiped her sweaty palms on her sides. Then she glanced at Takuma. He offered a reassuring smile but when he turned to face their new guests, it faded and was replaced by dread. Mark reached out and squeezed Susie's hand but she couldn't even summon a smile. Every time they tried to make progress the Divider threw something else at them. She felt so tired and wanted this over with. Orla straightened and glared menacingly at their newest threat. If she was going down, she was going down her way, scrapping 'til the end. Dearbhla caught her breath in sudden panic. Realistically, they had no chance against a mannequin army and three statues. Bearing that in mind, she observed the expressions of those who stood beside her and it gave her renewed courage. She would rather be here with these brave teenagers than with anyone else. Turning her attention back to the statues, her whole attitude and stance projected a simple message, 'Bring-it-on!'

They stood their ground when the statues drew to a halt directly in front of them. They each heard the distinct laughter of the Queen of the Mannequins. The rest of the army took their cue from their leader and joined in. The hilarity was fake and empty but the intent was clear. They believed the six were facing imminent destruction. As the last laugh echoed away, the mannequins joined the ranks. They stealthily moved into place behind the statues who hadn't uttered a single word. The Queen took her place beside the statues and sneered at the humans.

In a sudden change of position, the statues switched to stand in front of the six and took on a protective stance. The group were shocked by their change of intention. The Queen's face showed confusion as she addressed the statues.

"Why do you stand with our enemy?"

The Angel met her glare and smiled sweetly, "They are not *our* enemy."

This made the Queen twitch.

"Master will not appreciate your disloyalty," she delivered with an overly saccharine smile of her own.

"Ah, but you see, he is not *our* Master. The *Spellbinder* has our complete loyalty."

This infuriated the Queen who realised she had been outmanoeuvred.

"So be it," she announced briskly and walked back to join her army.

Meanwhile the six watched the exchange with fascination. They pulled excited faces at each other. They had reinforcements! The Soldier looked back at them and gave a cheeky wink, whilst the Sailor muttered something to the Angel. The Angel dropped back and addressed them.

"I hope we did not frighten you, but it is best to unsettle your enemy. My companions taught me that. Stay behind us."

Then she joined the other two statues just as the Queen issued a piercing cry of *"Attack!"* A mass of mannequins rushed towards them. The six took a retreating step but they needn't have worried. Their new bodyguards charged at the dummies and sent plastic bodies flying off in all directions. The Sailor lifted a car that had been abandoned earlier, and took aim at the crowd of dummies. It sailed through the air and crashed down upon the unlucky ones. The six humans cheered and shouted in delight. The dummies didn't get up.

Another band of dummies tried to encircle the Soldier. He laughed at their feeble attempt. Then grabbing the traffic light pole, he easily pulled it out of the ground. Mark and Takuma's mouths dropped open. Their awe continued as he swung the pole above his head and then spun around in a circle, annihilating his enemies with everyone he made contact with. At this stage, the road was covered in various plastic dummy parts including their wigs and accessories.

One of the dummies was a male dressed in pink shorts and a Hawaiian shirt. It had black floppy hair and wore sunglasses on top of its head. He kept carrying a fluorescent green picnic bag and seemed to be disorientated. Running from side to side, he screeched anytime a plastic limb or head came whizzing his way, ducking and then covering his mouth with his hand.

"Oh dear, Oh dear," he repeatedly cried out.

Leanne saw him and laughed out loud when the Soldier came his way. The mannequin froze and looked up at him. Before the Soldier moved, the mannequin lifted the green picnic bag and proceeded to beat the statue with it. Amused but unharmed, the Soldier stared at its futile attempts. He glanced over to the Sailor who was battling another horde of dummies. The Sailor caught his predicament, shrugged and returned to knocking dummies through the air and into the sides of buildings.

Hawaiian mannequin was running around the Soldier hitting him from all angles but it had the same effect as hitting him with a feather. His amusement faded as he spied four dummies sneakily coming up behind the humans. Reaching down, he grabbed the dummy by his leg and trailed him along the ground. The humans watched perplexed as he came striding towards them hauling the dummy. As he reached them he gruffly said, "Move!"

They parted and watched him swing his dummy weapon at four mannequins and knocked them all into pieces. The group were surprised they hadn't even heard their approach. Dearbhla shouted a "Thank you," as he began entering another fray. He turned, saluted her and began to lose speed as two mannequins launched themselves on to his back.

The Sailor had obliterated plenty of the army and the Angel had been equally as inventive. For her choice of weapon, she had broken off two parts of a railing and began swivelling them as she rotated her body. It became so fast she looked like a twister. Her path wreaked havoc through the plastic army and another wave of them lay broken. When she spun slowly to a stop, she straightened her halo and strode elegantly towards the Queen. The Angel and Queen faced each other but the Angel looked untouched, whereas the Queen had lost her blonde wig in the battle. Her right arm was missing and her face was scored black as if something had been dragged across it, or indeed, as if she had been dragged across the ground. Surveying the scene, Dearbhla concluded that was exactly what had happened.

The group watched the Angel converse with the damaged Queen. Then they were thrilled to see the Queen hold out her hand and the Angel take possession of their precious objects. The instant the objects changed hands, the Queen dropped to the ground lifeless. Every other remaining mannequin did the same and at last the war was won. The six humans hugged each other, relieved this part was over. Then they ran to the statues that had saved their lives. Deciding hugs were inappropriate for them, they praised their tactics and thanked them profusely for saving both the objects and themselves. Considering they were statues, they seemed quite flustered by the praise which made them even more endearing.

"I think these belong to you," said the Angel as she held out her palm. With heartfelt gratitude, Dearbhla carefully reclaimed the objects. The others cheered in relief and delight.

"Wait. Where's Orla?" asked Leanne concerned. As they frantically began scanning the area, Orla shouted out.

"I'm right here. Just settling an old score," she explained as she picked her way through the plastic remains, carrying a head. The group and the statues watched her, uncertain of her purpose. As she reached them, she slowly settled the mannequin head on the road in front of her. Then taking aim, she gave an almighty kick which sent the head flying into the distance. Dusting down her hands, she beamed at her audience.

"That was the fool that was carrying me like a sack of potatoes. I knew I'd get to kick him into touch."

They all broke out into laughter at Orla's revenge. It was time soon after for the statues to leave and for the group to complete the mission and find Ben. Saying their farewells, the statues repositioned themselves back on to their platforms. The group surveyed the scattered plastic and decided to make their way back onto the walls. Hopefully, the Spellbinder would make an appearance and show them what to do with the objects.

Chapter 52

Mark was increasingly worried for Ben's safety. The sooner they found him the better. He was sweating just thinking of the potential dangers his best friend was facing. They drew close to Ferryquay Gate and backed into each other when a lone figure appeared. It was a man dressed in old clothing. He was smiling and had his arm outstretched, dangling a key from his long fingers.

"Hello young friends!" With that warm greeting, the group relaxed but were intrigued at his appearance.

"A friend of ours, asked me to inform you that he shall meet you at the lookout point, which still has its own gate."

He inclined his head towards the walls.

As Dearbhla thanked him, he said, "I too looked after the gates, young lady. There were thirteen of us in fact."

Dearbhla recognised the reference to the Apprentice Boys and was truly amazed at the live history lesson both she and the rest of the group had experienced. If only they had more time it would have been insightful to bombard every single character they had met today with questions, but unfortunately, time was too precious to ensure their own moment in history.

He wished them good luck and walked up towards Artillery Street. His form began to fade but he continued swinging the keys, whistling a tune. The group were already speeding past him to ascend the steps back onto the walls.

"Follow me. I remember it," shouted Mark as he took the lead. He raced towards the Church Bastion eager to find the Spellbinder and help his friend. Mark stopped a couple of metres away from it when he spied the watchtower. He doubled over gasping for breath. At least he was right. Now they just had to wait on the Spellbinder.

"About bloody time!" shouted an irate Ben.

Mark's head shot up and he saw his friend cramped up inside the lookout tower with his face squashed up against the gate. Ben was glaring down at him.

"Get me out of here NOW!" he pleaded urgently.

Every part of his body ached being cooped up inside this dingy cell. He was beginning to lose hope anyone knew where he was. The air was musty and dry in this cage and he was completely dehydrated. Mark stood directly below him and started to laugh. Ben shot him a dirty look but it did nothing to quieten him. He let the tension leave him as he gazed upon his furious friend.

"Shut up Mark. When I get out of here, I'll put a dent in that face of yours!" he muttered. Then he caught sight of the rest of the group coming up behind Mark. He rolled his eyes and groaned. Great; now he was going to have to listen to the whole lot of them laughing like hyenas at his expense.

In fairness, the group glanced at Mark who was still laughing and tried to smother their own smiles. Orla, however, was watching Ben with glee.

"Well, well, well," she drawled as she walked up to stand beside Mark. Placing a hand on her hip she peeked in through the bars of the gate and tutted.

"Caught in a rat trap, Ben? How disappointing!"

Ben attempted to muster some pride and shuffled around his cramped quarters to fold his arms awkwardly.

"It's not too bad actually, Orla. I hear it's bigger than your bedroom so quite snug really…"

He let his voice trail off and ignored his muscles that were straining from being twisted into uncomfortable positions. Orla snorted and dug deep into her pockets. Then she made a show of being annoyed.

Shouting over her shoulder to the others, she said, "Aw Ben, if I had some cheese I could feed it to you. You must be ravenous!" She smiled sweetly.

Ben looked at her disgustedly, "Mice eat cheese, not rats, dumbass. Now go do something useful and entertain the Divider."

Orla laughed shrilly and swung away from the gate. Mark told his friend about the battle with the mannequins, the statues who fought on their side to reclaim the valuable objects and their victory.

"Oh goodie," Ben said sarcastically, "now get me out of here."

Mark turned to the group helplessly. They stared back, unsure of how to do so.

A sudden flurry of leaves and a strong breeze blew up. The leaves created a funnel shape until there was a flash of white and the leaves drifted to land at the Spellbinder's feet. He stood like a beacon of light and every member of the team felt both awe and pride at the events of the day. He smiled and bowed his head acknowledging their success. Somehow that was more meaningful than if he had heaped words of praise on them.

Gesturing at Ben, he said, "Gatekeeper, you have the key to free young Ben."

Dearbhla gasped and she quickly took out the key that was their second object. Throwing it to Mark, he opened the lock and pulled back the squeaking gate.

"At last!" said Ben but found he could hardly move. "Er… a little help, please!" he muttered.

Both Mark and Takuma helped him slide his body to the edge of the post. Then they took his weight when he weakly jumped out. They supported him while his body adjusted to being free of the confines of a tiny cell. He sucked in a breath when he slowly straightened his back. Although, he realised he would rather have the aches and pains, than to still have his legs nearly wrapped around his neck.

"You have all acted courageously and have earned the respect of every being in the light," announced the Spellbinder. Then he fixed Ben with his attention.

"Young Ben, you proved your loyalty and bravery to us all. I thank you."

Ben blushed but was delighted at his words. Then the Spellbinder looked at all of them.

"I thank all of you, my Guardian of the Gates, my Children of the Oak, on behalf of this city, who will never know of your battle against evil. You truly deserve your titles."

Orla stood beside Ben and nudged him. He looked at her and seen her megawatt smile. Shaking his head, he laughed and smiled back. They had done it! They had saved the day.

Dearbhla was about to ask what to do with the objects, when a sudden crack of lightning hit the walls near them. Repeated strikes had the group jumping with the sound. A black cloaked being stepped out from the multiple strikes. As he raised his head, he grinned maliciously. The Divider was not about to give up.

"I see the whole gang is back together," he snarled.

The group moved in closer together.

"Where is my dearest Leanne?" he asked with false interest.

Takuma grasped Leanne's hand and pulled her close. Leanne looked terrified as she met his keen gaze.

"A friend of mine wishes to reacquaint itself with you," he purred reasonably.

Leanne watched in horror as a thick black snake slithered its way out from under his cloak and wound its way up his chest until its head was level to his. It hissed and flicked its long skinny tongue out as it pinned her with cold black eyes; eyes that were as cold and black as its master's. Then, he too, joined the hissing. As he did so, a thick black tar like substance fell from both their tongues. It dripped on to the ground and bubbled like hot oil. More and more of it poured out and joined the bubbling, toiling mess before them.

Orla was petrified at the sight but was unwilling to let him see that. She glanced at Leanne's face. The stark terror on it fuelled her rebellious streak. How dare that feathered bully frighten them?

She gathered her courage and shouted, "Go brush your teeth with that feather that's sticking out of your stupid hat!"

He snapped his gaze to her but dismissed her as a nuisance. Dearbhla put a hand on her arm to pacify her. Now was not the time to enrage him, her quiet look communicated. Orla relented and nodded.

By this time, the tar like substance was beginning to writhe and change into various shapes. The group were so mesmerised by the scene that they failed to see the tar creep towards them. Only when some of it reached up and wrapped around Orla's leg, pulling her down, did they realise the danger. The tar tugged again and Orla screamed as it knocked her to the ground and began dragging her back towards the deep pool of writhing tar. Ben and the others desperately tried to hold her arms and pull her back but Orla screamed in agony at the tug of war on her limbs.

Leanne ran back to the Spellbinder who had remained silent.

"Do something," she shouted.

He put a calming hand on her shoulder and stepped forward. The screams and desperate attempts to hold on to Orla were mixed with the maniacal laugher of the Divider who was enjoying creating such distress. As Orla's leg entered the pool of black gore, her screaming became agonised. It seemed to be burning her as smoke was rising from where it touched her skin. She clutched at Ben.

"Don't let go," she screamed.

Ben was terrified as he saw her flailing leg burn every time it made contact with the tar.

"Hold on, Orla. Hold on," he shouted. "Get a stronger grip," he ordered the others as they all tried to improve their grasp.

"Release the girl," a voice boomed out.

The Divider didn't even look towards the Spellbinder. He continued his torturous attack on Orla, laughing wildly. A sudden flash of blue light blasted the Divider and his snake friend back. They were flung back against the ground. The tar began to shrivel and let go of Orla's leg. The Spellbinder followed the Divider and kept blasting him with the blue light shooting out from his hands. Each time the Divider was thrown backwards with the impact, until he lay exhausted in a heap.

"Leave here. You have been defeated, Divider. You lay no claim to this city, to these walls, to these people. Go!" ordered the Spellbinder, sounding as angry as the team had ever heard him.

The Divider picked himself up and glared at the group. Then he scowled at the Spellbinder.

"I'll go. But know this. It is not over. I *will* return."

He pulled his cloak around him and in a swirl of black smoke he had disappeared. A black snake suddenly fell at Leanne's feet with its throat slit. She screamed and covered her mouth. Laughter filled the air as the Divider gloried at his parting gift. He truly was a disgusting creature, thought Leanne.

The Spellbinder returned to them and placed his gentle touch on Orla's burnt leg. Immediately it healed and she released her breath.

"Thank you. That feathered idiot was lucky I didn't stick his feather up his ..."

"Orla!" interrupted Ben. "Maybe now is not the time," he widened his eyes at the Spellbinder and she sighed.

"Okay. Okay. Help me up."

Ben did, relieved she was back to her usual charming self. That had been a close call. He had thought she would be swallowed up by the quagmire of goo. He shivered and made an effort to fuss over her. She looked at him strangely but said nothing. The group followed the Spellbinder back to the watch tower.

Chapter 53

"Dearbhla, place the objects on to the stone," he invited, pointing to a particular stone in the wall.

She took the key from the gate and set it on the stone along with the oak leaf and the dove. When all three objects made contact with the schist, it caused a slow reaction. Sparks of golden light were shooting out of them. It was like watching a mini firework display. The sparks grew with momentum until such a strong light was being emitted they all had to screw their eyes up to continue watching.

It was a beautiful thing to see as the sparks seemed to be playing with each other, darting back and forth, creating patterns and enjoying their interaction with the three objects. Some of the golden sparks returned to caress the objects and before their watchful gaze, those same objects seemed to fuse into the sparks and into the stone itself. The atmosphere built up and offered more vigour, fuelling the light spectacle. It was as if there were hundreds of mini explosions as the flashes were overflowing with energy and needed to expel it rapidly. It became impossible to watch any longer.

As the brightness faded, they returned their gaze to the objects and were amazed at what they saw. The sparks had gone. The reaction was over. More importantly, the objects were no longer three dimensional, physical things. They were now gold carvings in the actual stone; part of the walls themselves; able to protect them forever.

"It is complete. The light has overcome evil and the walls are forever protected. It cannot be undone," said the Spellbinder.

Ben ran to the wall and looked over to see if it had worked. The people below remained like statues.

"It didn't change anything," he called out.

All eyes swung to the Spellbinder who seemed relaxed.

"Patience, young Ben, all will be well. Time must reset itself."

He smiled as he watched the Gatekeeper and the Children of the Oak embrace each other laughing and crying. He allowed them a few moments to enjoy their success. Then he approached Dearbhla.

"It is time." He fixed her with a penetrating stare and silently communicated what would happen next. Then he smiled a genuine smile of warmth. He glanced over at the six teenagers fondly and without ceremony, he turned and walked away.

Dearbhla stood aside from the others, watching his retreating form. There had been a few close calls but he hadn't let them down. More importantly, they hadn't let each other down.

The teenagers realised that the Spellbinder was departing. They took their place beside their trusted leader and silently watched the mysterious man. Tiny sparks began bursting out around his body. They danced and flirted with each other. Unlike the reaction of the objects, these sparks were a multitude of colours. It truly was like spectating a firework display, as the colours burst higher and left longer streams behind them.

The group cheered and laughed at the little show the Spellbinder was providing. As the lights got thicker and blocked him from their view, some of the colours began darting away into the walls themselves. It was an inspiring sight, to witness the stones absorb the colours and actually shine brightly, as that same colour, until returning to normal. The group couldn't help but gasp in admiration as the beautiful spectrum turned the walls into a magical, enchanted rainbow.

"He's gone," pointed out Leanne.

They weren't sure how because they were too entertained by the scene before them. Nearly all of the sparks had disappeared apart from seven. These different colours flitted towards them. Each of the group studied the spark which stopped in front of them. Orla reached out and touched her violet spark and reared back as it spread its colour through her finger. Then it travelled to her whole hand, up her arm and body, until every part of Orla shone a beautiful violet colour. She giggled and held her arms out to see the change in her skin tone. The others were amazed to see their friend change colour. Eager to see if it would happen to them, they each followed suit and touched their spark. They too soaked up the colour that was attracted to them, marvelling at themselves and each other.

"Ha ha. Cheer up Mark, you look a bit blue," laughed Ben, referring to his best friend's new look.

Mark grinned back.

"Yeah, well I hate to break it to you but you're princess pink!"

Ben frowned, "Am not. This is purple," he stated, affronted.

"Sorry Ben, I'm purple, you're definitely pink," said Orla, then burst out laughing as he started inspecting his hands and arms.

"Are you sure?" he asked unwilling to accept it.

The group were all entertained by his mortification at the colour shining out from his skin.

"Yip," said Orla, "But don't worry it looks good on you!" she added and wiggled her eyebrows at him. This placated him and he started joking that he was 'pretty in pink'.

Takuma was green, Dearbhla was orange, Leanne was lemon and Susie was red. A few minutes passed and the colours faded. The sparks went shooting out from their bodies and chased each other into the walls. The group chatted happily about the amazing exhibition of light; aware they had been involved in something unprecedented.

As they savoured their victory and deliberated over who had been the most frightening adversary, Dearbhla listened to them contentedly. When a static charge began to develop, she accepted that it was time to undergo their final and in many ways their most difficult challenge.

"Guys, it's time to go back to normal," Dearbhla broke into their revelry and braced herself, hoping to find the strength to say words that would change everything.

They all cheered, excited to see their friends and family.

"Wait 'til I tell Aunt Marnie about this. She'll think I'm a loon," laughed Ben.

Dearbhla shook her head, hating what she was about to explain.

"No Ben. When time is reset we each go back to the moment before time was stopped. We won't remember what happened today," she explained sadly.

They had all become so close; it was such a shame that they couldn't share the memory of how they had each contributed to saving their city. She saw the shocked expressions and felt awful. All of them had come such a long way. They had developed trust in each other and had been willing to do what it took to save this city. It seemed cruel that no one would know it, not even them.

Dearbhla felt a further change in the atmosphere around them and knew it was beginning.

"We don't have long. I just want to say thank you. We couldn't have succeeded if any one of us had been unwilling to help. I love you all. I hope that someday our paths cross again and that deep down we instinctively recognise our admiration and trust for each other."

She hugged each of them and felt herself being pulled by a force. Leanne was crying softly. Takuma and she shared a look and then they too felt the pulling force.

Ben saluted Dearbhla and said proudly, "It's been an honour. Even with you here," he added while looking at Orla. He smiled as she rolled her eyes and they too felt the pull.

They all watched hazily as Mark and Susie stood facing each other. Then Mark grasped Susie in a gentle embrace. They smiled tenderly at each other, ignoring a distant wolf whistle from Ben. As Mark leaned in close to kiss Susie, they were all sucked into a time shift. In seconds, the walled city was reset to the time just before the enchantment had taken place. The streets were cleared from the debris of battles that had been fought and won. Statues were replaced to their original location. It was as if nothing untoward had unfolded.

***

Miss Dunston glared at Ben, who shook his head as if to clear it. He felt strange but made a decision as he watched his teacher's face turn fifty shades of red. Jumping up with hands held out in supplication, he immediately apologised,

"I'm really sorry, Miss Dunston. That was a dumb thing to do. I'm an idiot."

His teacher closed her mouth in surprise and looked at him intently, unsure if there would be a catch. Ben noticed this and tried to reassure her.

"No, seriously, Miss. I'm going to say sorry to the wee girl now. No more bother from me, I promise."

He saluted her and then wondered why it felt as if he'd done that before. His teacher nodded quietly and wondered at his change of heart. Usually, he argued back and would swear on his life he'd seen a huge spider. She sighed but was glad to see Ben approach the girl who had fallen over in the panic about a spider. He helped her over to the wall and said he'd run to the shop and get her some plasters.

Susie had been watching the exchange and marvelled at the boy's ability to charm his way out of trouble. She felt in her pocket for a tissue to give the bleeding girl but weirdly found a packet of plasters. Frowning she wondered how they had gotten there. She didn't remember putting them in. Getting up she walked over to Ben and the injured girl. She handed him the plasters and he made a show of doing first aid. He had the girl giggling and fluttering her lashes at him by the time he had finished.

Susie walked away and passed by the boy she had noticed earlier. Their eyes met and she felt a tug inside. Looking quickly away, she returned to her project and tried to ignore him even though she stole sneaky glances at him now and again.

Mark had watched the strangely familiar girl offer plasters to his waster friend who was now flirting with the girl he had inadvertently caused injury to. She had beautiful eyes but there was just something about her. He got a warm feeling inside every time he looked at her. He also felt he knew her but was certain they hadn't met. Mark tried to meet her gaze again but gave up after his fourth attempt. He shrugged and got back to his work. It looked like Ben wasn't going to pull his weight on this project; typical.

Orla was sitting near Leanne and she continued to grumble to her teacher about sitting on the hard ground though she didn't feel as annoyed as she had earlier. In fact, now she thought about it, it wasn't a big deal. She looked at Leanne and smiled quickly not even sure why she did so. She didn't know her and usually couldn't care less about making new friends. A bit surprised at herself, she looked away from Leanne's answering smile and made a show of searching for chewing gum.

Leanne noticed the girl, Orla, smile at her and was taken aback. From what she had observed, she seemed a nasty piece of work but perhaps she was wrong to make such a quick judgement. She looked over and caught a young Japanese boy watching her intently. She offered a friendly smile and he appeared to shake himself awake. Returning her smile he coughed as if embarrassed and bent his head to his notes. Thinking he was shy like her she smiled to herself. It was good to know she wasn't the only person who was slightly awkward in social situations.

Takuma was startled from his daydream by the girl smiling at him. He hadn't realised he had been staring until she had smiled. He had smiled back but then immediately refocused on the project. His career plan did not include girls yet so he dismissed Leanne.

***

Dearbhla fixed her hair in the mirror of the bathroom in Austins. She was enjoying the sound of a toddler singing along with its mother. The door of a cubicle opened and the toddler came skipping out happily. He turned and waited for his mummy. Dearbhla exchanged smiles with the mother and left them behind to their singing.

Dearbhla exited Austins overwhelmed by a sense of pride as she stepped out onto Ferryquay Street in the bright sunshine. People milled about busily and cars passed by with radios and chatter momentarily filling the air. She took a deep breath of fresh air and closed her eyes. Opening them, she felt so contented. She really did love this city. Then she happily walked on out past Ferryquay Gate, with a hope that hadn't been with her that morning.

The End.

If you would like to find out more about Sinead Cox, follow her on Twitter: @CoxSinead or visit her author's page on Amazon:
www.amazon.com/Sinead-Cox/e/B00UKH0OJA
You can keep up to date with Sinead on Sinead Cox Author on Facebook.

Children of the Oak is also available on Kindle.

Other books by Sinead Cox

Bluebells and Lace – a collection of poetry available to download from Amazon Kindle.

The Billy Plant - a children's short story, written under the name Ena Macready. Available to buy from Amazon Kindle.

Printed in Great Britain
by Amazon